Shamra Divided

SHAMRA DIVIDED

By Barry Hoffman

Book Two Of
The Shamra Chronicles

EDGE BOOKS
■ 2010 ■

Shamra Divided
© 2010 by Barry Hoffman

Cover Illustration
© 2010 by Jen West

Interior Book Design & Cover Design
by Dara Hoffman-Fox
10-digit ISBN: 1-934267-16-3
13-digit ISBN: 978-1-934267-16-5

This book is a work of fiction. Names, characters, places and incidents are either the products of the author's imagination or are used fictitiously. Any resemblance to actual events or locations or persons, living or dead, is entirely coincidental.

Manufactured in the United States of America
All Rights Reserved

FIRST EDITION

Edge Books - An Imprint of Gauntlet Press
5307 Arroyo Street, Colorado Springs, CO 80922
Phone: (719) 591-5566
Email: info@gauntletpress.com
Website: http://www.ShamraChronicles.com

Acknowledgements

The Shamra trilogy wouldn't be possible without the assistance and encouragement I received from a number of people.

Dara, your layout, as always, is superb.

Jen West, your cover art for the entire series just blew me away.

Thanks, too, to Erika La Pelusa for her wonderful copy editing. She is the one who corrected all the inconsistencies I took for granted were not there.

And to Chris La Pelusa, who helped me more than I can describe with donating over 10,000 copies of *Curse of the Shamra* to schools (and others) in behalf of underprivileged children. Something that sounded so simple became a nightmare at times, but Chris persevered. Young girls and teens all over the country are profiting from his efforts.

Dedication

To my little Bauble (and granddaughter), Tyler. You're the inspiration for this series, and you know how much I love you.

Shamra Divided Pronunciation Guide

- **Dara** ~ *dare-a*; rhymes with *mascara*

- **Shamra** ~ *sham-ra*; rhymes with *mom* and *Tom* (not *ham* or *Pam*)

- **Pilla** ~ *pill-a*

- **Briana** ~ *brie-ann-a*; rhymes with *see*

- **Lexa** ~ *lex-a;* rhymes with *vex*

- **Galvan** ~ *gal-van;* second syllable pronounced like the word *moving van*

- **Lyna** ~ *lee-na;* rhymes with *see, he, me*

- **Screech** ~ rhymes with *peach, leech*

- **Shrieks** ~ *shreek*; rhymes with *leak, peek, seek*

- **Troc** ~ rhymes with *lock, sock*

- **Bauble** ~ *bawh-bull*

- **Tyler** ~ *tie-ler*; rhymes with *eye, sky, lie, bye*

- **Gren** ~ rhymes with *hen, pen*

- **Nyvia** ~ *niv-E-ah;* rhymes with *live, give*
- **Loran** ~ *lore-an;* rhymes with *sore, bore, door*
- **Drea** ~ *dre-a;* rhymes with *say, day, may*
- **Sera** ~ pronounced like *Sara* or *Sarah*
- **Jana** ~ *jan-a*
- **Ramorra** ~ *ra-more-ah;* like the word *remorse*
- **Kimra** ~ *kim-ra*
- **Dolor** ~ *dole-or;* rhymes with *molar, solar*
- **Baltar** ~ *ball-tar*
- **Atyra** ~ *at-tear-a;* rhymes with *leer, dear*
- **Lon** ~ rhymes with *Don*
- **Kril** ~ rhymes with *hill, pill, sill*
- **Bashra** ~ *bash-ra*
- **Cylia** ~ *sill-E-a*
- **Bly** ~ rhymes with *lie, sigh, my*
- **Malis** ~ *ma-lis;* pronounced like the word *malice*

Shamra Divided

- **Fangalas** ~ *fang-ga-las*
- **Dyann** ~ *die-ann*; rhymes with *lie, sky, bye*
- **Maritza** ~ *mar-it-zah*
- **Anis** ~ *a-niece*
- **Pror** ~ rhymes with *door, sore*
- **Kel** ~ rhymes with *fell, sell*
- **Tobin** ~ *toe-bin*
- **Sylar** ~ *sigh-lar*
- **Deedle** ~ rhymes with *needle*
- **Weetok** ~ *we-tock*
- **Bain** ~ rhymes with *pain, cane, lane*
- **Mya** ~ *my-ah*, rhymes with *lie, sky, bye*
- **Tergon** ~ *ter-john;* last syllable pronounced like *John*
- **Cid** ~ rhymes with *kid, did, lid*
- **Elna** ~ *el-na;* rhymes with *fell, bell, tell*
- **Lytle** ~ *lie-till*

- **Tweeble** ~ *twee-ble;* rhymes with *feeble*

- **Cheron** ~ *cher-on;* first syllable pronounced like *share*

- **Nyla** ~ *nigh-la;* rhymes with *sky, bye, lie*

- **Dedra** ~ *dee-dra*

- **Chaos** ~ *kay-ahs*

- **Kyle** ~ rhymes with *pile, style*

- **Kril** ~ rhymes with *pill, hill, Bill*

- **Jelon** ~ *jell-on*

- **Enron** ~ *en-ron;* first syllable rhymes with *hen, den*

- **Hoban** ~ *ho-ban*

- **Ishry** ~ *ish-ree;* first syllable rhymes with *fish, wish;* second syllable rhymes with *tree, see*

- **Meeko** ~ *meek-o;* rhymes with *leek, seek*

- **Janis** ~ *jan-is*

- **Regor** ~ *reg-or;* rhymes with *Meg*

- **Cym** ~ *sim;* rhymes with *Tim, gym*

SHAMRA DIVIDED

- **Garn** ~ rhymes with *yarn*
- **Dahlia** ~ *dall-yah* or *dahl-yah*
- **Tron** ~ rhymes with *Don, Ron*
- **Reva** ~ *ree-va;* rhymes with *peeve, Steve*
- **Gwin** ~ rhymes with *fin, kin*
- **Tillery** ~ *till-er-E;* rhymes with *hill, pill, dill*
- **Kronin** ~ *crow-nin*
- **Tokar** ~ *toe-car*
- **Enwee** ~ *en-wee;* rhymes with *hen, fen, Ben*
- **Zyr** ~ *zeer;* rhymes with *fear, deer*
- **Nephyr** ~ *nef-fur*
- **Kalin** ~ *kay-lin;* rhymes with *say, may, day*
- **Nedir** ~ *ne-deer;* second syllable pronounced like *deer*
- **Darcy** ~ *dar-see;* rhymes with *car, far*
- **Tobor** ~ *toe-bore*
- **Corina** ~ *core-een-na;* rhymes with *Maureen*
- **Allegra** ~ *a-leg-ra*

Prologue

Dara was pulled out of the murky waters of the swamp by an unseen hand. She ran as squat, bulbous plants pummeled her with a gelatinous goo that sapped her energy. Her breathing became labored as she fought to move forward. Suddenly, the same invisible hand pushed her in the back, and she was sent sprawling out of the forest, into a clearing. Having escaped imprisonment, death, or maybe something far worse, Dara tried to make sense of this latest assault.

The swamp had seemed benign when she'd entered. Though hungry, Dara hadn't picked from any of the plants for nourishment. Many forests and swamps she had traveled through had turned out to be living organisms. Everything in them was connected. Eating from one plant had repercussions for entire portions of the forest or swamp, and she could become its prey until she navigated her way out. So Dara was careful where she chose her food.

Dara had come to a stream of luminous green water. She had to shield her eyes from its brightness. She found a branch that had fallen from a tree and poked it into the water. Not deep at all, she thought. And the water did no damage to the branch. There was no getting around the stream. Cross or turn back. Retreat was a last option for Dara. Midway through the stream, the water had turned a sickly green, then to mud, and Dara was trapped, unable to move. She felt herself being sucked from below. It was then that the invisible hand had plucked her, none too gently, from the stream. Moments after escaping the stream, the plants that had appeared harmless during her journey through the swamp turned treacherous. The liquid that spat at her was sticky and smelled of decay. It didn't harm her, but Dara couldn't wipe it off. It stuck to her like a garment. She was soon slowed by the sheer weight of the substance. She knew if she fell, she would be devoured by the swamp. Yet, as her strength failed her, she was again saved by a hand she felt but couldn't see.

Why? she thought, as she caught her breath. Had she passed some test? Or maybe failed one? Had the swamp rejected her? Was she too small or weak to be worthy? Or maybe something about her might sicken, even kill, the swamp. Or possibly the swamp was comprised of dueling entities. One desired her to succumb. The other came to her aid for unknown reasons.

Dara would never find out. When she had first begun her journey from her Shamra homeland, she often became frustrated when answers eluded her. Now she merely accepted the fact she had again survived and could move on to her next challenge. Not everything could be explained, she had learned. And that wasn't necessarily bad, she knew. She would spend the night replaying the adventure and conjure all manner of reasons she was still alive.

Her travels had been as exhilarating as she had anticipated. Any number of times, she had faced injury or death yet had prevailed. Unlike the Shamra of her homeland, she embraced danger. She had no death wish. On the contrary, she had too much to live for. But being bored to death as a housewife had no appeal to her. The unknown beckoned. She couldn't remember being more content, even if she now smelled of decayed food.

A pond suddenly appeared in the clearing. It was as if the earth had opened to reveal what it usually kept hidden. Maybe those who survived the swamp were rewarded. The pond itself was only twice the size of her body. The water smelled sweet and alluring. The water beckoned, and Dara couldn't resist. Not only did she reek from the swamp, but she had little water remaining in her canteen. Dara had no fear of the water. Nothing so beautiful could be deadly.

A loud squawk startled Dara out of the fog that had enveloped her mind. She looked skyward and saw Screech, her Shriek, who appeared to be warning her not to approach the water. Shrieks were bird-like creatures covered with black scales instead of feathers. They were fearsome, with talons that could tear their prey apart, and teeth as sharp as knives. Totally loyal to those who provided for them, they had been soldiers of the invaders of her homeland. Screech, though, hadn't been brought to her homeland by the Trocs who had sought to enslave the Shamra. When Dara and another resistance fighter, Heber, had fled their homeland to locate allies, Screech had attacked them. The creatures were predators, and Dara and Heber, much smaller than these creatures, appeared the perfect prey. But Screech had been thwarted, captured, and injured. Dara had nursed him back to health, and he had become loyal to her, just as the Shrieks were to the Trocs. Screech could soar above the dangers of swamps and forests. If Dara rode Screech, she would be safe. But the thrills she encountered would have eluded her. So she trudged through the swamp while Screech flew above.

Now the creature sensed something amiss, and its shrill scream pierced the stillness. Dara stepped back, picked up a stone, and tossed it into the pond. It plummeted endlessly.

The water was an illusion, the pond, a bottomless pit with hypnotic powers. If Screech hadn't warned her, Dara would have disappeared forever or possibly been devoured by yet another living entity. Dara moved back even farther. She was still a gooey, putrid mess, but she was alive. Ahead lay a forest. Maybe there she'd find real water and be able to bathe.

Dara entered the forest and heard a loud noise, as if a door had closed behind her. She attempted to leave the forest, a sense of foreboding surrounding her, but there was no longer any exit.

Dara shrugged and moved forward. What else could she do? And, as always, her curiosity overcame her fear. The deeper Dara entered into the forest, the darker it became. She could see just a few feet ahead of her. Around her was a cacophony of voices. Screams of terror, torment, and despair, yet Dara saw no living creatures. Then it began to rain. A sudden downpour. Dara thought it was a mixed blessing. The sticky substance was washed off her, but the rain fell with such intensity, it was like needles striking her flesh. She sought shelter under a huge tree whose trunk pulsed as if it were breathing. The tree wanted nothing to do with Dara. Its leaves and branches began swatting her, warning her off. She ran from the tree, back to the path, and slipped on some wet vines. The rain continued to fall steadily, and Dara felt herself being sucked into the wet ground. She heard other voices calling out to her, but still saw nothing.

"Stay down."
"Don't get up."
"Join us."

At times thunder drowned out the voices.

Then Dara did see something that made her skin crawl. From the mud, figures arose. She didn't recognize any, but each seemed a different species. Some stumbled toward her on two, four, or even six legs. Several of the creatures had one eye, while others had as many as a dozen. Some had as

SHAMRA DIVIDED

many arms as a tree had limbs. Yet, different as they were, Dara could understand their plea.

"Join us. Join us," they spoke as one. *"Become one of us."*

"And lose myself?" Dara yelled back. "No, never!" She tried to get up but sank deeper into the muck. The creatures moved toward Dara as one, as if linked by a rope. She was utterly helpless.

Two figures rose from the mud in front of Dara. With swords, they began hacking and thrashing at the creatures, their backs to Dara. With difficulty, Dara freed herself from the mud and joined the battle. She was able to see that one of those who fought by her side was Pilla. Her lifelong friend, Pilla had died during the occupation of the Shamra homeland. She had become a prophet upon her death and had saved Dara's life on several occasions. Just as important, Dara felt Pilla's presence wherever she ventured. It was always a comfort to her. Dara didn't get a good look at Pilla's companion but knew she, too, was female. Her face seemed shrouded in a mist. It didn't hinder her, however, as the three of them fought for survival…at least Dara's survival. As the creatures were struck by their swords, they howled in pain, despair, and frustration. Just as suddenly as they had appeared, they allowed the mud to swallow them to escape death. Impossible, Dara thought. Somehow she knew that, like Pilla, they were already dead. But Dara had long ago learned to accept the impossible during her journey.

With the threat gone, Pilla and her companion disappeared. Now the only sounds to be heard were the rain that continued to pelt Dara and the sound of thunder. Without warning, a bolt of lightning filled the sky, felling the tree Dara had sought refuge under. Then, like arrows, more lightning struck nearby Dara—first to her left, then her right, in back and in front, as if to imprison her. Then silence. No rain. No thunder. A swirling light appeared above Dara, and a bolt of lightning struck her, knocking her down.

CHAPTER 1

"Are you all right?" a voice said, laughing.

Dara opened her eyes. She was no longer in the forest, but on a mountain. There were no trees, just the midday sun that forced her to shield her eyes. Above her loomed a horse.

"I told you riding a horse was more difficult than it seemed. He threw you. You took a nasty spill. Now will you let me show you—?"

"I know you," Dara said, her voice weak.

"Of course you do."

"Briana," Dara said. "From my dreams."

"Yes, you told me about your dreams. The Gift of Sight. It runs in our family."

"*Our* family?" Dara asked, confused.

"Yes, *our* family. We're related," Briana said. "I told you. A distant relationship, but you are part of our clan and the family that rules the clan."

"Why do you speak as if we know one another?" Dara asked.

"You've been here for five days," Briana said.

Dara shook her head. "I've never seen you...other than in my dreams."

"Are you sure you weren't injured in the fall?" Briana asked, and Dara could hear the concern in her voice.

"I didn't fall," Dara said, her voice rising. This is so frustrating, she thought. "I was struck by lightning. I assume you found me—"

"You found *us*," Briana said. "Five days ago. You said you were looking for the original Shamra homeland, where your people had lived, then abandoned. You found that and more. You found us—descendants of Shamra left behind. We were banished," Briana said, then paused. "I'm going to get Lexa. She's a healer, in case you forgot."

Dara grabbed Briana before she could leave. "Listen to me. I was struck by lightning. I don't know how I got here or why I was on a horse. In my dreams, I saw you on...on a hill of stones. Such a structure doesn't exist in the Shamra homeland where I lived."

"Stone Mountain," Briana said. "It's where we live now."

"You said we were related," Dara said, then paused. She looked at Briana, who appeared to be the same age as Dara, sixteen. Oddly, Briana looked more like Dara did than the females from where Dara had spent all of her life as an outsider. Like all Shamra females, Briana was short. Thin and wiry. Her lips and nose were thin. Her features, angular. But there the resemblance to others from her homeland ended. Briana's eyes were brown like Dara's, where all but a few Shamra from her homeland were born with blue eyes. Briana's fingers were stubby like Dara's. All other Shamra females Dara knew had long, delicate fingers. Dara's fingers had made her feel even more of an outcast among her own kind. But this female had fingers like hers.

The differences between the two were few. Briana's white hair was longer than Dara's, running halfway down her back, something that had been forbidden where Dara came from until after the Trocs were overthrown. Dara's shoulder-length hair had been frowned upon in her homeland. She had refused to cut it short but wore it in a bun when out in public. Briana's face wasn't smooth like Shamra females but weather-beaten from being out of doors. Faint scars crisscrossed one of Briana's cheeks.

Briana wore a necklace with a red stone hanging from a leather string. Dara wore a necklace of her own. Dara's necklace had no stone but bore an animal's bone that was a faded red. No other Shamra except Pilla, who had a necklace similar to Dara's, wore necklaces. Before Dara left her homeland, she had given Pilla's necklace to Rhea, Pilla's younger sister. Wearing jewelry was frowned upon by the clerics who spoke for the prophets.

"Your necklace?" Dara asked, not waiting for Briana to answer her other question.

"After our first kill, we go to the top of Stone Mountain and pick a stone. A rite of passage, I guess you'd call it."

Dara also noticed that Briana wore a bandana similar to hers. Where Dara's was red with black polka dots, Briana's was yellow with black polka dots. Wearing colorful clothing also made others where Dara had come from uncomfortable with her. Shamra, both male and female, wore earth tones. Wearing a colorful bandana had been passed down in Dara's family generation to generation. She had no idea why. Her parents had died from a fever when she was two. Her mother had told her stories from the day she was born, but Dara remembered just fragments. The bandana, necklace, and long hair she and Briana shared reminded Dara just how different she was from those in her homeland…and how similar she was to this female she had met face to face for the first time.
"I have so many questions," Dara said. "I still don't understand how I got here."

"I was going to answer your questions about your heritage today," Briana said. "You told me your parents died when you were two. You could only recall scraps of the stories they told you."

Dara nodded. Briana seemed to know far more about Dara than seemed possible. Dara still refused to believe she had been on Stone Mountain for five days. Everything about the forest where she had been struck by lightning was so vivid. Too graphic to have been a dream.

"You were restless, cooped up on this mountain that has become our home," Briana said. "I was going to take you hunting. I was going to tell you about your heritage. But maybe you're injured worse than I thought."

"No," Dara almost shouted. She stood up, tentatively. She had a slight headache, but what was she to expect after being hit by lightning. Actually, she expected far worse. "I'm fine. Let's go...hunting."

"If you're up to it," Briana said, brightening.

As they got on their horses—Dara following Briana's instructions carefully—Dara looked at Briana. "I know you think I've been here five days and that I've learned a lot about...our clan. And you obviously seem to know a great deal about me. But I remember nothing. I feel like a fool, but indulge me, and start at the beginning. I do know I wanted to find the land where the Shamra had originally settled. I know we fled...well, fled this place, I guess after we had been invaded and enslaved three times. But that's all I know."

"You were almost slain by the Galvan," Briana said, pointing to the lush farmland that stretched as far as the eye could see. "We used to live there, but that's a story for later. We...I guess you can say we coexist with the Galvan. It's a tenuous truce. They try to storm the mountain every so often. When food is scarce in the forest, we raid some of their farms for animals. Lately they've been more aggressive. Stone Mountain is impregnable, but we number less than one hundred, while there are thousands of Galvan. We can't afford many casualties." Briana paused. "You remember none of this?"

Dara shook her head.

"Our family has led our clan for three hundred years. We're hunters and warriors—"

"Hunting is forbidden among the Shamra where I come from," Dara said. "And we had no warriors—no militia—until after the invasion. Edicts from our religious leaders who have since been discredited forbade establishing an army, even for self-defense."

"I'll explain why *your* Shamra had no army later," Briana said. "What I told you several days ago is that in the past six months, my two brothers and three sisters have been slain by the Galvan. It was like they were looking specifically for *us*. Others in our clan were spared, but our family members were pursued and slaughtered." Briana touched her cheek where Dara had noticed the scars. "I was severely injured. For weeks there was doubt whether I'd survive. Now when we're attacked, I'm forbidden to engage in battle. Guards accompany me into a cave."

"The last of your family?" Dara asked.

"My mother Lyna leads the clan. She's too old to bear any other children. If I died…well, when she dies, there will be a battle among the other families for leadership. But then you arrived. A descendant of *our* family. Now, if I die—"

"Oh, no," Dara said. "It was thrilling to lead an army. Well, it wasn't much of an army, but there were those who would sacrifice their lives for freedom. But then I had to govern with another. I wasn't born to rule. I'm not one for compromises, the endless bickering or boring day-to-day decision-making. Actually, I've been most content exploring the unknown. No offense, but I could never be cooped up on a mountain for the rest of my life." Dara paused. She wanted to change the subject. "You said I was almost killed by the Galvan."

"Yes. We rescued you, and you joined us on this mountain that has been our home for close to two hundred years. And days ago, you told me the same thing. You plan to leave.

You have no desire to head our clan. I won't try to convince you otherwise, but you were destined to lead. Who knows what the future holds?"

"Where's Screech?" Dara asked, suddenly aware she hadn't seen her Shriek.

Briana looked at Dara oddly. "Screech?"

"A mammoth bird-like creature with scales," Dara said.

"You came alone."

Dara put her hand into her stomach pouch. Her Bauble Tyler wasn't there. Baubles were worm-like creatures given to Shamra children on their first birthday. Tyler was over a hundred years old and quite wise. For sixteen years, Dara had relied on Tyler often. Tyler could be stubborn, cantankerous, and ornery, but other than Pilla, there was no one Dara was more fond of than her Bauble. Dara told Briana what Tyler looked like. Dara asked if Tyler had been injured.

Briana shook her head. "You arrived alone," she said again.

"I couldn't have lost both Tyler and Screech," Dara said, tears welling in her eyes. They had turned gray from despair. A Shamra's eyes changed color according to their mood. Something was terribly wrong, Dara knew. None of this made sense. For now, though, Dara had to put Tyler and Screech from her mind.

Briana led Dara through caves and passageways, and they finally emerged from the mountain through a cave at its base.

"Why do you live on a mountain and not in the valley below?" Dara asked.

"We have a two-hour ride to the forest where we hunt. Let me start at the beginning—two hundred years ago. Your many questions will start to make sense.

Chapter 2

~ Coming of Age ~

200 Years Ago

Gren, of the farmer's clan, rode up on his horse in a cloud of dust and asked to see Nyvia, head of the hunter's clan.

"What do you want of me?" Nyvia asked. Nyvia stood in the doorway, a stick in each hand to keep her from falling.

"I have a message for the leader of your clan," Gren said.

Nyvia's laugh was interrupted by a fit of coughing. She spit a thick glob of mucous on the ground, then wiped her mouth with the sleeve of her shirt. She looked at Gren with a twinkle in her eye. "Do I look like a leader?" she asked before coughing again. "I am old and infirm, certainly a poor excuse for the leader of our proud clan. Never mind," she said, before Gren could answer. She waved one of her sticks at him and almost toppled over. "Let's hear your message. I'll pass it on."

"I didn't mean—" Gren began

"I don't have time to listen to apologies," Nyvia interrupted. "Your message."

"Members of the four clans are to meet tomorrow to discuss our leaving this land. You are to send four representatives to speak for your clan."

"We're being summoned, are we?" Nyvia said.

"I'm only a messenger. I mean no offense," Gren said. He seemed clearly uncomfortable in Nyvia's presence. "You're not being—"

"Who demands our presence?" Nyvia asked, waving her stick once again to silence Gren.

"Nobody demands—"

"If we don't come, we have no say, isn't that right?" Nyvia asked.

Gren said nothing.

"So it's not an invitation, is it? Who summoned us?" Nyvia demanded, raising her voice.

"Loran, of the religious clan, sent me to deliver the message."

"So the religious clan speaks for us now?" Nyvia said, making no attempt to keep the disdain from her voice. "Where was Loran at the Massacre at Monument Gate? Where was he and his clerics during the uprising? Holed up in their temple praying for us." Nyvia spat on the ground. "My people and yours died to gain our freedom while Loran prayed. And now *he* commands, and the other clans follow." She shook her head in disgust.

"Will you attend?" Gren asked, his voice hardly above a whisper. "The meeting will be at the temple."

Nyvia walked toward Gren. Needles of pain accompanied her every step. At fifty-two, she was considered ancient. Few Shamra lived past forty-five. She grabbed Gren's arm, which was heavily bandaged. "You fought during the uprising, young Gren," she said.

"Yes," he said, making eye contact with Nyvia for the first time.

"Your parents?" Nyvia asked.

"My father perished. Your clan protected my mother and sister at Monument Gate. I will be forever grateful."

While Gren and Nyvia were talking, other members of the clan had gathered outside Nyvia's hut.

"I will not set foot in Loran's temple," Nyvia said, and coughed again. It was as if she had a fur ball stuck in her throat. She saw the look of concern on Gren's face and smiled a toothless grin. "Our clan shall attend," she added, and laughed at the look of relief on Gren's face. "Now go, and let me rest my weary bones."

"We are indebted to your clan," Gren said as Nyvia turned from him. "Your people suffered far more than anyone."

Nyvia turned quickly and almost fell. "Memories are short, young Gren. Yes, we have suffered." She paused. Her breathing was labored, and talking was a chore. "You owe your freedom to those of our clan who gave their life. Let's see how we're repaid. Now go and tend to your wounds."

Gren got on his horse and rode off. Nyvia turned to the large crowd that had gathered. "Tonight we meet," she said. "Come with me, Drea," she said, speaking to her granddaughter, who had gathered with the others. Nyvia hobbled into her hut. "Pour me some water, child," she said when Drea entered. Drea sat on the ground on a bed of straw and sighed deeply. At fifteen, other than Nyvia, Drea was the oldest remaining member of her family — a family that had ruled their clan for five generations. Sera, Drea's mother and the clan's leader, had perished at Monument Gate as had Jana, Drea's older sister. Upon Sera's death, Jana would have become leader of the clan. She had been groomed for the responsibility since she was a child. With her death, there was a void.

"You will speak for our family tonight," Nyvia said to her granddaughter. "How do you plan to conduct yourself?"

For a moment Drea said nothing. "I will listen and learn," she finally answered.

"Wrong!" Nyvia said, raising her voice. In her day, Nyvia had ruled with an iron fist for twelve years. Her prowess as a hunter was legendary. As a warrior, she had no peer. Yet on her fortieth birthday, she had gladly passed leadership of the clan to her daughter. One didn't lead the hunter clan until death. Now Nyvia had to impart strength to her granddaughter. "You now lead our family. You lead our clan. Show weakness, and Ramorra will swat you like an irritating insect."

"I am only fifteen, Grandmother," Drea said.

"Yes, far too young to lead our clan in normal times," Nyvia said. Before she could continue, she suffered through another bout of coughing.

Drea remained silent.

"Your mother and sister are dead. I am old and frail. It's been twelve years since I turned leadership of the clan over to your mother. My time has passed. Your time has come. You have no say in the matter," Nyvia added.

"What would you have me do?" Drea asked.

"Lead, child."

"What about Ramorra? She is far wiser than me," Drea said.

"Because she's older?" Nyvia asked. Without waiting for an answer, she continued. "She's not of our blood. She's ambitious, vain, and self-centered. She is certainly not wiser than you, just more…experienced. She is a threat to us, yes, but she doesn't inspire loyalty."

"And I do?" Drea asked. "I am little more than a child."

"A child who has proven herself in battle. Stories of your valor have already spread among the clan. You are held in high esteem because of your fearlessness in combat. When children of the clan reenact the Massacre at Monument Gate, who do you think they choose to be?" Again, Nyvia didn't give Drea the opportunity to speak. "Your exploits have already become legend. Your prowess will be spoken of for generations." Nyvia paused to catch her breath. "You lead, child, or our family will be challenged. You put Ramorra in her place tonight, when she gives you the opportunity. Force her to challenge your authority or accept you as the clan's leader. She is no warrior. She will back down."

"If I am to lead, advise me, Grandmother," Drea said.

Nyvia shook her head. Instead she asked Drea question upon question, demanding Drea think for herself.

"At some point, all eyes will be on you. As the youngest, do you make or avoid eye contact?" Nyvia asked. "Do you raise your voice to Ramorra or answer calmly?"

Finally Nyvia nodded in satisfaction. "You are a worthy successor to your mother. She taught you well, child. Now let me rest. You will make us proud, Drea. Those of our clan who remain and those who have passed over will smile upon you. Now off with you," she said, and closed her eyes.

♦♦♦♦♦♦♦♦♦♦♦

Drea went to her hut. She withdrew her sword from the sheath she wore on her back. Few in her clan had a metal sword. Her clan used bows and arrows and spears to hunt. Swords had been forbidden by their oppressors. The craftsman clan feared they would be caught and punished if they made metal weapons for Drea's clan. So most weapons were fashioned from wood. Even those had to be hidden from the Kimra. A male from the craftsman's clan who was Drea's age had had a crush on her. Drea was amused, but didn't take Dolor seriously. She was a hunter and warrior. He was persistent and had asked her what he could make for her that she would forever treasure.

"A sword of metal to slay my enemies," she had answered with a laugh, then put it out of her mind. Three days later, Dolor had given her a sword and sheath to hold it.

"I will treasure this, Dolor," Drea said, swinging the sword and marveling at its balance. "I will think of you with each Kimra I slay." She kissed him on the cheek and laughed as his face turned the red of a tomato. Dolor had perished during the uprising. He had been more of a warrior than Drea had given him credit for.

Drea closed her eyes and replayed the Massacre at Monument Gate and all that followed. This first disastrous battle in the war to free the Shamra was why she was now supposed to lead her clan at the age of fifteen.

The Kimra had invaded the land of the Shamra twenty-five years earlier. It was the third time in recorded history that the Shamra had been conquered and enslaved. The valley where the Shamra resided was lush with fertile fields for the farmers, the largest of the clans. There was an abundant supply of animals in the surrounding forests that were prey for the hunter clan. So bountiful was their country that it had proven a bit too enticing. Travelers were welcomed with open arms, given food and drink, and invited to the many celebrations that marked Shamra life.

Peaceful and trusting by nature, the Shamra had been easy targets for invading armies. The Kimra towered over the elfish Shamra, who stood no more five-feet tall. While the Kimra walked on two feet like Shamra, their bodies were reptilian. Scales that covered their bodies afforded them protection the Shamra lacked.

Unlike most Shamra, the hunter clan wasn't content to wait for disease to destroy their enemy, as had occurred before. They preached that the Shamra must fight for their freedom.

In the past few years, the Kimra had grown slothful, complacent, and careless. Drea's clan had watched and observed.

Shamra Divided

While Kimra were scattered throughout the country, a great many had taken refuge in the Shamra's largest town. Rather than watch over their subjects, more and more of them waited for the weekly offerings of food, clothing, pottery, and jewelry each clan was forced to deliver. Baltar, leader of the Kimra, lived in a huge palace constructed by the craftsman clan. As more of the Kimra gathered in the city, Sera, leader of the hunter clan, had sensed that the Kimra could be taken by surprise and defeated.

Once the Shamra had been conquered, they had exhibited little resistance against the Kimra. Previous invaders had been felled by diseases that the Shamra were immune to. The vast majority of Shamra simply waited, reasoning that, once the time was right, the Kimra would feel the wrath of the prophets who watched over the Shamra. Sera privately scoffed at such talk but held her tongue in public. She secretly had her clan forge weapons and train. Members of her clan had infiltrated the town, looking for weaknesses in the Kimra's defenses so that Sera could overwhelm Baltar and his guards with a surprise attack.

Sera had kept plans of the attack secret from all but her clan. She was distrustful of the other clans, who meekly succumbed to the Kimra or prayed for deliverance. A plan was devised. Weeks of intensive training followed.

Only females delivered the weekly offerings to the Kimra. Females were considered inferior to males among the Kimra. They were for breeding, raising their young, and tending to the homes of the males. The Kimra hoped to pass on their wisdom and customs to the Shamra. The weekly procession of females to the palace was to show all Shamra that females served males, whether they be their own kind or the Kimra. On the day of the Massacre at Monument Gate, Sera and two hundred of her clan's females mingled with the other clans as they entered the compound to the palace.

Sera's plan was simple. She and two dozen of her warriors would lead a frontal assault on the palace, which was not heavily guarded. Slay Baltar, and the Kimra, without a leader, would panic. Her daughters, Jana and Drea, would engage the larger number of guards at the gate so they couldn't attack Sera's warriors from the rear. Ramorra and her family would remain outside the gate to repel any Kimra from the countryside who rallied to Baltar's call for reinforcements. No matter how swift Sera's attack, the Kimra would attempt to summons help with their horns.

Once inside the gate, Sera raised her sword, and her warriors stormed the palace. Without warning, dozens of Kimra stood on the roof of the palace and rained arrows at Sera and her soldiers. Sera had never been told of these marksmen and was completely taken by surprise. Sera was among the first to fall.

Knowing the attack was doomed, Drea and Jana, standing back to back, fought the Kimra guards who attempted to close the gate and trap the Shamra army within. Females from other clans ran in panic. The guards swung their swords at defenseless females, thinking all were in on the plot. Before the guards could figure out whom the enemy were, Drea, Jana, and members of their clan had killed several dozen guards. Still, it wasn't enough to keep the gate open. Retreat was now impossible.

Side by side, Drea and Jana battled on. Drea, with her metal sword and quickness, felled Kimra after Kimra in an effort to protect those from other clans who had no weapons or will or ability to fight. From the palace, the Kimra archers shot arrows at them once the few surviving members of Sera's group had retreated in disarray. As the gate was far from the palace itself, arrows hit Shamra and Kimra alike. Finally the archers were ordered to cease. Dozens of guards poured from the palace to join in the slaughter.

Shamra Divided

"We must get the gate open," Jana shouted to Drea, "or we shall all perish. Can you climb to the top and get to the other side?" Drea's older sister asked.

"I will, or die trying," Drea said. "Take care, sister."

Drea climbed the wooden gate. Halfway up, several arrows hit the gate on either side of her. She was no easy target. Near the top of the gate, an arrow found its mark, embedding itself in Drea's leg. She was pinned to the gate by the arrow. If she couldn't free herself quickly, other arrows would claim her life. Crying out in pain, Drea broke the arrow in half and yanked her leg from the half of the arrow still lodged in the gate. She scampered to the top, then dropped onto the soft dirt outside the gate.

Ramorra and her family stared at Drea in surprise. The Kimra hadn't sounded the horn, because there was no need for assistance from the countryside. Ramorra's family had no idea of the carnage within the gate.

"The attack has failed," Drea said. "We open the gate or all inside perish." Drea took off a red bandana with black polka dots from her head and wrapped it around her leg to stop the bleeding. Her long white hair streamed past her shoulders. Ramorra seemed paralyzed, as if she didn't know what to do. Drea barked instructions.

With heavy wooden posts left outside to fortify the gate, Ramorra's clan pounded the gate until it finally collapsed inward.

"Rescue all you can, and retreat into the woods," Drea said, as she limped back into the fray. She noticed Ramorra now issued orders but never stepped foot inside the gate.

Drea saw Jana fighting off four palace guards. She was on one knee swinging her wooden sword to keep the guards from falling upon her. Limping, Drea came to her sister's aid. She killed three of the guards, then, too late, saw the last guard lunge at Jana. His sword pierced Jana's chest as Jana's struck him down. Drea dragged Jana, who was barely conscious, to the gate. Two females from the farmer's clan took Jana from Drea.

"We will take her to safety," one said. Drea nodded and watched for a moment as the two led Jana away. Filled with dread and fury, Drea rejoined the battle, intent on killing every Kimra who crossed her path. Her eyes, like all Shamra's, changed color with her mood. Drea's now blazed red with anger. It was hopeless, she could see. For every Kimra that fell, several others emerged from the palace to take his place. Drea gathered six of her clan, and they formed a wall to keep the guards at bay while those from the other clans retreated. Atyra, Drea's lifelong friend, finally grabbed Drea after Drea had felled yet another Kimra. Atyra wore a yellow bandana with black polka dots.

"It's senseless to stay and die," Atyra said. "We must live to fight another day."

"But what of the others?" Drea shouted. "So many defenseless—"

"There are no others," Atyra said, cutting Drea off. "We've rescued all we could. We're yours to command, but to die now is senseless."

Drea nodded and sounded the retreat, then ran. She stepped over the bodies of those who had perished. What a disaster, she thought. She couldn't even count all the dead from her clan and from the other clans, there were so many. And punishment against all the clans by the Kimra would be swift and brutal.

In the woods, where Drea fled, she saw members of her clan gathered in a circle. Bursting through them, she saw the body of her sister. Drea collapsed. Grief and loss of blood from her wounds hit her like a fist.

Word of the massacre spread, and with each telling, the bravery of the Shamra was magnified and the slaughter of unarmed Shamra was exaggerated. It was as if a chain had been severed. Grief-stricken Shamra throughout the countryside

SHAMRA DIVIDED

began to fight their oppressors. At first there was no plan. See a Kimra. Attack the Kimra. Kill the Kimra.

When Drea awoke, Lon, a leader of the male warriors, stood over her. Both of his arms were bloodied, and dirt covered his face. "All across the land, the Shamra have risen to fight the Kimra," he told her. "It's a wonder to behold. And Baltar has made a grievous error. He keeps his soldiers gathered behind the gates of the town to protect him. Those outside are outnumbered and leaderless. Soon all will be dead or captured. The craftsmen are forging swords and other weapons. The farmers give us horses. In three days, Nyvia herself will lead an attack on the palace. Freedom shall be ours."

Though still weak, Drea led the attack on the palace three days later. Nyvia rode with her but assured Drea she was there solely to give moral support. "With these tired bones, I can barely sit on a horse much less raise a sword," she told her granddaughter.

With hundreds of Shamra descending upon the palace, Baltar surrendered without a blow being struck. The palace belonged to the Shamra. The oppressors were defeated. Nyvia, with Drea by her side, stood at the entrance of Monument Gate and said a solemn prayer for those who had fallen.

The religious clan, which had been silent during the uprising, suddenly called for an assembly to discuss what to do with Baltar and his followers.

While they talked and talked and talked some more, Nyvia sent Lon and fifty of their clan back to the palace. Baltar and every remaining Kimra was killed, and the palace was burned to the ground. Drea had remained in her clan's village tending to the wounded and had no knowledge of the attack. Of the two hundred warriors who had been at Monument Gate, only fifty survived. Many of those were badly wounded. Atyra had led attacks during the uprising while

Drea recuperated from her wounds. During one assault, Atyra had received a nasty wound to her neck and was feverish. Drea wiped Atyra's brow with a bandana, which she'd dipped in water mixed with healing herbs. Atyra was delirious. Drea spoke to her in soothing tones, hoping to get through to her friend.

"I never felt so alive as when I was in battle, Atyra," Drea said to her friend. "I was born to be a warrior. It's not the killing. *That* I could do without. But the danger and excitement. It's in our blood, Atyra." She took off the bandage on Atyra's neck on put on a salve of herbs, then covered her friend's wound again. "I could see it in Jana's eyes when she was surrounded. I've never seen her eyes so blue." Blue signified happiness and excitement. The more intense the blue, the greater the satisfaction. "I'm certain Jana didn't welcome death, but when the guard struck the blow that felled her, I saw no fear." She lowered her voice. "In a way, I'm sorry the battle is over. I know it's a terrible thing to say. So many have died. It will take years for our clan to recover. But they all died gloriously. I know a part of you wants to join those who have passed over. Peace will bring boredom. You must recover, Atyra. I need you." She continued talking to her friend, hoping to reach something within that would overcome the fever.

Drea felt a presence behind her and saw her grandmother standing over her.

"Baltar and his guards have been put to death," she said. Drea wondered if Nyvia had intentionally kept the attack from Drea, who had been tending to the wounded.

"Was that the decision of the assembly?" Drea asked.

Nyvia spat on the ground. "They continued to talk," she said. "We could not allow any to survive. Some might have eventually fled for reinforcements. We couldn't take the risk. So while the others did what they do best, we acted. The battle is over. Rest, child, and grieve for those who have fallen."

SHAMRA DIVIDED

Drea said nothing as her grandmother hobbled off, but she was troubled. Nyvia had done what was necessary, but at what cost? There would be resentment against their clan, rather than the praise they deserved. Her clan had planned and led the uprising. Her people had suffered the greatest. In killing Baltar, though, they had defied the assembly. Repercussions would surely follow.

♦♦♦♦♦♦♦♦♦♦

That night when Drea took her seat at the Circle of Families, there was a hushed silence. All heads turned toward Nyvia, who sat outside the circle, surrounded by the remaining children in her family. There were eight, none older than eleven. Their parents had all been slain.

One member of each family sat in the circle. Discussion was allowed, but all decisions were made by the ruling family. With Sera and Jana dead, it was thought Nyvia would assume leadership again. Sera, as head of the clan, had begun all meetings. Though aware of the custom, Drea, who had taken Sera's place in the circle, remained silent. She saw a brief smile pass over Ramorra's face. Ramorra rose to speak. She was all but challenging the rule of Nyvia's family.

It was the tradition of the hunter clan to rule until challenged. A family was only challenged when it showed weakness. There had been just three successful challenges in the history of the clan. In the first, a fight to the death by the head of each family was required. The vanquished family was then put to death. Generations later, with the second challenge, there was again a fight to the death by the leader and challenger. But this time the defeated family was banished, not killed. They had joined the farmer's clan. When Drea's family had challenged, seeking to overthrow a weak leader, the clan was more civilized. Leader and challenger fought until one surrendered. If the vanquished family pledged allegiance to the new rulers, they were welcome to remain in the clan.

37

Now Ramorra seemed ready to challenge the rule of Drea's family. Before Ramorra could utter a word, Drea stood. She unsheathed her sword and thrust it into the ground before her. "Our family rules this clan," she said, looking around the Circle of Families, her blood-red eyes finally resting on Ramorra. "Unless, of course, we are challenged. In Nyvia's name, and in the name of my mother Sera, I now lead our family."

Ramorra looked at Drea, then at Drea's sword, then back to Drea again. She sat down.

Nyvia's right, Drea thought. Ramorra was ambitious but all bluster. Drea was young to lead her family, but none could deny her bravery or skill with a sword. Ramorra would not challenge this day or ever.

"There will be no discussion," Drea said. "We are Shamra. If after three occupations there is the will among the others to move to a safer location, so be it. As warriors and hunters, we will be needed more than ever if the Shamra are to survive. We will abide by the will of the majority. In the meantime, we must tend to our wounded. We must become strong again. That will only come with time." Drea pulled her sword from the ground and sheathed it. "Any comments?" she asked.

There was silence.

"Ramorra, Lon, and Kril will join me tomorrow at the assembly. This meeting is over." She looked at Nyvia, who nodded slightly. Lead, Drea had been told. Lead, she had.

Alone in her hut, Drea knew her mother and sister would have been proud of her. How she missed them. She missed her mother's quiet strength. Sera was a leader of few words. Her actions spoke for her. Whether during a hunt or in battle, she took the lead heedless of the danger. Drea missed her mother's guiding hand. Her mother had patiently taught Drea to be a warrior and hunter. She had taught Drea loyalty to her family, clan, and people. She had taught her self-sacrifice for the good of the many. Yet there was so much Drea had yet to learn. There was so much more her mother would never be able to teach her.

Jana had been more like Nyvia. She had been outspoken. She teased, taunted, and provoked confrontation. Still, she never held a grudge. She never allowed a heated argument to linger. After a quarrel, she was often seen laughing with the target of her venom. A reckless streak ran through Jana. She leaped, *then* looked. And Jana could be stubborn, even talking back to her mother when she disagreed with her. But it was always in private. In public she endorsed her mother's every command. As with all in her family, loyalty was Jana's strong suit. For as long as Drea could remember, Jana had been by her side, even though Drea was four years younger than her sister. Jana would go hunting with Drea, patiently teaching her how to track and attack her prey. Jana camped at night with Drea in the forest, telling Drea stories of evil spirits out to feast on young Shamra. And Jana had stood by Drea's side at Monument Gate. Drea never felt like Jana's little sister. In battle Jana trusted Drea as if she were the most battle-tested warrior.

Drea now cried for the first time since her mother's and sister's deaths. She felt as if her heart had been wrenched from her body. She so wanted to share her confrontation with Ramorra with her mother and sister. And she wondered just who she'd become. In many ways she was like her mother. In some ways she was like her sister, like Nyvia. But she didn't know just who she was. She would have to learn about herself alone, and she was terrified.

She wasn't aware Atyra had entered. Atyra sat down next to Drea and said nothing. Drea put her head on her friend's shoulder and cried for what seemed an eternity. Finally, all cried out, she wiped tears from her eyes.

"I was so proud of you tonight," Atyra said. "You are a true leader of our people."

Drea shook her head. "I only did what Nyvia suggested."

"Nyvia told you to plunge your sword in the ground?" Atyra asked.

"No. She told me to force Ramorra to challenge me."

"So Nyvia told you to wait until just before Ramorra was to speak?" Atyra said.

"No, she told me to—"

"Lead," Atyra finished. "She advised you, but you instinctively knew when to make your move. You didn't do Nyvia's bidding. You proved yourself leader of our clan. So, yes, I am proud of you."

"You're all I have left," Drea said. "More than ever, I need your friendship. I need your counsel."

"You'll have both forever," Atyra said.

"I wanted you to accompany me tomorrow," Drea continued. "But I had to let Ramorra save face. She cowered before me. But we need her if our clan is to recover. And I don't need her as a sworn enemy. Do you understand?"

"I would have gladly stood by your side tomorrow, but there's no need to explain yourself. You must do what is in the best interest of the clan. Don't worry about sparing my feelings." Atyra paused. "Still, you must tell me everything when you return," she said, her eyes gleaming a bright blue of anticipation.

Drea laughed. "I can trust you to bring me back to reality if I get too full of myself. And no one makes me laugh like you can. Don't ever be intimidated by me. Speak your mind freely. It's what I need."

For the next ten minutes Atyra mimicked Ramorra at the clan meeting. Drea laughed until her sides ached.

"Get some sleep," Atyra said finally. "That's an order," she added with a smile. "You can't be yawning at the assembly tomorrow."

SHAMRA DIVIDED

Drea fell asleep knowing she wasn't alone. Much as she missed her mother and sister, she still had Atyra. She held her bandana in her hand knowing that in her hut, Atyra was doing the same with hers. Only those in her family wore a bandana. It signified their leadership. Atyra had always been family to Drea. While giving a bandana to Atyra had been frowned upon, Drea's stubbornness had prevailed. Her best friend would wear a bandana—though a different color than those in her family—and even Sera couldn't convince Drea otherwise. Aware of the unique bond between the two, Sera had relented.

♦♦♦♦♦♦♦♦♦♦♦

The next day, Drea entered the assembly hall without looking at the crowd that had assembled to watch the proceedings. A murmur spread through those gathered as she entered. Drea knew Nyvia's absence had been noted. Drea waited to enter until after the other clans had been seated. She exaggerated her limp from the arrow that had pinned her to the gate the day of the Massacre at Monument Gate. She had instructed Lon and Kril not to remove bandages from wounds they had suffered. She wanted all to remember who had led the battle to free the Shamra from their oppressors. She wanted all to acknowledge which clan had suffered most. Yet, as she walked down an aisle with all eyes on her, she sensed something amiss. Something about this entire event seemed staged. They should be meeting in private, not in front of others. Drea had the uncomfortable feeling that decisions had been made without her clan's consultation.

Loran, leader of the religious clan, sat at the head of a long table. He had been drumming his long, delicate fingers on the table as Drea and her clan made their way through the hall to their seats. The other clans seemed to acknowledge him as their spokesman.

Drea was aware that the religious clan, though far fewer in number than the others, had grown in stature during the twenty-five-year occupation. The religious clan felt the Shamra themselves were responsible for their own misfortune. When free, the Shamra hadn't paid proper homage to the prophets. They were not pure in thought. They were not deserving of the bountiful land the prophets had provided them. Their insolence and lack of piety had brought the Kimra.

The Shamra had to embrace the prophets in all aspects of their lives, the religious clan preached. The prophets had spoken through the priests of the religious clan, who spent their days in meditation and prayer. The words of the prophets filled a massive book that was to guide all Shamra life.

Drea's mother had been wary of the growing influence of the religious clan over the past several years. Her clan did not attend the daily prayer vigils at sunrise and sunset. The religious clan preached acquiescence and obedience, so during the occupation, the Kimra allowed and even encouraged the religious gatherings. Sera had heard that as many as half of the farmer's clan and one-third of the craftsmen clan regularly attended the religious services.

Drea recalled Sera reading passages to her and Jana of the new version of the holy book, which the religious clan had supplied. All copies of any other text were to be turned over to the religious clan to be destroyed. "This book distorts the history of our people," Sera said as she finished a passage and closed the book.

"What do you mean, *distort*?" Drea remembered asking.

"They lie," Jana said, raising her voice in anger, before her mother could answer. Jana, four years older than Drea, could read, and there was little she needed explained to her.

"They're not the stories I remember being read to me by Nyvia and her mother," Sera said, smiling at Jana. "The religious clan has revised them," she said. She seemed to sense Drea still didn't understand. "They have been rewritten. Changed. Reading these, one would think only males were heroic. Only males are prophets. These passages could have been written by the Kimra."

Drea again seemed confused.

"Only male Kimra are warriors. Only male Kimra may serve in their army. Only males guard Baltar and his palace. Females must be submissive—" Sera said, then stopped, as if she knew Drea was going to ask her what that word meant. "Females must be *obedient*, just as we have to do the bidding of the Kimra. Actually, Kimra females aren't treated much better than the Shamra."

Sera had then told Drea and Jana stories that had been passed down by the clan. "I'm sure our stories exaggerate the importance of our clan, Drea, but they're far closer to the truth than what's written in this book."

Sera took out an old, tattered copy of the holy book written before the Kimra invasion. While copies had been confiscated by followers of the religious clan, Sera had hid hers. She knew others in her clan had done the same. She read some passages to Drea and Jana, then explained, "We acknowledge the prophets. Their words guide us. There are females who were prophets in the older version." She held up the book she had read from. "In the original text, it was never said we should wait for the prophets to rid our country of oppressors. The prophets never opposed resistance to enslavement. Religion didn't govern our daily life. The new text preaches patience, prayer, and obedience."

Drea smiled at the recollection. She recalled Nyvia telling her very much the same, but Nyvia would be pacing the room, her voice raised in anger, her chubby fingers pointed at Drea for emphasis. The hunter clan was the only clan to have plump fingers. And only members of her clan were born with brown rather than blue eyes.

Nyvia didn't just relate stories from the holy books. It had seemed like Nyvia demanded the old text be heeded. Sera said the same thing, but the way she said it was far more convincing than how Nyvia said it. Drea knew she had to carve her own identity. She didn't want to be just like her mother, but she was no Nyvia. And at the assembly today, more of Sera was required than the bluster of Nyvia.

Drea watched as Loran led the assembly of the clans. Challenging Loran's authority to lead was out of the question. The religious clan were pacifists. A challenge at this meeting would not be settled by armed conflict, as in her clan, but through discussion and voting. This, too, was new. Before the Kimra, there had been no assembly of clans. Drea also didn't underestimate Loran. The diminutive priest was certainly aware the hunter clan was a shell of itself. Overthrowing the Kimra had taken its toll. Loran would take full advantage of their weakness.

"The prophets have spoken," Loran began. "The Kimra enslaved us because we didn't heed the words of the prophets. The violent uprising against the Kimra is not condoned by the prophets," Loran said, looking at Lon. "The butchery of Baltar and his guards is contrary to the teachings and will of the prophets. It is only a matter of time before an even stronger enemy conquers us because we lack the patience and discipline to wait for the prophets to vanquish our enemies. We can—*we must*—leave this land and the blood we have spilled. We must start anew, following the teachings of the prophets."

Drea saw others around the table nodding their heads. As Drea had instructed, Ramorra, Lon, and Kril sat stiffly, listening but saying nothing. Only Drea would respond when it was appropriate.

"The question before us is, do we heed the prophets and leave this land we have defiled?"

Drea knew Loran already had his answer. She saw it in Loran's eyes, which blazed red in anger, then turned a deep shade of blue as the others nodded in agreement. The eyes of the others at the table were differing shades of blue, where before the uprising, they had been the gray of dejection and resignation. Eyes don't lie, Drea knew. Drea now felt the dread of betrayal.

Loran went around the table, asking the leader of each clan to cast the clan's vote. The farmers agreed to leave. So, too, did the craftsmen.

"Lon, what does your clan say?" Loran asked.

Only now did Drea rise. "You will address me, Loran. Daughter of Sera, granddaughter of Nyvia, I now lead our clan."

"You may lead your clan in battle, child," Loran said, "but—"

"I lead our clan, *period*," Drea said. "I don't disrespect you, Loran, who prayed in this very hall while my mother, sister, and countless others from our clan gave their lives so we could be here today. Don't trivialize my accomplishments and the losses our clan has suffered. Regardless of my age, I am no child. My clan accepts me as their leader. Will you show me the same courtesy?"

Loran looked at Lon, who remained silent. Drea saw Loran looked uncomfortable. Passages from the new text of the holy book flashed through Drea's mind, and she understood. It wasn't her age that bothered Loran. It was that she was a female. She was being disrespected because she wasn't a compliant female. "Very well," Loran said when Lon refused to make eye contact with him. "What does the hunter's clan say?"

Drea was aware Loran hadn't accepted her as leader. Nevertheless, she now spoke for her clan. "We accept the will of the majority," she said.

"The clans have spoken," Loran said. "We leave this land in seven days." He paused for a moment. From the way the other clan leaders looked at Loran, Drea knew they had already agreed on something more. "When we leave, we travel as one. There shall no longer be four clans, but one group united by a common heritage and one set of laws as set down by the prophets," Loran continued, clasping his hands together to emphasize his words.

A member of the religious clan gave a copy of a slim book to the head of each clan at the table. He held out a copy to Lon, who refused to take it. The cleric looked at Loran, then placed the book in front of Lon, refusing to acknowledge Drea. Drea said nothing and ignored the book.

"Our holy book is our guide," Loran continued. "For the understanding of all, the priests have listed rules that shall guide us as we become one." Loran read from his copy of the book that had been handed out. Females were to be revered as vessels from which future generations would spring forth and flower. As such, they wouldn't share the burden males bore.

Drea heard the words praising females but knew their true meaning. Females were to be submissive, as it had been for the Kimra female.

An army, which the hunter clan had urged to have long before the Kimra arrived, was forbidden, as were the use and possession of weapons of war. The Shamra would be pacifists. If the Shamra were pure in heart and deed, the prophets would protect them from oppressors. Finally, the members of what used to be the religious clan would interpret the words of the prophets, as the prophets had spoken to them through prayer.

"We vote now to accept these laws to govern us as the Shamra become one family," Loran said. As before, the farmers and craftsmen joined the religious clan in supporting the new order.

SHAMRA DIVIDED

"Will the hunter's clan make it unanimous?" Loran asked, for the first time acknowledging Drea by looking at her. Drea thought she could almost see a smile on the priest's face. He looked comfortable, confident, and smug. She might speak for her clan, but he knew that under the new order, she would speak no more after she cast her vote.

Drea stood. She could have asked for time for her clan to confer. That would show weakness, she knew. She could almost feel her mother and sister by her side. She could hear words of encouragement from Nyvia and Atyra. Lead, she had been told. Lead, she would.

Drea took out a book she had brought with her. "We support the rules of the law passed down for generations. We affirm the words of the prophets from the beginning of time, as told in the Book of Ages." She began reading a passage from the original holy book, as read to her by her mother.

"Stop!" Loran commanded, rising from his chair, pounding his fist on the table. His eyes were once more red with rage. "What you hold is blasphemy." He picked up the new version of the holy book and held it high for all to see. "These are the true words of the prophets."

"The new text is *not* the words of the prophets but of your clan," Drea said, without raising her voice. "You want to rewrite history to suit the needs of your new order—"

"That is heresy," Loran interrupted her. "We will listen to no more," he shouted, his hand trembling as he pointed at Drea.

"This is the path we shall follow," Drea said, holding her book aloft. "The true will of the prophets." She began reading another passage when Loran again interrupted her.

"Then your clan is banished," he said, his voice drowning out Drea's. "Adhere to the words of the prophets," he said, raising the revised text in his hand, "or remain in this accursed land."

"We will not follow false gods," Drea said, then left the hall. Ramorra, Lon, and Kril rose and followed.

"You are banished," Loran yelled at their backs. "*Banished!*"

Outside, Drea looked at the other three, who look stunned. "Not a word," she said. "Not now, and not to anyone in the clan. We meet tonight. Then we talk."

Later, in her hut, Drea spoke only to Atyra. She would have told Nyvia what had occurred, but Nyvia stayed in her hut. Drea understood. Drea was now the clan's leader. Nyvia was showing her the same respect she showed Sera when power had passed to her.

Drea told Atyra of the banishment. She told Atyra to pepper her with questions and to find flaws in her logic. After an hour, she looked at Atyra. "There was nothing else I could do, was there?" she asked. "Be honest," she added.

"Not without abandoning what has driven our clan since the first Shamra," Atyra said. "We shall survive. Even thrive."

"But what of the Shamra? They're our people too."

"As you said, they follow false prophets. What *can* we do?" Atyra asked.

Drea shook her head. "We can't just abandon them." She told Atyra of an idea she had been considering. After another hour of give-and-take, Drea was satisfied. Her confidence had been restored. She smelled herself and smiled. After a hunt or battle, those of her clan gave off what others would consider an offensive stench. The odor was strong now. "I was going to bathe and rest. I need my strength for tonight's meeting. But I'll just nap now. I want the clan to smell my scent. It will comfort them."

They met at dusk. At Atyra's suggestion, Drea wore her bandana, as if she were preparing for a hunt or battle. Drea was too keyed up to sit once the meeting began. As she told of the banishment, she paced back and forth, making eye contact not only with the leaders of each family but everyone in the clan. When she finished, she asked if there were any comments or questions. "These are unusual times," she told them. "I lead, but on this matter, you are free to object without offending my authority. Our destiny shall be shaped by what we decide tonight."

There was silence.

"I will not force my will upon you. Any of you who want to leave with the others may do so. Are there any who wish to go?"

Again she was met by silence.

"Some *must* go," Drea said. For the first time, Drea sensed restlessness.

"We are united," Ramorra said. "I admit, when you became leader of the clan, I was opposed. But you not only possess valor. You have shown wisdom. We have no desire to split the clan."

"Thank you, Ramorra," Drea said, "but that's not what I meant. I have thought long and hard about this. Some *must* go to represent our clan wherever the Shamra settle. We are all Shamra. All that we are will be lost forever with those who leave unless some of our clan accompany them. It won't be easy. You will be viewed with suspicion. You must adhere to their new order," Drea said with disdain. "But in the privacy of your home, our clan shall remain alive. Two families must go. Are there any volunteers?"

Drea saw members of the clan looking at one another, then Nyvia raised her hand. Then more hands went up until all were raised.

"We will have a drawing of the sticks," Drea said. Lon and Bashra drew the short sticks. "The other clans leave in seven days," Drea said, looking at Lon and Bashra. "Tomorrow you will go to Loran. Beseech him to allow you to go with him. He'll agree. It will please him to no end to think our clan is divided. Three days from now, you will leave us and make camp with one of the other clans. Lon, your mate perished in the uprising. You must choose another, someone who desires to go on this quest with you."

Lon nodded.

"We will persevere," Drea said. "We will thrive." She longed to say more to rally them for the hard times that were sure to follow, but she sensed it was unnecessary. "This meeting is over."

♦♦♦♦♦♦♦♦♦♦♦

Three days later, Drea entered Atyra's hut. Several others who had been talking to Atyra quickly left without making eye contact with Drea.

"I don't know if I'll ever get used to that," Drea said with a sigh. "You're the only one who treats me as I was before I became the clan's leader. To the rest, I've somehow changed. It's infuriating."

"You're babbling," Atyra said.

Drea laughed. "Show me some respect," she said, and they both broke out in laughter.

"Tell me not to go," Atyra finally said.

Lon had asked Atyra to be his mate, and Atyra had agreed to go with him. The two, along with Bashra and her husband, were to leave that night and set up camp with the farming clan. Loran had been elated, Lon had told Drea, that there was dissension within the hunter's clan. As long as they agreed to abide by the new order, they were welcome to join in the exodus.

"Tell me not to go," Atyra said again. "I can't bear to think of us apart."

"I will be alone without you, is what you mean, though you're too much of a friend to utter the words. I can't deny it. I *don't* want you to go. I can't bear the thought. But I remembered what you told me when I became the clan's leader. I had to consider what was best for the clan. It will pain me to no end, but you must go."

"Lon can choose another," Atyra said.

"Not as strong as you." Drea met her friend's gaze. "Lon's strong, but he's no leader. When you get to your final destination, you will lead the hunter clan."

"There will be no hunter clan," Atyra reminded Drea. "We are to be one."

"It's up to you to keep the spirit of our clan alive, if only in your home. Lon and the others...I don't have faith in them. With the passage of time, we will become but a dim memory to them and their descendants. Our future rests with you."

"Have you had one of your dreams?" Atyra asked. Nyvia had told Drea of dreams where she saw the future. Nyvia's grandmother had the same power. It seemed to skip a generation. Sera had had no such dreams, but Drea and her sister had been born with the gift.

"Last night I dreamed that far into the future, in a land foreign to me, a female leads her people in a battle for survival. She wears a bandana similar to ours. So you see, the destiny of *all* Shamra is in your hands." Drea stood and brightened. "No more gloomy faces. I come bearing gifts." She unsheathed her sword and held it out to Atyra.

"I can't," Atyra said. "Dolor made it especially for you—"

"To do with as I please. It has served me well. Your journey will be perilous."

Still, Atyra hesitated.

"Look, Atyra, we have friends among the other clans. Not all agree with this new order the religious clan has devised. There are craftsmen forging weapons for us. Farmers have given us seeds. I shall have another metal sword."

"We're not allowed weapons," Atyra said.

"We're building a false bottom to the wagon you'll be taking."

Atyra laughed and took the sword.

"But there's more," Drea said. From a sack she carried, she took out a holy book with the original text. "This, too, you must hide. You must tell your children of our heritage. The problem is, with time, the stories become distorted. This is the legacy of our people. I have added pages at the end telling of Nyvia, my mother, and sister, of Monument Gate, and the uprising."

"I shall cherish it," Atyra said, holding the book tightly in her hands.

"One more gift," Drea said excitedly. She went outside and returned with a baby wrapped in a blanket.

"Mya, your niece. I don't understand," Atyra said.

"I told you of my dream. You and Lon will no doubt have children of your own. But someone with the blood of my family must go with you. Jana gave birth to her third child just a week before Monument Gate. No one from the other clans will suspect this isn't your child. Raise her as you would your own. When you think it's wise, let her know her heritage. That female I saw in my dream. She shares my family's bloodline."

Atyra took the child. "She has your bandana," Atyra said, seeing it wrapped loosely around the baby's neck.

"My gift to her," Drea said.

Atyra untied her bandana and gave it to Drea. "My gift to you. I shall sew a new one for myself. When you feel utterly alone, the bandana will remind you I'm by your side no matter how many miles separate us."

♦♦♦♦♦♦♦♦♦♦

On the seventh day, Drea and her clan stood watching a procession of wagons and carts heading east. Doubts gnawed at Drea. Had she done right by her clan or had she been too obstinate? She wished she could speak to Atyra. More than ever, she felt completely alone. She felt a presence by her side. She thought it was Nyvia, but it was Ramorra. Drea wiped her eyes so Ramorra wouldn't see her tears.

"I had my doubts about you, Drea," Ramorra said. "I was wrong. I pledge you eternal allegiance," she said, then paused. "And friendship, if you desire."

Drea looked at Ramorra. Maybe she wasn't alone after all. She put her arm around Ramorra's shoulder. "I'd like that," Drea said. "Very much."

Chapter 3

~ The Present ~

The forest was in sight. When Briana finished her story, Dara was silent for several moments, taking it all in. "So we *are* related," Dara said finally. "And this Drea saw into the future and saw *me*?"

Briana nodded. "A warrior named Dara, with a red bandana with black polka dots, who led her people to freedom."

"How could my mother know I was the Dara whom Drea had seen in her dreams? If the Gift of Sight skipped every other generation, there was no way she could have known."

"There are two possibilities," Briana said. "Your grandmother might have seen the future. She would have had the Gift of Sight." She then paused. "But I have another thought. The story of our clan wasn't written down, from what you told me."

Dara nodded. "It would have been too dangerous. Writing down the story you just told me, for instance, would have been forbidden by the clerics. The consequences of a written history of your...I mean *our* clan being discovered could have been dire." Now Dara paused. "But what's your point? The stories were passed down by word of mouth."

"That *is* my point. As children, we played a game. My brothers and sisters. We would whisper a secret and tell it to one of the others. It would be repeated to each of my brothers and sisters. The last would say it aloud. It was *never* the same message the first had told. Through the telling, it had been distorted."

"And what does that have to do with me?" Dara asked irritably.

"The story of our clan, our banishment, and the prophesy of Dara leading the resistance to an invasion was repeated countless times over a period of two hundred years. I can't begin to imagine how much it changed with each telling. I doubt after that long a period of time the name of the savior of your people was Dara. Maybe she had no name at all. Your mother named you Dara for reasons of her own, is what I'm saying, not knowing you were the reason the story of our clan was repeated for two hundred years."

Dara shrugged. "Since I can't remember much of what my mother told me, I can't argue with you. What you say makes sense. I always felt like an outsider. An outcast. I didn't look like other Shamra females, and I certainly didn't act submissive, as the clerics preached. It's now clear to me, seeing our clan, that I *was* different." Dara paused a moment. "Is there more? What happened to Drea? Why did we leave the valley for Stone Mountain?"

"Patience, Dara," Briana said and laughed. "You *are* from our family. Patience was never a virtue we practiced. But first, there's the hunt."

"I've no need to hunt," Dara said. "I want to know—"

SHAMRA DIVIDED

"But I do," Briana said. "It's a different story. One from the here and now. I'm after a particular creature. A pack of them actually. It began nine months ago…"

Chapter 4

~ The Present ~

Briana, her sister Cylia, and her brother Bly made their way through the woods on foot. While Briana was the youngest of Lyna's six children, she led the way. She was the best tracker in the clan and arguably the fiercest hunter.

With no prey on Stone Mountain, small groups of hunters would sneak out of one of the many caves at the base of the mountain and ride to a forest teeming with animals. It was a two-hour trip each way, and the results had always been rewarding. Lately, however, some Shamra had returned empty-handed.

"Some of the animals have fled the forest," Cylia said, after returning from a fruitless hunt. "We saw tracks leading *away* from the forest. We have nothing to show for our efforts."

A few days later, Malis returned with his group of hunters with even more disturbing news. "We found the remains of three boars. Just bones. Every bit of meat had been devoured. Tracks of six four-legged creatures led away from each boar."

A week later, Briana tracked them down. It wasn't difficult, as the creatures either weren't overly intelligent or had no fear of anything in the forest, thus had no need to cover their tracks. Briana thought it the latter. Since there was no opposition in the forest, they had grown careless. Having seen their kills, Briana would never underestimate her prey. From a tree she and Cylia climbed, they saw what they had to contend with. The creatures weren't particularly large. They were half the size of a Shamra. They walked on all fours. It was difficult to make out their faces because they were completely covered with fur. They looked like huge fur balls at first glance and not particularly dangerous.

Briana and Cylia watched as the pack of six cornered a boar. One brought it down, and then all six were upon it. Cylia gasped at their efficiency and brutality. The creatures tore at the boar with fangs far out of proportion to the size of their heads. Their claws were just as deadly. In fifteen minutes, the boar was reduced to a pile of bones, and the creatures were licking themselves and one another. The fur that covered lethal weapons was camouflage.

"Fangalas," Briana said.

"You've seen them before?" Cylia asked. She knew Briana had journeyed to forests that other Shamra hadn't.

"No, but their fangs are what make them deadly. Fangalas."

Cylia nodded.

Briana, with other members of her family, tracked the Fangalas several times. Unchallenged, the six Fangalas hunted together without attempting to conceal themselves. A cave served as their lair.

SHAMRA DIVIDED

Briana planned the attack. Cylia was deadly with a slingshot and Bly lethal with a bow and arrow. Briana liked to fight up close. She carried a spear, sword, and knife. They made their way to the den at dawn. The Fangalas wouldn't emerge for several hours, Briana knew. Cylia and Bly hid behind trees.

"Wait until all six are out of the cave," Briana instructed. "If any get back to the cave, pursuit will be difficult…possibly deadly."

The six emerged appearing lethargic. They stretched, not yet fully awake. Two of the smaller creatures groomed one another. Upwind, the Shamra wouldn't be detected.

Briana gave the signal, and the attack commenced. Cylia felled the largest with her slingshot. Bly brought down another with his bow and arrow. Briana rushed from behind a tree and impaled one of the creatures with her spear as it lunged at her. Bly wounded another with an arrow. Briana beheaded the fifth with one swipe of her sword. The last ran for the cave, but Briana blocked its path. The Fangala looked left and right, then growled. Cylia emerged from the trees to block its retreat. The creature bared its fangs and ran toward the cave Briana blocked. She held her ground. The Fangala, Briana could see, wasn't going to attack her but merely knock her down and make its escape. Briana stuck her knife in its soft underbelly as it attempted to bowl her over. It collapsed in a heap.

The three Shamra split up to make sure all the Fangala were dead. They would skin them. The fur would make warm coats and blankets. Each would take one of the claws for a necklace they wore that marked particularly satisfying kills. They would leave nothing behind. Bones could be used for cooking and eating utensils as well as weapons. The intestines would serve as strings for their bows.

Briana later blamed herself for her arrogance. She led the attack. She should have told Cylia and Bly to start with the Fangala farthest from the caves while she worked from the cave outward. As each skinned one of the predators, the Fangala closest to the woods, who had been hit by a rock from Cylia's slingshot, rose and dashed into the forest. It was the largest of the six and had probably been knocked unconscious. Seeing the rest of the pack slaughtered, it had feigned death until it could make its escape.

Briana tracked the Fangala for half a day, but the creature was clever, climbing rocks so it would leave no trail and crossing streams so Briana would lose its scent. When it became dark, Briana finally gave up. She had no desire to become its prey.

When she returned to the others, all that remained were pools of blood. Briana was given a bone that had been cooked over an open fire and saved for her. The rest of the meat would be brought back to Stone Mountain for the others.

Cylia and Bly were exuberant as they left the forest. It had been a glorious hunt. They congratulated Briana on her plan and themselves on its execution. They would have a wonderful story to tell that night.

Only Briana was silent. One had escaped, and she was to blame. She wouldn't excuse her carelessness. And she couldn't rid herself of the feeling she hadn't seen the last of her foe.

CHAPTER 5

"So we're after the elusive Fangala?" Dara asked.

"A pack," Briana said. "For eight months, there was no sign of the one that escaped. I tracked the creature, but it appeared to have left the forest. Animals returned. Our hunters prospered. Then, a month ago, our hunters noticed the forest had thinned again. Animals who had returned once again fled. The bones of a boar were discovered. Some tracks were found, but fewer than before."

"There were less of them," Dara said.

"No, they were being more crafty," Briana said.

"A new pack?" Dara asked.

Briana shrugged. "There are any number of possibilities. The Fangala that escaped may have been a female. And pregnant. The new pack could be her offspring. That would explain the months of inactivity. Or the Fangala who escaped left the forest to find another pack. Regardless, it's returned with a pack of five others. By the time we discovered them,

Cylia, Bly, and the rest of my brothers and sisters had been killed by the Galvan. I was wounded, too feverish and weak to hunt. A group of three tracked the Fangala to their new den. Two were from Dyann's family. One from Ramorra's.

"Not as good as you, if you're still after them," Dara said.

"They were careless," Briana said. "Maritza, from Ramorra's family, stood guard where the Fangala might flee when drawn out. Maritza wasn't a particularly good hunter. Her lack of vigilance led to her death. The other two hunters made their way to the den. They carried torches. They would smoke the creatures out, then kill them. Not a bad plan, actually. However, the Fangala knew they arrived. One of them circled behind Maritza and attacked her from the rear. Like I said, she wasn't being vigilant. She should have been aware of its approach. It ripped her stomach open, then fled. When the other two came to Maritza's aid, the Fangala in the cave escaped."

"The one that injured Maritza—?" Dara began.

"Was the one who had escaped our ambush. It ran with a slight limp. I saw that Fangala before."

"And Maritza?"

"She died a slow and painful death," Briana said. "She lingered for three days, but there was nothing that could be done for her. The Fangala, I believe, had no intention of killing her outright. It wanted her to suffer. Retaliation for the slaughter of the first pack. I blame myself."

"So what are we doing here?" Dara asked. "The two of us are going to take on a pack of six?"

"No. I'm going to destroy the pack myself," Briana said. "This is my burden."

"And die in the process?" Dara said.

"I'll take my chances," Briana said.

"Because you feel guilty about Maritza?" Dara said. "That makes no sense at all. You die for what? It won't bring Maritza back."

"I was responsible for the escape of the Fangala when we first had them cornered. So, yes, I'm responsible for Maritza's death," Briana said. "But it's more than that. I was a hunter and warrior, but because all of my brothers and sisters have been killed by the Galvan, I can no longer fight when they attack. Hunting is my only outlet. Think how you would feel if you had to stay in your homeland and rule. If you couldn't explore. It would be like a prison for you. That's just how I feel."

"The difference is, if you die, your family will no longer rule when your mother passes. That's selfish of you," Dara said.

"You could rule," Briana said.

"I told you I wouldn't…days ago," Dara said.

"Life is full of surprises," Briana said.

"I won't let you fight them alone," Dara said. She took out her sword and the knife made of Shriek scales. "We fight side by side or not at all."

"It's your choice," Briana said. "I won't force—"

"You've given me no other option, Briana, and you know it," Dara said. "You claim to have known me for five days. You know I'm no passive observer. Two against six. I don't like the odds, but you are determined to fight alone. I will not hide behind a tree and watch you perish, which is precisely why you brought me here. You knew I wouldn't abandon you."

They came to a clearing. The forest surrounded them on three sides. To their back was a wall of rock, too high for even a Fangala to leap from. With her knife, Briana cut into the palm of her hand and let blood drip to the ground. "We make our stand here," Briana said. "They will sniff us out. For now, we wait. If you wish, I will tell you the fate of Drea."

CHAPTER 6

~ THE WATERFALL ~

196 years ago

"I'm going hunting," Drea said as she passed Ramorra. "Alone."

"Seems like that's how you spend most of your time," Ramorra shouted at Drea's back. "Hunting. *And* alone."

Drea spun around, anger etched on her face, her eyes blazing red. "Do you have a problem with that?"

"You lead our clan," Ramorra said. "Yet you spend more time in the forest than in the village. *Alone* in the forest."

"There's precious little for me to do as far as leading," Drea said. "So I might as well hunt."

"I meant no disrespect," Ramorra said. "You've told me to speak freely…as your friend. As your advisor. If you'd rather I didn't—"

"Then talk," Drea interrupted. "But get to the heart of the matter."

"Fine. You don't go hunting," Ramorra said. "You seek danger. You hunt the most dangerous animals. You fight with a knife when it's a bow and arrow you should use. I've seen you take on a wild boar as big as you with only your sword. And you wait until the last second, as if you want to feel its tusk on your flesh. We need your strength as a leader, but it sometimes seems you'd almost welcome death. That's fine for you, but not for the clan."

"You've had your say," Drea said. "Satisfied?" Without waiting for an answer, Drea said sarcastically, "Blow the horn if we're invaded. I'm off."

Drea stomped into the forest without another word. She'd heard enough. She wasn't upset with Ramorra. She *was* angry because Ramorra was aware of her discontent. Drea was a hunter and a warrior. The boredom of the past four years was draining her life from within. She had no death wish, but, yes, she sought danger. And, yes, she intentionally put herself in harm's way.

She came to a stream and sat on a rock. She always came here alone. It was her place and hers alone. She'd sit as the water flowed past and reflect on her life and the choices she had made. She often thought of the water as her life, rapidly passing her by. At the age of nineteen, she didn't fear growing old. She led an ordinary life. She wanted to lead an extraordinary life, even if it meant premature death. She threw a stone into the stream and watched it sink. She was that stone. Going nowhere.

An apparition of Atyra rose from where the stone Drea had thrown landed. Drea had been without her closest friend for four years. Sending Atyra with the rest of the Shamra to find a new homeland had been necessary. Of all her choices, it had been the most important, yet it was the one she regretted most. Atyra, she now knew, was a soulmate, not a mere friend or someone to confide in. Without Atyra, she felt utterly alone and often inadequate.

The figure made its way toward Drea. This wasn't really Atyra, Drea knew. Drea had conjured her years ago, when loneliness threatened her sanity. She would talk to this spectral image who helped her accept the dreariness of her existence. Like the real Atyra, Drea's creation wouldn't let Drea wallow in self-pity.

"Are we pouting again?" Atyra asked, sitting next to Drea. The water on her skin reflected the sunlight, so she seemed to shimmer and glow. "Life for you has been good."

"Uneventful. Unsatisfying," Drea countered.

"You live in peace. You have a family."

"*Your* journey to a new homeland was filled with peril and adventure. How I envy you," Drea said.

"You took a husband. You have a child. You even named her after me," Atyra said.

"Yes, Anis," Drea said with a smile. "If it weren't for her…" she started, but let the thought hang. "But I didn't marry for love."

"Did I?" Atyra asked. "I agreed to marry Lon for our journey into the unknown. He was looking for someone with the strength to endure the dangers we'd face. There was no courtship. No romance."

"And love had nothing to do with my marriage," Drea said. "Pror was a fearless hunter, and he fought valiantly against the Kimra. The clan all looked upon our marriage with favor. He's been a good husband and father, but I haven't learned to love him. Nyvia said he would grow on me. She was wrong."

"You don't love your daughter?" Atyra asked.

"I don't have the makings of a mother," Drea answered, avoiding the question. "Yes, Anis is special. One day she'll lead the clan. She has a reckless streak like Nyvia, the spirit of Jana, and the wisdom of my mother."

"And nothing of you?" Atyra asked.

Drea shrugged. "My impatience," she said, and smiled weakly.

"So you do love her," Atyra said.

"She's almost four. A child. I see her potential. When she gets older, maybe we'll bond like Jana and I did with our mother."

"The words stick in your throat. Is it so difficult to admit?" Atyra asked.

"Yes, Atyra, I love my daughter," Drea said, feeling exasperated. "But I can't devote my life to her. I have needs motherhood won't satisfy. I loathe the life I lead now."

"Ramorra couldn't replace me as a friend?" Atyra asked.

"No one could replace you, Atyra," Drea said, aware she was crying. She shrugged. "Ramorra has been a friend, but I sometimes long for the Ramorra of old. I remember the Ramorra who plotted to take control of the clan. She has seen what the responsibilities of leadership have done to me and has no desire to rule. She is content with her lot, married with four children."

"So what *do* you want?" Atyra asked.

"If I can't have a soulmate like you, I almost wish for a rival. A worthy adversary. Someone to plot against me. Someone who poses a threat. Someone to relieve the tedium."

"An enemy to vanquish," Atyra said.

"But a worthy one," Drea added.

"You won't find one in the clan," Atyra said.

"So I remain miserable," Drea said, her eyes turning a dull gray of dejection and despondency.

"There are alternatives," Atyra said.

"What are you suggesting?" Drea asked.

"I've overstayed my welcome," Atyra said. She rose and walked into the water.

"What are my alternatives?" Drea shouted after her.

"The hunt," Atyra said. "Don't go back empty-handed. You never do."

Atyra disappeared beneath the water. Still, Drea felt less irritable. She had identified her discontent. No, that's not true, she admitted to herself. She had always known the cause of her dissatisfaction. She just had never uttered the words aloud. Now that it was out, she would mull it over in her mind. Understanding her unease, though, did nothing to end it. Feeling restless, she went out to hunt. She killed a small boar that put up little resistance. Her clan had killed the most dangerous animals in the forest. There was little to challenge her even here. She might have to put a stop to the hunts temporarily or else there soon would be no prey left.

Drea returned to the village, the boar over her shoulder. She saw a crowd gathered in a circle. Those nearest her parted as she drew near.

Kel and Tobin, Jana's sons, were wrestling. Kel, who was fifteen, was taller than most Shamra, but not particularly muscular. Tobin, only eleven, was husky and determined. The two often fought to a draw. Both were aware that one would someday lead the clan if Drea died or gave up power before Anis was old enough to rule.

"Enough," Drea said, throwing the boar on top of the two wrestlers. They looked up at her in surprise. The blood of the boar dripped onto both of them. Drea's clan settled arguments with their fists, though they seldom held a grudge. The wrestling today, though, seemed far more ferocious than usual. The two brothers seemed to want to harm one another. Competition was one thing, Drea knew, but what she saw could fester and grow into hatred. It could split Jana's family or cause blood to be spilled. Like her, the boys needed an outlet for their true nature.

And then it came to Drea. Atyra's words. *The hunt*. It *was* an alternative. Not a hunt in the depleted woods she had just left. No, Drea would organize a hunt to uncharted territories, where there would be worthy adversaries. It would be a great adventure. She and those she chose would be gone for a month, maybe two. Those who remained could protect themselves. While the clan appeared defenseless, they had spent months constructing obstacles for any enemy who might attack. Pits covered with roots and branches held deadly sticks that would impale any who fell onto one. Rocks from the mountain to the north would crush any enemy if the tree trunks that held them in place were dislodged. Lookouts were posted on the mountain. An enemy could be seen miles away. If a warning was sounded, one hundred warriors would burrow into shallow holes that had been dug. When the enemy was between holes, to the east and west the warriors would rise, and their foes would be cut down from the front and rear. All over the country, there were other traps and weapons for defense.

Yes, Drea thought, she could take a party on a grand hunt. Upon their return, she would lead another group, then yet another.

The next morning, Drea and twenty of her hunters set off. Kel and Tobin were among them. She kissed Anis on her forehead. "One day you shall accompany us on a wondrous hunt," she told her daughter. She tied the bandana Atyra had given her around her own head, covering her long white hair. Anis had a bandana of her own. Drea tied it around the child's head, then smiled. One day, she thought, my daughter and I will travel to the unknown together…and alone. It would be their special time. Drea got on her horse and led her party south.

Ramorra had insisted on joining them. Drea had looked at her oddly. She knew Ramorra had no great love for the hunt, nor did she desire to leave her children for such a long period of time. So why was Ramorra so adamant?

"To curb your excesses," Ramorra said. "To protect you from yourself."

Drea was in too good a mood to even think of putting Ramorra in her place.

Drea could feel the excitement and anticipation of the others as they rode, then made camp the first night. Our village—*our entire country*, Drea thought—has become a prison. But they had escaped, and the lure of the unknown thrilled each and every one of the hunters. In just one day, Drea could see the change in their eyes. They were now sky blue, where they had been gray before. And the eyes of those who had been somewhat content were an even deeper blue. Drea could also once again smell the pungent odor her clan gave off during battles and hunts. It was unpleasant to the other clans but sweet nectar to Drea and her people. Intoxicating. Invigorating. Contagious. It was as if they had awakened from a deep sleep. For the first time since her confrontation with Loran, she felt like a true leader of her clan.

Around the fire that first night and every night thereafter, the hunters told stories of the uprising against the Kimra. Those too young to have participated, like Kel and Tobin, listened in rapt fascination. Of those present, only Drea and one other had taken part in the Massacre at Monument Gate. Drea told of the bravery of her mother Sera and how she and her sister Jana had fought back to back as Kimra guards attacked from all sides. Drea saw the pride on Kel's and Tobin's faces as she recounted their mother Jana's valor. She downplayed her own heroics. She was not one to boast or sing her own praises.

Then Sylar took up the story, and all eyes were on Drea as Sylar told how Drea had saved countless lives with her heroism.

"You should have seen young Drea, just fifteen at the time, climbing Monument Gate. If she couldn't get to the other side to tell Ramorra's family to batter the gate down, every single Shamra within would perish. We fought, but had one eye on Drea. Guards from the palace fired arrows at her. One hit her in the leg," Sylar said, showing on her own leg where the arrow had struck Drea. "Unable to move, other arrows would have found their mark and struck her dead," Sylar continued. "Our hopes sagged. But Drea broke the arrow in half, then unstuck her leg from the other half that pinned her. Moments later, she scaled the gate and was on the other side."

A hushed silence had fallen among the others.

"We heard the pounding, but would the gate fall?" Sylar continued. "How long could we hold out?" Sylar clapped her hands together. "Some began to panic, but Atyra, Drea's lifelong friend, rallied those giving in to despair. Suddenly the gate crashed inward. Ramorra's family ushered those from the other clans to safety."

There was a cheer, and Drea looked away, embarrassed at the fuss being made over her.

"But Drea wasn't done," Sylar continued. "It was as if she were possessed by the spirit of her fallen mother. She hobbled in and made her way to Jana. Her bandana was wrapped around her leg and dripping blood, but she fought to get to her sister. Jana was badly injured, but it was only because of Drea that she was taken to safety. And still, Drea fought until every surviving member of the other clans had been led through the gate. She would have fought to the death," Sylar said, looking at Drea, "if Atyra hadn't forced her to retreat. Drea might say I exaggerate, but I saw it all with my own eyes. Fifteen, and she was willing to take on the entire Kimra on her own. A truly horrible day for the Shamra, but also our finest moment."

Again, cheers rose for Drea.

While the others slept that night, Drea relived the battle once more. Sylar hadn't exaggerated...at least not much. Long after Drea was dead, she knew the story would be retold. Over time, she knew, her exploits would be further embellished. She smiled. Even in death she would live forever. It was all a Shamra in her clan could wish for. Not a life after death, as the religious clan promised, but immortalized in stories handed down from generation to generation.

Drea sometimes wished her country would be invaded by some new enemy. Yes, many of her clan would fall. But far better to die in battle than of old age. Far better to taste your own blood and that of your enemy than to pass day after day toiling in fields farming, as so many in her clan had to do so there would be food for all.

Thinking of the battle, Drea also recalled her grandmother who had died six months after the uprising, just a week after Drea had given birth to Anis. Nyvia had been fifty-two, ancient by Shamra standards. Her body had long ago betrayed her. She couldn't walk without the use of two sticks. Her breathing was labored when she spoke. She couldn't speak more than a few sentences without being interrupted by a fit of coughing. In her day, Nyvia had ruled the hunter's clan with an iron first.

The day she died, Nyvia had summoned Drea to her hut. "The responsibilities of leading our clan robbed you of your youth," Nyvia wheezed. Her voice, which could put the fear of the prophets into those who drew her wrath, was now barely audible. "My time has come—"

"Nonsense, Grandmother," Drea interrupted. "You'll outlive me."

"Now you talk nonsense," Nyvia said, raising her voice before she was struck with another bout of coughing. "Listen to me, and don't utter a word. I'm still your elder."

Drea had smiled and held Nyvia's hand, which was cold to the touch. Inside, Drea knew her grandmother was dying.

"I've lived too long as it is. Seen my daughter and granddaughter die before me. I'm a warrior," she said proudly, then paused to catch her breath. "Yet I now need help just to get out of bed. It's no life for a member of our clan. Better to have died in battle or on a hunt."

"You'll live forever in my heart," Drea said when Nyvia stopped talking and closed her eyes as if sleeping. "Anis shall be told of your heroism. She'll tell her children, and they, their children."

"You've made your point," Nyvia said, surprising Drea. "Now hush. I robbed you of your youth, child," Nyvia said and waved at Drea before Drea could protest. "I can't regret something I had...no control over. You...you were our family's last...hope." She closed her eyes for a moment, then continued. "There's something I must tell you. I've seen you...far into the future." She paused again, breathing heavily.

Like Drea, Nyvia had the Gift of Sight. And, like Drea, Nyvia had seen Dara, a descendant from their family's bloodline who would one day lead the Shamra against oppressors in a faraway land.

"You mean you saw Dara," Drea said. Drea had seen Dara with a bandana similar to hers. Her grandmother must have gotten them confused.

"No. I saw you *both*...together. Here. Not in some faraway land. For all I've taken from you...this is my gift. I may...live in...stories of my exploits," Nyvia said, struggling to speak. "You shall live...again. Don't ask me how. I only know what...I've...seen. Now...let me rest," she said, and closed her eyes.

She still held Drea's hand. As Drea pulled away, Nyvia opened her eyes, which were now almost white. "Try to find joy...in...this...life," she said, then shut her eyes once more.

Drea had left her grandmother's hut. A question had struck her. How old had she appeared when Nyvia had seen her with Dara? She walked back into Nyvia's hut and found her grandmother dead.

This hunt reminded Drea of her grandmother's words. *Try to find joy in this life*. So far, she had failed miserably, but with this hunt, maybe there was still a chance.

Three days passed before Drea's hunters came to a forest. It was full of creatures Drea had never seen before. The hunt was on, and the clan ate well that night. Upon their return, they would hunt here again to bring food back to the others who had been left behind.

It was another week's ride before they would hunt again. This time the animals were even more fearsome than before. Drea's hunters prevailed, though they suffered their first casualty. That night, there were no prayers for their fallen comrade. Instead, Drea and others recounted stories of the departed so she would remain alive in the minds of the rest of the clan forever. Then, as was their tradition, the hunters celebrated into the night with food and song. Death, especially a heroic demise, was not to be feared or mourned.

Three days later, it was Kel and Tobin's turn to venture ahead of the rest to scout. All were given the honor. Kel and Tobin, who had quarreled so often in recent months, had healed any rift between them. The hunt, as Drea had hoped, had brought them together. Now they were riding furiously toward Drea and the others.

A wide-eyed Kel began babbling as soon as he and Tobin had stopped. "There's a country up ahead. Rich farmland. Small, stocky people. And Kimra."

"Kimra," Drea said, instantly alert and no longer amused by Kel's nonstop banter.

"Yes," Tobin added, just as excited. "We saw Kimra. These people are enslaved by the Kimra, just as we were."

Drea said nothing for several moments.

"What are you thinking?" Ramorra asked, and Drea looked at her with blue eyes full of excitement. "You're not thinking of—?"

"No, not yet," Drea said, reading Ramorra's thoughts. But she *was* thinking just what Ramorra feared. The hunt had been exhilarating. But combat with the Kimra again… In her wildest fantasies, Drea had never dreamed of anything so invigorating. She urged herself to remain calm. "We'll take a look," Drea said, unable to hide her smile.

They rode in silence for twenty minutes. Half a mile from where Kel and Tobin had seen the Kimra, Drea and her warriors dismounted. They would approach on foot. On a hill overlooking a lush valley, Drea saw dozens of farms and the people Kel and Tobin had spoke of. She saw Kimra. She looked at Ramorra and smiled.

"You're not—?"

"But I am, Ramorra," Drea interrupted. "First, though, I've got to speak to one of these people. I'm no fool, Ramorra. Twenty Shamra warriors are no match for the Kimra. We need those who are enslaved to rebel, just as our fellow Shamra did, if we are to prevail. I'm going to speak to one of the farmers."

"Let me go," Ramorra said.

"Would Nyvia or my mother let you go in their place when they led our clan?" Drea asked. Before Ramorra could answer, Drea continued. "Kel and Tobin must learn from my example. I expect nothing more of my warriors than I would of myself. I risk my safety to instill confidence in them. Only then can I ask them to risk their lives and be taken seriously."

Drea saw a solitary farmer working his land. She waited for the Kimra guard to appear again, then counted. She sent two warriors to track the Kimra's movements. The Kimra appeared twice more before Drea acted. Her warriors reported back that the Kimra patrolled several farms. He obviously had a set routine.

"I have thirty minutes to speak to the farmer," Drea said. She looked at Ramorra. "If the Kimra deviates from his routine, whistle three times in succession. I'll meet you in the trees," she said, pointing.

She summoned two of her best archers. "You shoot *only* if I'm seen. There will be no battle today." She looked at Ramorra. "Don't look so glum. I have no desire to be hunted and killed like the prey we hunt in the forest. I will be cautious."

"Today," Ramorra said, "but I can read your mind. I can smell your stench...and that of the others."

"We're warriors, Ramorra." She thought to say more, but those two words said it all.

Fields of wheat hid Drea as she made her way toward the lone farmer without being seen. She was within a few yards of him before he spotted her.

"I mean you no harm," Drea said, speaking the language of the Kimra. "I just want to talk to you."

"How do you speak the language of the Kimra?" the male asked, looking around as if expecting the Kimra to come charging at the two of them.

"My people were enslaved by the Kimra. What is your name and your tribe?" Drea asked.

"I am Deedle of the Weetok. We, too, are ruled by the Kimra. Did you escape?"

Deedle was short, round, and squat. A round head atop a round body atop short muscular legs. One of his eyes was green, the other blue. He kept licking his lips. Drea didn't know if this was because he was nervous or if the licking served some other purpose.

"I didn't escape. My name is Drea. My people are the Shamra. We defeated the Kimra. Killed them all."

Deedle's round eyes opened wide. "Your people are free?" he asked.

"Have been free for four years after twenty-five years of oppression by the Kimra," Drea said.

"The Kimra have ruled here for twenty-nine years," Deedle said.

"We can help you, if you want," Drea said. "Do you have a leader of a resistance group I can speak to?"

Deedle looked around, as if afraid of being overheard. He licked his lips several times before answering. "Bain leads a small group who fight the Kimra. Not actually fight them. He helps some of our people escape."

"Can I meet him?" Drea asked.

Deedle again looked around, as if fearful of being caught talking to this stranger. "At the wood's edge," Deedle said, turning so Drea could see where he meant. "Be there three hours after the sun sets. Bain may not come today. I may not even be able to speak to him right away without arousing suspicion."

"I will be there for three nights," Drea said. "It's important he be cautious."

"How many are you?" Deedle asked.

"I've got to go now before the Kimra returns," Drea said. "I'll answer all Bain's questions."

Before Deedle could reply, Drea began crawling away from the farmer. She had five minutes before the Kimra would return. Plenty of time.

The next night, waiting where Deedle had instructed, Drea saw a solitary figure approach.

"The creature with the bandana," the male said when Drea stood up. "I am Bain. Deedle forgot your name. He was shocked to see you and even more shaken by your words."

"I'm Drea of the Shamra," Drea said

"And you defeated the Kimra?" he asked, as if needing to hear the words himself.

Drea noticed that he, too, licked his lips with his tongue. "We led the attack. The rest of our people joined in the battle. The Kimra are not easily beaten, but we outnumbered them and fought them with the will of one."

"Many of your kind died," Bain said. It wasn't a question.

"That I can't deny," Drea said. "Freedom comes with a steep price."

"You say you will help us fight the Kimra. Why?" Bain asked.

"We're warriors." Again, Drea decided not to elaborate.

"You enjoy killing," Bain said.

Drea shook her head. "We were born and bred to fight when necessary. We take no joy in killing. But we find the battle exhilarating. We will help you, but your people must do their part," Drea said.

"We are farmers, not warriors," Bain said.

"You'd rather remain enslaved?" Drea asked. "Look, most of the Shamra who joined in our uprising were farmers and craftsmen. They were not trained fighters. Still, the smell of freedom is sweet. It's precious and overpowering. It numbs the fear. You outnumber the Kimra. With our help, you can conquer them."

"How many warriors do you command?" Bain asked.

"Not enough. We were on a hunt. I can send for more. We can be one hundred strong, all on horseback, and all with weapons. We can be ready in four weeks. Is that enough time for you to prepare your people?"

Bain nodded. "You will tell us what to do?" he asked.

"Yes, but first you must tell me about the Kimra. She peppered Bain with questions for twenty minutes until she was satisfied she had enough information to formulate a plan. "We will camp several days from here and post guards so we won't be seen. My warriors will be here every day, learning the lay of the land. Don't worry, we'll remain hidden," Drea said when she saw concern on Bain's face. "We will meet here once each week. Let me know of your progress. I'll have more questions. When the rest of my warriors arrive, we'll have a plan."

"You sound so confident," Baid said. "I wish I could share your enthusiasm."

"Just remember, we fought the Kimra. We defeated them. I don't underestimate the Kimra, but we know them well. These Kimra know nothing of my people. Our attack will come as a surprise. Remind your people what's at stake.

Freedom. For the first time in twenty-nine years, your people have it within their grasp."

The next four weeks were among the happiest in Drea's life. Kel and Tobin were sent back to return with eighty-one reinforcements. Drea sent some of her warriors back to the forest they had last visited to hunt for food. Daily, her warriors stayed hidden but observed the movements of the Kimra. And each week, Drea met with Bain. The Weetok were fearful of reprisal, but they craved freedom, Bain told Drea. They would rise up when Drea's warriors struck. They would fight knowing some, even many, would die. They wouldn't let the Shamra down.

At one of their meetings, Bain told Drea, "My people have one fear." He seemed to be choosing his words carefully. "Actually, many fears," Bain said, shrugged, and licked his lips. "But one in particular. If we rid ourselves of the Kimra, some think your people will replace them. They want to know if we are trading masters we've come to know for others who might be far worse? I don't meant to offend—"

"It's a fair question," Drea said, not letting Bain apologize. "We are hunters and warriors. It's not in our nature to have others toil for us. You have come to know me. Do your instincts say I'm deceiving you? What does your heart tell you about our intentions?"

"I trust you," Bain said. "But I've met you. The others are more suspicious."

"Then you must convince them," Drea said. "My mother was the leader of our clan when we attacked the Kimra. She and my older sister perished in the first attack. My grandmother was too old to rule. If our family was to lead our clan, she said it was up to me. I was fifteen. Old enough to fight, but young to command my clan. I did what had to be done. I led. It's what you must do, Bain. Rally your people. Convince them we mean them no harm. You and I will meet once more before the attack. If your people desire we leave,

SHAMRA DIVIDED

we will abide by their will. We are not the Kimra. What more can I say?"

Bain was able to convince the Weetok the Shamra's intentions were honorable. Kel and Tobin returned with warriors excited at the prospect of battle. Drea held a counsel with four warriors who had led the uprising after the Massacre at Monument Gate. Drea's decisions would be final, but she knew to lean on the wisdom of others. If they helped plan the assault, she also knew they would be even more committed to its success. In this regard, she was different from her mother. Sera had planned the attack on Monument Gate with no other counsel. It had led to her death.

Just as in the Shamra's country, the majority of Kimra had moved to a village and lived in a palace built for them by the Weetok. Drea's plan called for the village to be isolated before being attacked. Her warriors and the Weetok would first attack those who lived and patrolled the countryside. Half of her warriors, along with the Weetok, would keep the Kimra pinned within the village. When the countryside was clear of all Kimra, the Shamra and Weetok would advance on the village.

The day of battle was overcast, but Drea's spirits couldn't have been brighter. Ramorra came to get her. Ramorra had surprised Drea over the past four weeks. She would never be the most valiant warrior, Drea knew, but her organizational skills were second to none. Drea dreamed up battle scenarios. Ramorra made them a reality. She knew the strength and weakness of every warrior. She knew the best riders, the best archers, and the best hand-to-hand fighters. Drea's plan called for five groups of warriors. Drea chose the leaders for each. Ramorra suggested who should be included in each group. Curious over the choice of a warrior to accompany her, Drea asked Ramorra to explain.

"Dyann is headstrong," Ramorra said. "She's never been in battle. She will do what she thinks is best, though it may not be prudent. However, she worships you. She will follow your orders without question. And she would rather die a thousand deaths than disappoint you."

Drea asked Ramorra about several other choices she had suggested. She was amazed how familiar Ramorra was with each of the warriors.

"I underestimated you, Ramorra," Drea said, "and for that I apologize. A battle can't be won with simply a plan and valiant fighters. You have already proven your worth before the fight has begun. I am proud to call you my friend and comrade. When this is over and we're home, you must go on a hunt with me. Just the two of us. I've had no one to confide in since Atyra left. I've tried to make sense of my life on my own. I've been pigheaded and foolish. Maybe it's time I listened to someone else. I can't think of anyone I've learned to respect more since we've come to this land than you."

"I'd be honored," Ramorra said, blushing, her eyes turning purple. She seemed not to know how to respond. "After the battle is won," she said, then quickly left to make sure all was ready.

Drea gathered her warriors to rally them. The air was pungent from the odor of her troops. Some had waited for a day such as this all their lives. They had been bred to be hunters and warriors. She carried her bandana in her hand. "Some of us were lucky enough to have fought the Kimra four years ago. We didn't fear death then. We don't now. What the past four years has taught us is death in battle is far more desirable than the boredom of farming the fields of our homeland."

She paused when the warriors laughed and nodded. "For those who roll your eyes at our stories because you were too young to fight, you are in for the greatest experience of your life this day. Savor every moment. You may never see another battle in your lifetime. For those of us who fall today, there can be no greater honor. Your exploits will be passed down for generations."

SHAMRA DIVIDED

Only now did Drea tie her bandana around her head. She raised her sword. "For our clan. For those who fight today and those who have passed over and look upon us with pride."

Drea got on her horse and led her group of twenty warriors. As had her mother, Sera, Drea would lead a frontal assault. She refused to remain tucked away, watching her plan unfold while her clan was fighting for their lives. For her, as with Nyvia, Sera, and Jana, the battle itself was life-sustaining.

Archers on the hillside would add support. Two other groups would isolate the village with the aid of the Weetok. One group, led by Sylar, would be held in reserve. Sylar would deploy her troops as events dictated. Sylar's instincts were second to none. Drea trusted her judgment completely.

Drea's band of fighters met no resistance as they entered the Weetok homeland. They rode across open fields, toward a cluster of farms, where they would encounter a dozen Kimra, Bain had told her. Outside the first farm, the Weetok would join them. As they rode, Kel's horse stumbled, and he fell to the ground. Then a second and a third horse became entangled, and their riders were thrown. Drea reined her horse and raised her arm to signal the others to stop. On the ground, Drea saw a rope of vines had been laid to slow Drea's attack.

As Drea ordered her warriors to dismount, several dozen Kimra rose from holes that must have been dug the night before. There was not a Weetok to be seen. The Kimra had been warned, Drea knew. The element of surprise so pivotal to their success was gone. The Kimra had prepared. It was Drea's troops who had ridden into an ambush. Drea wondered if Bain had betrayed her. As the Kimra advanced on Drea's group, a horn sounded. Drea could see in the distance Kimra on horseback pouring from the village. One group of at least fifty veered to the left to meet Shamra soldiers emerging from the woods to isolate the village. Her warriors would be too late, and no Weetok would join them. Another group of Kimra swerved to the right, where Drea's other troops were advancing on the village. A last body of soldiers of at least one hundred Kimra marched toward Drea and her small band.

As the mass of soldiers drew closer, Drea saw three horsemen holding poles aloft, as if they were battle flags. Drea's heart sank. The poles bore no flags, but the heads of Bain and two others. Drew knew no Weetok would join the battle.

Outnumbered, Drea knew her warriors could be in for a rout. Still, she rallied her forces. If they could hold their own, maybe the Weetok would regain their courage. Shamra who had never fought had risen as one after the Massacre at Monument Gate. The slaughter of so many females from all the clans had finally awakened the anger most Shamra felt.

Still, Drea had planned for the possibility of failure. Monument Gate had taught her that lesson. There would be no slaughter of her warriors on this day. Nor would her warriors surrender to be enslaved. If the battle was lost, each group had instructions to retreat. Those Drea commanded would head for the forest, where the Kimra seldom ventured.

Drea led her soldiers on foot against the first wave of Kimra who had risen from the ground. If they could be defeated, the larger group that approached on horseback might not be so bold. If Drea could hold her ground, Sylar would provide reinforcements. Her archers would come down the hills and be more effective. She thought the battle was far from lost.

Drea's warriors fought valiantly, but the Kimra kept retreating, waiting for support. Before they could all be killed, the mass of Kimra from the village were upon Drea and her warriors. The arrows from the advancing column of Kimra archers found their marks. Drea saw five from her group fall as arrows rained upon them. Those who remained inflicted heavy casualties on the first group of Kimra. But it was too little, too late. A second barrage of arrows left her with just seven warriors. Drea herself had been hit in the shoulder, making it difficult to wield her sword. Kel, with arrows protruding from both his legs, fought on one knee.

The battle lost, Drea sounded the retreat. She dragged Kel toward the woods. She looked back and saw Dyann still fighting Kimra, which gave Drea precious moments to make her escape. Almost at the forest, she felt two arrows whip by her head. A third hit her in the back. She stumbled. Kel fell with her. She got up, and she and Kel made it to the trees. She looked back and saw the Kimra advancing. Would they follow? So far, nothing had gone as planned. Just because they hadn't entered the woods before didn't mean they'd be too afraid to follow Drea into the forest now.

"Can you make it on your own?" Drea asked Kel. "It's best if we split up."

Before Kel could answer, Drea heard the sound of more arrows. These, though, came from the forest and were not aimed at her. Sylar and two others rushed toward them. Sylar told the two with her to carry Kel to safety while she helped Dara into the woods.

"We saw it was hopeless," Sylar said. Though Sylar was disheartened, Drea could still hear the excitement in her voice. "If we had come to your aid, we would have been cut down."

Drea nodded. She understood. She agreed.

"Instead, we split into groups to cover your retreat," Sylar continued. "We've spent the past month becoming familiar with this forest. We know it better than the Kimra do. Hit-and-run," Sylar said, smiling. "In the forest, we can pick the Kimra off one by one. They'll flee."

"I'll stay and fight with you," Drea said.

Sylar shook her head. "You're of no use to us, Drea." She gave Drea her crossbow. "Fire an arrow," she said.

Drea couldn't. The arrow that was lodged in her shoulder made her arm useless. "I can still fight with my sword," Drea said.

"No more hand-to-hand combat today," Sylar said. "It's time for us to inflict damage from behind trees, without being seen, so the Kimra won't follow. We hit-and-run so the Kimra have to be cautious and take their time. Then we vanish. That was your plan. Then we regroup. I'm only following your orders."

Drea nodded. She longed to continue the fight. It hadn't been much of a battle. With the Kimra alerted and no Weetok rising to fight with them, her attack had been doomed. If she hadn't been wounded, she would have remained with Sylar's archers. Leaders didn't flee leaving others to sacrifice their lives for them. But wounded, Drea would have been a hindrance and a distraction. Others from her clan would give their lives to protect her. Just as at Monument Gate, there was a time to fight and a time to flee.

"You know where to go," Sylar said. "We'll join you when we can. When the sun sets, we'll rejoin the others." Drea saw Sylar look at her and smile. "It's been a glorious battle, Drea. We did our part. You said all along this was the Weetok's fight. We could help, but we couldn't defeat the Kimra alone. You and your warriors were magnificent. We have nothing to be ashamed of. Now go before I order my archers to lead you away."

Drea smiled at her compatriot. "Take care, Sylar," Drea said and fled.

Bleeding from her wounds, Drea became lightheaded. She thought she was heading in the right direction, but nothing looked familiar. She came to a clearing, then to a cliff with a river flowing below. She knew she was hopelessly lost. Across a ravine, she saw a waterfall. It seemed to beckon to her. She could almost hear voices imploring her to enter. She heard the voices of Nyvia, of her mother, of Jana, and of countless others.

SHAMRA DIVIDED

She stepped off the cliff onto a large rock that appeared out of nowhere. She took another step and found herself on another stone that was big enough for her to stand on. She kept walking. As she approached the waterfall, she looked back. A bridge of stones had formed from nowhere. Water cascaded around Drea, but she wasn't wet. She walked through the waterfall into…

♦♦♦♦♦♦♦♦♦♦

…Drea found herself standing in a forest, surrounded on all sides by the waterfall. Water from the falls crashed around her, yet neither she nor the forest was wet. This forest seemed somehow different from the one she had just left. A Shamra child, just a few years older than Anis, stood at a crossroads of three paths. She held a wormlike creature in her palm. She was lost. She said something to the creature. Tyler, she called it. Then, to Drea's surprise, the creature answered her. The child wore a bandana like the one Drea wore, except it was red with black polka dots, whereas hers was yellow with black polka dots, given to her by Atyra before she had left. The child then put the small creature into her stomach pouch. All Shamra had an extra layer of skin covering their stomach. Drea kept her bandana in her stomach pouch when she wasn't wearing it. Drea recognized the child.

"Dara," Drea said aloud.

Dara didn't respond. She didn't seem to hear Drea. The child ventured onto one of the paths. It was like when Drea had one of her visions of the future. She could see and hear those speaking, but she couldn't interact with them. Had she fallen asleep? Was she dreaming? Drea had the sense Dara was in no danger.

Voices called to Drea again, and she walked through the waterfall. She found herself in the same forest. Actually, it was less a forest and more a swamp. This time she saw two figures. Both wore bandanas. Dara thought it was her and Atyra. No, one was Dara, she could see. Dara was a few years older. Drea had no idea whom the other female was. Dara stepped into a plant, and it swallowed her whole.

Drea screamed. She reached out, and her hand went through the plant. She was watching Dara die, and she was helpless to do anything. Suddenly, there was a piercing scream. The plant unfolded, and Dara walked out, a smile on her face. A knife in her hand dripped with green blood. Dara had known what she was doing, Drea now understood. Still, it had given Drea a scare.

Drea walked through the waterfall a third time. Part of her wanted to get out. She had to meet her warriors who had survived the failed attack. Another part of her wanted to wander through this endless maze of the future, which all seemed to center around Dara. She knew Dara was a descendant of Mya, Jana's daughter, who had accompanied Atyra when the Shamra had fled to a new homeland.

This time Drea stepped into a forest. It wasn't a swamp, and it looked nothing like where she had been before. There was Dara with her bandana, in a cage, feeding a worm to a giant bird-like creature. This Dara had aged several years, though she was still a few years younger than Drea. It appeared Dara had befriended this creature, who could have torn Dara to shreds. Again, Drea sensed no danger.

Drea herself felt totally lost. She had no idea where she had entered the waterfall. She wondered if she would wander through scenes of Dara's life for eternity. Drea was enjoying this little tour, but not being able to interact was frustrating. She had no desire to just watch scenes unfold. What if Dara was in danger and Drea could help her? And Drea still felt the urge to return to her people. They needed her. Yes, battle had been energizing, as Sylar had said. But many of her warriors had perished. Those remaining needed her strength now more than ever.

Unseen voices interrupted Drea's thoughts. She went toward them and stepped through the waterfall once again. She was back in her homeland, in the mountains, yet she knew this was still the future. Looking down, Drea saw fertile fields. On the mountain, she saw a number of Shamra. They looked like the ragtag remains of an army. In their midst, she saw Dara, maybe a year or two older than when she had been with the bird-like creature. Dara was speaking with another female about her age. Dara called her Briana. Drea felt as if somehow she knew this Briana. But how could that be? It was all so confusing. And Dara was no longer with her people, but in the abandoned Shamra homeland. How did she get here? And why was she here? She remembered the words Nyvia spoke the day she had died. Nyvia said she'd seen Dara and Drea, but she had been mistaken. She had seen Dara and Briana. And their meeting, Drea knew instinctively, would determine the fate of her clan…close to two hundred years into the future.

Suddenly Nyvia was standing beside her, watching Dara and Briana talk. "You were called, child," Nyvia said. "Not just once, but many times."

"What do you mean, I was called?" Drea asked.

"Summoned in times of need," Nyvia said.

"Why me?" Drea asked.

"Memories fade, child," Nyvia said. "I am long forgotten. Your mother and Jana, all dim memories. All but you."

"But why me?" Drea asked again.

"Because you led such an extraordinary life. Stories of your valor and sacrifice have kept your memory alive. When nothing but despair is in the air, it is you they remember. They persevere because of the example you set. They summon you, and you appear."

"How?" Drea asked. She had so many questions.

"Patience, child," Nyvia said. "You'll learn with time. Now let an old lady rest." Nyvia seemed about to disappear, then was back again. "It's time for you to return to your time," she said. She pointed to a spot in the waterfall, then was gone.

Drea walked through the waterfall. She saw Ramorra and several other warriors standing over a body. The bridge of stones was gone. Drea called to her comrades, but the raging waterfall must have swallowed her words. She began to call out again, and Ramorra bent down. Lying face down was a body, its shirt covered in blood, an arrow sticking out of its back. Drea felt a chill run through her when she saw the bandana on the head of the fallen warrior. Ramorra pulled the arrow from the warrior's back. She turned her over and cradled her in her arms. It was Drea that Ramorra held. Drea knew she had taken an arrow in the back, but it was her shoulder wound that had given her the most pain. She must have collapsed and bled to death.

Drea stood at the waterfall as others from her clan arrived. Sylar told the others of Drea's heroics at Monument Gate. Ramorra recounted Drea's confrontation with Loran of the religious clan. Kel, leaning on Dyann's shoulder, shared how Drea had risked her life to carry him to safety.

As they spoke, Drea heard Nyvia's voice in her head. "There is no death for those who have lived extraordinary lives."

"Do I have a choice?" Drea asked aloud. "Our people need my leadership."

Drea again heard the voice of Nyvia in her head. "They will survive without you. But, yes, you can cross the river and return to your body. You will be badly wounded, but alive. You might live to be as old as I," her grandmother said.

"But would my life be extraordinary, or would I loathe growing old as you did?" Drea asked. "Would I be summoned or forgotten?"

SHAMRA DIVIDED

"There are many futures, child," Nyvia said. "You have a decision to make now. Whatever your decision, there are consequences. Choose well, Drea."

Drea had so many more questions for her grandmother, but she sensed Nyvia was gone. Cross the river and live. Rally her people. Be there for Anis. Or enter the waterfall to the unknown. She'd been given a peek at what was in store if she chose to enter the waterfall.

Drea turned and walked back into the waterfall.

Chapter 7

~ The Present ~

Dara shifted uneasily where she had been sitting after Briana told her of Drea's fate.

"Something is bothering you," Briana said. "Out with it."

"I can understand how our ancestors knew of the ambush by the Kimra," Dara said hesitantly. She didn't want to offend Briana, whom she'd only known for a few hours. "But how would they know Drea chose to pass from this life to another? What you refer to as fact seems to me to be...I don't know...legend, or folklore, I guess."

Briana smiled. "A hole in my logic, possibly, except that Drea appeared to us—"

"In dreams," Dara said with disdain.

"Not just in dreams," Briana said patiently. "She was summoned, just as I told you. When things were bleakest for our clan, Drea was summoned and appeared. That's how we knew details about your life almost two hundred years before they occurred. Not just that you were a freedom fighter, but the other incidents from your life, as well. Did they occur?"

Dara nodded. What could she say? It seemed impossible.

"When Drea appeared, she told our ancestors she chose to pass from this existence to another. That's why we no longer believe in the prophets. A scared people needed to believe they would be saved by divine intervention. Our people had been enslaved three times. Each time, belief in the prophets grew stronger."

"Drea isn't a prophet?" Dara asked.

"Hardly. She said so herself," Briana said. "When Drea was summoned, our people wanted to elevate her to the status of a prophet. She would have none of it. According to Drea, our people don't die. They only pass from one existence to another. Any Shamra could be summoned, but Drea lived such an extraordinary life, her exploits were passed down generation to generation. In times of crisis, it's only natural it's she, above all others, that they feel can offer solutions to their problems."

Dara again fell silent. Briana's revelations were difficult to accept. Dara had never believed in the prophets as the clerics in her land described them, but she never denied their existence in some form. Pilla had helped her numerous times. If Pilla wasn't a prophet or messenger of the prophets, why was she by Dara's side at times of peril? Had she summoned Pilla without even being aware of doing so? It was a lot to digest. Now she could understand how many of her people in her homeland had trouble abandoning their long-held beliefs. She felt a bit of a fool for ridiculing them for holding on to what had been proven untrue. She was in the same position now. Yet how could she deny what Briana told her? Briana clearly knew of incidents in Dara's life that Drea had seen almost two hundred years before they occurred.

Before Dara could voice her concerns, Briana tensed. "I smell their scent. I feel their presence. They are close, assessing whether this is a trap or two foolish Shamra to be devoured."

"You really want to go through with this?" Dara asked, knowing the answer. There was a pungent smell from Briana's body that told Dara her friend was excited. She relished the encounter that awaited. Dara recalled that others in the resistance in her homeland commented—behind her back and quietly—how Dara had given off a rancid odor before an attack on the Shrieks. The others didn't. It was another bond Dara shared with *her* clan and not the Shamra who had banished her people.

Briana looked ahead. "No turning back now," she said, her eyes fixed on something.

Dara saw three of the creatures emerge from the woods. Then two more appeared, one blocking the escape to the left, the other to the right. They were as Briana had described. Fur balls. Only by looking carefully could Dara see their talon-like claws. And only as they began to growl in anticipation did she see their fangs. Behind the first five, a sixth appeared. It was somewhat larger than the others and walked with a limp.

Dara saw Briana put something to her lips, but her attention was drawn back to the Fangalas as the first five charged all at once, as if on cue.

A high-pitched whistle pierced the air. Dara quickly glanced at Briana. She had put a whistle to her lips. But why? The Fangalas continued to move forward, but they appeared disoriented. Their growls turned to howls of pain. Two flung themselves at Briana but seemed distracted. Briana's spear was sharpened at both ends. She impaled one of the Fangalas with one end of the spear, then swung the other end at the second creature, gutting its soft underbelly.

A third Fangala made a half-hearted attack on Dara. She cut off its head with her sword.

Briana now went on the offensive, and Dara followed her cue. Briana used her sword and felled the fourth. Dara sheathed her sword and attacked the fifth with her knife made of sharpened Shriek scales. The Fangala swiped Dara awkwardly with its paw. Dara sliced off its foot with her razor-sharp weapon, then stuck the blade of her knife into the creature's skull.

Now there was only one remaining. It was the largest and had held back as the others were butchered. It growled in pain at the sound of the whistle, just as the others had, and even took a few steps back, as if to retreat. Then Briana stopped blowing the whistle. She threw it aside and held out her arms, as if inviting the Fangala to attack. The Fangala nodded as if the two were communicating. Briana stepped back and retrieved her sword.

"This one's mine," Briana said. "One on one."

Before Dara could protest, the Fangala charged and lunged at Briana, its fangs bared. It didn't move awkwardly like the others. Briana tried to strike it with her spear, but the Fangala batted it away with its powerful paw. Briana fell, and the Fangala was on top of her, its fangs going for her neck. With one hand, Briana grabbed the hair that surrounded the Fangala's head. With the other, she produced a knife and slit the throat of the creature. It died on top of Briana, its blood splattering her face and clothing. Briana smiled and licked the blood from her face.

"We won't make the same mistake again," Briana said. She pushed the Fangala off her and rose.

"You're bleeding," Dara said in alarm, seeing a deep gash on the side of Briana's neck.

"The Fangala's blood," Briana said.

"No," Dara said, gently touching Briana's wound.

Briana grimaced. "I felt nothing. I deflected its blow." Then she smiled. "It left its mark on me. A fitting and lasting reminder."

"Let me cover your wound," Dara said.

"Later. We're not done yet," Briana answered. With her sword, she sliced open the belly of the Fangala who had wounded her. Five unborn Fangala spilled from its midsection to the ground. Dara could see them move. Alive, she thought. Briana stabbed each with her spear. "Start with the one closest to the forest. Make sure they're dead. Then we skin all but this one," she said, pointing to the pregnant female. We bring the meat for the clan, as well as the claws and fangs."

"And that one?" Dara asked, looking at the pregnant female.

"She's the one I allowed to escape nine months ago. She killed Maritza. We return with her to the clan. We'll bury her next to Maritza."

Dara looked at Briana oddly.

"She was a worthy adversary. As cunning as a Shamra warrior. A leader of her pack…her children. This one, we treat with respect. We cook it in the presence of the clan. Everyone eats a part of it, ceremoniously consuming its courage, ferocity, and guile, making it a part of them. Then we bury the remains next to Maritza."

Dara shook her head. "Your eyes are no longer the vibrant blue they were during the battle. You'll miss stalking her and matching wits with her. It's back to hunting boar."

Briana sighed but didn't challenge what Dara said. Briana poked at one of the unborn Fangala with her spear. "Speaking of children, do you want to know of Mya, whom you are descended from? It will pass the time as we skin the Fangala."

Dara nodded. As much as she'd been intrigued by Drea, she had wondered if Briana had stories of the Shamra that ventured to her homeland. Was Mya as heroic as Drea? What challenges had she faced?

"Start your story while I dress your wound," Dara said. When she saw Briana begin to protest, Dara continued, "Some hero you'll be if you die of an infection."

Briana laughed. "Make sure all the Fangalas are dead. Then do with me as you wish."

CHAPTER 8

~ Survivor ~

200 years in the past

Atyra was sitting under the shade of a tree, reading the holy book of the New Order, when she spotted Loran approaching. The clerics had given them the name: the New Order of the Shamra, or New Order for short, since leaving their homeland. Atyra thought it pompous but held her tongue. Loran held a toddler by the scruff of her collar. The child's feet were kicking the air as if she were in a race with her captor. Mya wasn't crying, but Atyra could see the look of defiance on her face. The bandana around Mya's head had slipped and was covering her eyes. It was all Atyra could do to keep from laughing. Mya was in trouble, which meant Atyra was to blame, yet again. This was not the time for Atyra to be laughing, as Loran possessed no sense of humor.

Loran deposited Mya at Atyra's feet. He was none too gentle about it. Still, Atyra remained silent. She put the holy book down on the ground and stood. Loran looked at her with disapproval.

"One *never* puts the holy book on the ground," Loran said, as if scolding a child. "It disrespects the words of the prophets. It shows your lack…"

Atyra wasn't listening. If Loran wasn't grouchy, he was cranky or ornery or ill-tempered. He was also long-winded and prone to lengthy lectures, as if he liked the sound of his voice. Atyra had long ago learned to tune the cleric out. She picked up the holy book and wiped its cover with the sleeve of her shirt. Still, Loran prattled on about Atyra's many shortcomings. Loran was head of the religious clan of the Shamra. Actually, there was no longer a religious clan under the New Order. Or a farmer's clan. Or a craftsman's clan. And Atyra's hunter's clan had been banished before the Shamra had begun their journey to find a new homeland.

Shamra were now *one*, governed by rules of the New Order, which had been written by the religious clan but agreed upon by all. By all, that is, except for her hunter's clan. Rejection of the New Order and rewritten holy book had resulted in Atyra's clan being exiled. The hunter's clan remained in the old Shamra homeland while Loran led one thousand Shamra to find a new country to settle. Atyra's family and one other family from her clan had been allowed to accompany the Shamra. They had agreed to abide by the New Order and turn their backs on their disgraced clan.

Atyra looked down at Mya. She had picked up an insect that had crawled by her. Whatever she had been caught doing hadn't seemed to upset her. Atyra fought the urge to yawn. She knew the only way to keep Loran from spouting gibberish for the next fifteen minutes was to ask him a question.

"What has my daughter done now?" Atyra asked.

SHAMRA DIVIDED

Loran seemed to have momentarily forgotten about Mya, as Atyra's offense seemed to preoccupy his mind. A little mind, Atyra thought. Loran was narrow-minded, close-minded, and intent on having his own way as well as the last word. Like all the priests, and unlike most Shamra, Loran's face was chalky and smooth, while Atyra's was flesh-toned and weather-beaten from working out of doors. Loran's eyes were gray, while, even on this arduous journey, most Shamra's eyes were varying shades of blue. This journey had been exhilarating for Atyra. While the natural color of the hunter's clan's eyes was brown, her eyes had been a rich blue until Loran's approach. Now they were a dull gray, knowing she would draw the wrath of Loran. Unlike the other Shamra, the priests lived a solitary existence and didn't look like the typical Shamra. Loran's eyes were often gray, like the other clerics'. Atyra wondered if the priest enjoyed being miserable. Only when angry, as Loran was now, did they flare red in anger or fury, or orange in irritation or frustration. And while the Shamra as a whole had long white hair, the clerics were bald.

Loran now looked at Mya with distaste. At three-and-a-half months, Mya couldn't yet talk, but like most Shamra children, she could walk and run. Mya, Atyra knew, could do much more. Mya seemed to sense she was again the focus of attention. She closed her fist around the insect, careful not to crush it, Atyra noted.

Loran glowered at Mya before he spoke. Atyra picked Mya up, adjusted her daughter's bandana, and held her tight.

"Your daughter climbed a tree," Loran said, pointing to a grove of trees. "She tossed fruit to the other children. She could have injured one of them."

Atyra noted Loran said nothing about the possibility Mya could have fallen and hurt herself. Not that she would, Atyra knew. Mya had been fascinated with the trees since the

Shamra had entered this land. Atyra had climbed a tree to get fruit for Mya. She had to go deep into the forest, not the nearby grove, so she wouldn't be seen by the others. It was forbidden for Shamra females to climb trees, one of the rules of the New Order. It seemed new rules were dictated every time a female did something that displeased the priests. Soon Mya was attempting to climb trees herself. Atyra always watched her. Twice Mya had fallen into Atyra's arms. The third time she had scaled a small tree and rewarded Atyra with a smile. Mya seemed to be able to sense when climbing any higher might pose a danger to herself. Over the next three days, Mya had become adept at climbing trees. Atyra no longer feared Mya would fall.

"She's a disobedient child," Loran continued. "Not at all like other children. She sets a bad example for all. None her age should be climbing trees. Females most of all. She's not too young to learn respect," Loran finished.

"You mean that I should take a switch to her?" Atyra asked.

"If that's what it takes for her to follow rules. And I don't approve of that scarf she wears around her head," Loran added.

Atyra wore one just like her daughter's. It was a symbol of independence. Actually, it was much more, but Atyra couldn't think of Drea now.

"Is it forbidden to wear a bandana?" Atyra asked, wondering if a *new* rule had been written just for her and Mya. She held up the holy book in one hand, holding Mya with the other. "I study the writing of the priests—"

"The words of the prophets," Loran corrected her.

Atyra again held her tongue. She could have debated that last sentence with Loran, but it would have gotten her nowhere. Atyra knew you had to pick your battles. Arguing over the holy book was not a battle Atyra would ever win. And it could bring the wrath of Loran and the rest of the

Shamra on her and her family. "Yes, the words of the prophets," Atyra said. "I study them, as you can see. I am no scholar, and maybe I misinterpreted them, but I can't find any prohibition to wearing a bandana."

"The prophets say Shamra are One. There are no more clans. We are a collective. A unity. *One*," Loran said, talking to Atyra like a teacher to a wayward child. "The scarf you and your daughter wear don't conform to the dress of other females. If we are to be One," he said, clasping his hands together to make his point, "we toss out the old. We dress as One."

"My bandana is not meant to be a symbol of division or disrespect. The hunter's clan didn't wear bandanas. It's merely a family tradition. Surely the prophets don't ask us to turn our backs on our ancestors," Atyra said.

"Personally, I think you would be better served dressing like the others," Loran said, seeming to choose his words carefully. "But the prophets would never ask you to forget the wisdom of those who have passed over."

"Then the bandana is not forbidden," Atyra said.

"You daughter's behavior is what upsets me and offends the prophets," Loran said. Atyra could see he was uncomfortable and would never admit Atyra was correct, so he changed the subject instead. "We are guests in this country. We agreed not to plunder the trees. Males provide food. Females prepare the meals, so say the prophets. I tire of returning your child to you for disobeying rules we have all agreed to."

It was true that this hadn't been the first time Loran had brought Mya to Atyra for having broken what Atyra felt were foolish edicts. Three days before, Mya had attempted to race against several male children. Loran had dragged Mya back, the child's legs kicking the air. And a week before, Mya had gotten into a fight with a male who had taken Mya's bandana. Again, Loran had returned Mya to Atyra with a stern lecture.

"She is just a child," Atyra said.

"Children follow the example of their parents. Rather than have her wear a scarf, you should teach the child to wear flowers in her hair like the other females…"

Tuning him out for a moment, Atyra was struck by the fact that Loran never mentioned Mya by name. She wondered if he even knew her daughter's name.

"... She should stay in the company of other female children, not mix with males," Loran was saying when Atyra listened to him again. "You should keep your eye on her, and teach her right from wrong. You and your daughter have not followed the will of the prophets as closely as we had hoped."

"I study daily," Atyra said, again holding up the holy book. "I will try to do better," she said, hoping to end the lecture with contrition.

"It's fine to study, but even more important to heed the words you read." Loran paused, then smiled. It was the kind of smile Atyra dreaded. Loran was about to tell Atyra something that would greatly distress her, and Loran found this amusing.

"The council met last night," Loran said. The council was made up of members of the former clans. But before the council met, Loran and his fellow clerics would interpret the words of the prophets. The council was convened simply to accept the edicts of the priests. "We have been studying the words of the prophets, and it has been decided no Shamra shall wear hair past their ears."

Atyra knew this was another rule directed at Shamra females, as the hair of males was short and never grew past their ears. And of all the clans, the hunter's clan wore their hair the longest. While hunting, her clan even colored their hair with stripes from the blood of creatures they killed. A member of her clan might hunt with a red streak, a blue streak, and a green streak. Atyra knew she would have to tread lightly. She was intent on abiding the rules of the New Order, but there was a limit to what she would accept.

"Females will cut their hair," Loran said, and for a second, his eyes almost turned a shade of blue. "Uniformity. We are One."

"No offense, Loran," Atyra said, thinking as she spoke, "but like our bandana, the way we wear our hair has been passed down by our ancestors." She knew the female farmers wore their hair short. Working in the fields with their husbands was tiring. There had been little time for a farmer's wife to bathe and comb her hair after preparing an evening meal for the family and putting the children to bed. Short hair for them was practical.

"I have already allowed you far too much leeway out of respect to your ancestors," Loran said. "I can't…" he started and paused. "The council has made a decision. You will abide by it, or there will be consequences."

Loran often spoke of *consequences*, but he never elaborated. Atyra wondered just what he would do if she refused. Atyra decided to be conciliatory instead. "What if we wear our hair up," she said, then demonstrated so her hair didn't fall past her ears. "I can then honor my ancestors without being disrespectful to the New Order. Others can do the same. You know how females feel about their hair. For me, it's a family tradition, but I agree that for many it is pure vanity. If we all wear our hair up, you have uniformity."

Loran looked ready to speak, but hesitated. "We…we will read again the words of the prophets. I make no promises, but it's possible what you suggest isn't contrary to their will. Until we make our decision, you are to wear your hair up, as it is now. The same with your daughter," Loran said, turned, and left.

Atyra's eyes shined a vibrant blue when Loran's back was to her. She had made a convincing argument. While most other females had accepted their new submissive role, there might be some who would openly rebel if the clerics went too far. Loran was crafty, something Atyra had to always remind herself. He might eventually demand females cut their hair, but for now, a compromise might dispel dissatisfaction. Atyra sighed as she tied Mya's hair so it didn't fall past her ears. It was going to be exceedingly difficult to live with the rules of the New Order, especially if the others females put up no resistance.

Mya took a berry out from her stomach pouch and handed it to her mother. Atyra had to keep from laughing. She ripped the berry in half, ate one piece, and gave the other to Mya, who smiled and ate hers.

Later, when Lon returned, he looked at Mya with disapproval. Mya wasn't really Lon and Atyra's child.

Drea, head of the banished hunter's clan, had asked Atyra to take Mya to continue the bloodline of her family in the new Shamra homeland. Mya had been the newborn daughter of Drea's older sister, Jana, who had been killed at the start of the rebellion against the Kimra.

Atyra had learned to love Mya as if she were her own. Like Atyra, Mya was a free spirit, feisty and curious. Atyra knew that, like her, Mya would never submit to the will of others. She would follow her own path regardless of the consequences. Lon had never totally accepted Mya. The older and more mischievous Mya became, the more Lon distanced himself from the child.

"Word has spread about Mya's latest foolishness," Lon said irritably over dinner. "We are the butt of jokes for not being able to control our child."

"*Our child*," Atyra said. Shamra females under the New Order were to be submissive and respectful to males. Atyra was respectful to males in public, but she was not about to grovel before a male in her own home. "You have nothing to do with Mya."

"She's not my daughter," Lon said.

"You've made that clear. She's too young to understand, but I can tell she wonders why her father shows her no affection."

"Every day she acts more like Jana," Lon said, referring to Mya's mother.

"No, every day she acts more like *me*," Atyra said. "Oh, I'm the obedient Shamra in public. But Mya's only acting out her true nature. The blood of our clan courses through her veins. She's only acting as any child in our clan would."

"That's the problem, Atyra," Lon said. "We are already looked upon with suspicion. I'm trying to make a life for us, but you don't even make an effort to be accepted by the other females. Worse, you allow Mya to do as she pleases."

"Have you forgotten why we're here, Lon?" Atyra asked. She continued before Lon could respond. "Yes, we adhere to these new oppressive rules, but our mission is to keep the spirit of our clan alive. Have you so quickly forgotten why Drea chose members of our clan to join the rest?"

"It's easy for Drea to say. She's not here with us," Lon said. "She hasn't suffered as we have. We have more in common with those we have joined than those who stayed behind. I want us to be accepted by the rest, not looked upon as outcasts. I have gained the trust of the others. So have Tergon and Bashra. Why do you find it so difficult? Why can't you learn the art of compromise?"

"You mean be like *them*? Accept the New Order?" Atyra asked. "You want an obedient wife who will bend to your will, tend to the children, and do menial chores. I won't embarrass you in front of others, but I'll never *be* like the others. Neither will Mya."

Lon stomped off, as he often did when he didn't get his way. He knew he could never convince Atyra to accept the new role of females under the New Order. And in Mya, he saw a young Atyra who would grow up to be defiant of the new rules the rest had agreed to follow.

That night, when Lon and Mya were asleep, Atyra snuck into the forest. Atyra was happiest when the Shamra camped near a wooded area. In the old homeland, the hunter's clan spent hours each day in the forests. It was almost a second home. Wherever they traveled now where there were woods, Atyra would feel almost as if she were back with her clan. She always sought out a tree that stood out from the rest. Sometimes it was bigger than the others. Other times it was stunted and dwarfed by those around it. Atyra would sit by the tree and be joined by Drea. It wasn't really her best friend and leader of the hunter's clan. Still, this apparition Atyra conjured would talk with Atyra, and for a little while, she didn't feel so utterly alone. Drea now joined Atyra, both sitting at the foot of a tree, which was horribly bent. An outcast among the others in the forest, just like Atyra.

"That drawing of sticks to choose who would leave the clan wasn't such a great idea," Atyra said to her friend.

"Ya think?" Drea answered.

This Drea was far more lighthearted and irreverent than the Drea Atyra had known. *That* Drea had the burden of her clan's survival on her shoulders. It was a lot to handle at only fifteen years of age. The Drea that visited Atyra made light of her own blunders.

"You should have anticipated the ostracism we would face," Atyra said. "You should have known how lonely we would become. You should have foreseen the seduction the New Order would have on Lon and Tergon."

"And Bashra?" Drea asked.

"Don't get me started," Atyra said, but she spoke her mind anyway. "Bashra was no great warrior, Drea, and she has become the model Shamra female to gain acceptance. You should have chosen those who would resist the lure of the New Order instead of leaving it to chance."

"Not a bad thought," Drea said. "Maybe my closest friend should have pointed that out to me *before* I acted so foolishly."

Atyra knew Drea was referring to her. It was the truth. Atyra hadn't objected to the drawing of sticks. She really wasn't angry at Drea. She was upset with herself for not anticipating the hardships that would face the two families chosen.

"You cut to the heart of the matter, don't you, Drea?" Atyra said. "Yes, I share the blame."

"Is it as bad as you speak, or are you blowing it all out of proportion?" Drea asked.

"Lon and I argue constantly. Seems I can do nothing right," Atyra said. "The distance between us grows daily."

"Is that your problem or Lon's?" Drea asked.

"What do you mean?"

"It's he who wants to conform. It's he that accepts the New Order," Drea said. "You and Mya are the future of our clan. I wish the others had your strength and resolve. You stubbornly follow our heritage and traditions. Is that so wrong?"

"I guess it *is* Lon's problem," Atyra said. "You must think me foolish."

"You're lonely," Drea said. "I miss you, too, but at least I am among my own kind. It's you and Mya against the world. And Mya is an infant. You are not foolish to desire friendship. Oddly enough, it's you I envy."

"What's to envy?"

"You're on a grand adventure," Drea said. "Each day opens a door to the unknown. The perils you face and overcome are far better than the tedium you've left behind."

"It's not so glamorous, Drea," Atyra said. "We enter a new land and Loran gives precious supplies to the rulers to guarantee our safety." Atyra shrugged. "I'm not saying we should take without asking, but there are those we meet who would gladly share some of their bounty. Loran simply wants to avoid confrontation. So he gives more than necessary, with no idea how long we must travel. The prophets will watch over us, he tells us. They won't abandon us. We'll find a new homeland before we starve. I don't believe him for a moment."

"You know you and Mya won't starve," Drea said with a smile.

"Yes, but the hunting I do I must do in secrecy. Any animals I kill I must devour in the forest and leave the rest behind. You know it's not the way of our clan to be wasteful. That's why I bring Mya with me. I want to give her a taste of the hunt. I want her to taste meat forbidden by the priests. And I long for a battle, but I fear Loran would rather see us butchered than raise a hand in self-defense."

"You can always return, Atyra," Drea said. "You and Mya, flee and return to me. I'd welcome you with open arms."

"*Never!*" Atyra said, almost shouting. She put her hand over her mouth. Soon she and Drea were giggling, just as they had as children. "Taunt me all you want, Drea," Atyra finally said. "I know my destiny. I will honor your faith in me. I won't turn tail and see our clan die in the new Shamra homeland."

"Ya think?" Drea said, and the two laughed again.

"You *do* make me feel more like the warrior I am, even if you're a figment of my imagination. I do miss you, Drea, more each day."

"Don't get sentimental on me," Drea said. She got up. "You fight battles every day. The battle to keep your identity; it's the most important battle. Think on that," Drea said, winked, then walked into a mist that swallowed her.

❖❖❖❖❖❖❖❖❖❖

Two weeks later, Atyra was with child, and suddenly Lon was far more attentive and less argumentative. He still ignored Mya, but he beamed at the thought of having a son he could raise. And he was certain Atyra would bear him a male.

As word spread that Atyra was pregnant, there seemed to be a thawing toward her from other Shamra females. A dozen Shamra females had become pregnant since the journey began, and they spent a good deal of time together. Cid, who had been a member of the farmer's clan, already had eight children and was carrying her ninth. She took those who were with child for the first time under her wing. She chided others that were pregnant who kept their distance from Atyra. Atyra spent more and more time with Cid and slowly gained acceptance among the others.

Even Bashra warmed up to Atyra. Bashra had two young children of her own. She joined Atyra one day by a pond they had come upon. Atyra was washing her clothes, along with Mya's. She had grudgingly agreed to wash Lon's clothes as well. Back home, he would have washed his own clothes or walked around in his own stench.

"It's good to see you with others," Bashra said to Atyra. "I get along with the rest, but I share little in common with them. Maybe we can talk."

"About what, Bashra?" Atyra asked. She kept the anger and hurt out of her voice. It would be good to talk to someone who shared common interests, but until now, Bashra had shunned her, just like the others had.

"About how we should raise our children," Bashra said.

"Do you remind your children of the heritage we share?" Atyra asked.

"Not as much as I should. Tergon—"

"Insists you follow the laws of the New Order," Atyra finished for her.

"I sometimes feel torn," Bashra said. "I haven't forgotten the old ways. I'm just not openly defiant."

"And I am?" Atyra asked.

"It appears to others you are. You seem aloof, and your bandana is thought to be a symbol of our clan rather than of the unity they preach."

"You know otherwise," Atyra said.

"But they don't," Bashra countered. "And Mya is such a handful—"

"Mya acts no different than any child of the hunter's clan," Atyra interrupted, finding it difficult not to chastise Bashra. "Should I stifle the spirit within her? Look, Bashra, I won't deny who I am. I won't tame Mya. But I do understand the lure of the New Order to our males. And being pregnant, I don't have the energy or desire to be alone. There's no reason you and I can't get along."

Atyra and Bashra chatted often. Atyra didn't think she and Bashra would ever become close, but alone, they could talk of their people, hunts, and battles fought.

Two weeks later, as the Shamra traveled across uninhabited plains, a sense of unease came over Atyra. As a hunter, Atyra had learned to anticipate danger and not to wait for it to appear. Survival depended on vigilance. She wasn't surprised, then, when a cloud of dust was seen in the distance. She wasn't alarmed when she saw what must have been an advance scouting party from a group of nomads who scoured the countryside for easy pickings. The dozen creatures seemed no threat. They were half the size of the Shamra, covered from head to toe in fur, riding horses half the size of the ones the Shamra rode. It wasn't dust Atyra had seen when they approached. They were enveloped in a mist that seemed to follow them.

Atyra didn't understand the sense of dread, even panic, that gripped the Shamra at the presence of the creatures. What were they afraid of?

"Kimra!" Atyra heard Bashra cry to Tergon. Both Tergon and Bashra looked shaken, referring to those who had enslaved the Shamra for twenty-five years. But these weren't Kimra, Atyra knew. She looked at Lon and saw the color drain from his face.

"What do you see, Lon?" Atyra asked.

"Kimra. Hundreds of them, all armed," Lon said, his voice trembling.

Atyra looked at Mya, who stared at the creatures wide-eyed. She, too, looked frightened. She was still too young to speak. Atyra described the Kimra to Mya. "Is that what you see?" she asked.

Mya nodded.

Atyra saw Loran and seven other clerics from what had been the religious clan approach the creature who had come closest to the Shamra travelers. Atyra could hear the creature issue his demands.

"You require safe passage through our lands," the creature said. Its voice was an irritating whine. It certainly didn't inspire fear in Atyra, but looking at the Shamra around her, she could see them cower. "Leave your animals, and you won't feel the wrath of our army," it continued. "Defy us, and we slaughter your males and enslave your females and children."

Loran tried to reason with the creature. He offered the creatures one-third of the animals, plus grain, pottery, and jewelry.

"We have no need for your trinkets," the creature talking to Loran screeched. "*All* of your animals. You have until sunset, or face slaughter."

Loran called an assembly of a dozen males who were consulted on such matters.

Atyra remained puzzled. Was she the only one who saw the creatures for what they were? There was no army. And they certainly weren't Kimra. Even if they had been Kimra, giving up all their animals meant sure death for the Shamra, unless they settled in this uninhabitable land. Animals pulled the wagons. The milk of some animals fed the young and was used in the preparation of food for all. Some animals were killed for their hides, which was used for clothing and blankets, their bones for bowls and cooking utensils.

While the assembly met, Atyra walked among the Shamra who had set up camp as if it were night. Everywhere she went, Shamra whispered about the fearsome army of Kimra.

Atyra saw Cid whispering with Elna, another Shamra female who was pregnant. The look on their faces showed concern, but not fear.

"Do you see Kimra?" Atyra asked.

"Do you?" Cid asked in return.

"You see what I see," Atyra said. "No more than a dozen creatures half our size on miniature horses. Not a Kimra among them."

Cid nodded. "Surrounded by a mist," she said.

"But if everyone else sees Kimra, who are we to say we aren't mistaken," Elna said.

"Do you see Kimra, Elna? Do you even see an army?" Atyra asked.

Elna shook her head.

"It must be the mist," Atyra said. "It makes the others see what they fear most. The Kimra."

"But why don't we see them?" Elna asked.

Atyra was about to shrug. She had no idea. Then Cid spoke.

"The three of us are pregnant," Cid said. "That's what we share in common. The mist must not affect us."

Atyra smiled. "You are indeed wise, Cid. The thought hadn't crossed my mind."

Cid smiled, almost as if she were a warrior, proud of seeing what should have been obvious to the others.

"How are we to know?" Elna asked.

"Gather all the pregnant females, Elna," Atyra said. "Do it quietly. We'll test Cid's claim."

The other pregnant Shamra females acknowledged they saw what Atyra, Cid, and Elna saw.

"We should tell Loran," Lytle said.

"He won't believe us," Atyra said, holding back her bitterness toward the cleric. "We are a thousand strong, yet all

SHAMRA DIVIDED

but twelve see a mighty army of Kimra. And we twelve are *females*. We don't speak our minds, do we?" Atyra asked. "And we don't question what Loran sees. He's guided by the prophets, after all."

"So we do nothing?" Cid asked. "We give all of our animals to these..." she threw up her hands, as she could find no words to describe what were a dozen harmless creatures, not the Kimra. Atyra heard anger, restlessness, and rebellion in her voice. If she didn't know better, she would have thought Cid a member of her clan.

"We confront them, the twelve of us," Atyra said. "Get a horse and a weapon. A pitchfork, a shovel, a carving knife," she added, when the others looked at her without comprehension. "They are no match for us."

"What about Loran?" Lytle asked.

"We twelve must take a stand. Only we see what truly confronts us," Atyra said. "Anything else would be a betrayal of our people."

"You will lead us, Atyra," Cid said. It wasn't a question.

"Yes," Atyra said.

"Then I am with you," Cid said. "What of the rest of you?" she asked.

The others nodded, though Atyra could sense reluctance from several.

"We meet here in fifteen minutes," Atyra said.

Atyra went to her wagon, and from a false bottom that had been constructed before she left her clan, she withdrew the sword in a sheath that Drea had given her. It was one of several parting gifts. Drea must have sensed that Atyra would one day need the weapon. Atyra considered asking Bashra to join them, but she didn't have time to convince Bashra that what she saw was an illusion.

Atyra and her eleven warriors rode out to meet the leader of the army that didn't exist. Cid, who was plumper than most Shamra, rode by Atyra's side. "Bear eight children, and see what happens to your figure," she had told the others, laughing. Looking at Cid now, Atyra could see she was also more muscular than the others. A farmer's wife, she had worked side by side with her husband in the old Shamra homeland. She would have made a good warrior, Atyra thought. Atyra could smell a strong odor from Cid's body. Only the hunter's clan gave off such a pungent scent when a great hunt or battle was at hand. Other Shamra usually found it offensive. Atyra could see that her aroma comforted her comrades. Atyra wondered if Cid might have some warrior blood in her. There had been little intermingling between the clans, but it was possible.

The creature who led the charlatan Kimra army looked at Atyra and her warriors with disdain as they approached. "Have your leaders sent you to beg for mercy?" the creature whined in its squeaky voice.

"We come with demands, not to grovel," Atyra said.

"Only males speak for your kind," the creature said, its voice shrill.

"How do you know that?" Atyra asked, and then understood why they appeared as Kimra. They could somehow read minds. They *knew* it was the Kimra the Shamra feared most, just as they knew males under the New Order spoke for all Shamra. With the mist, they had cloaked themselves as Kimra.

"Leave before my troops make an example of you," the creature shrieked.

"We see you as you truly are," Atyra said. She described their appearance and looked down at the creature, making eye contact. If she were talking to a true Kimra warrior, she would have had to look much higher. She then unsheathed her sword. "Are you prepared to take me on in battle?" Atyra asked. A part of her wished the creature would accept her challenge.

SHAMRA DIVIDED

The creature looked at Atyra and her sword. Its own sword was made of wood and was one-third the size of Atyra's. "We Tweeble will withdraw and allow you to pass through our land," the creature said. Atyra heard fear in its voice.

"You'll do more than that if you value your lives," Atyra said. "I long for a battle, even if you're not a worthy opponent. You will give us your horses, and leave on foot. You will rid yourself of this mist that masks you from the rest. And this is not open for negotiation," Atyra added. "One word of protest, and I strike you dead where you stand, and my warriors will slaughter your puny army."

The creature sheathed its sword and dismounted, telling the others to do the same. "One question: How could you see through the Mist of Illusion?" it asked.

"We are guided by our prophets," Atyra said. "They are not fooled by your trickery."

The Tweeble waved his hand, and the mist was gone. Atyra could hear other Shamra murmur as they saw that no Kimra and no army surrounded them.

"Leave us," Atyra said, "before we have a change of heart." She brandished her sword. "Spread the word of the power of our people."

Atyra's warriors retrieved the small horses and, with Atyra in the lead, made their way back as the creatures fled on foot. Shamra were cheering until Loran, surrounded by members of the assembly, appeared. All fell silent.

Atyra saw Loran smoldering. He had been humiliated, by females no less. Atyra thought to make a peace offering before Loran could speak. "We deliver these horses to you, Loran. The prophets allowed those of us who were pregnant to see through the veil of those creatures."

"The prophets spoke to you?" Loran asked, his fury unabated by the offering. "I think not. This was a test by the prophets, and once again, we failed because you didn't truly believe." Loran spoke in a booming voice so all could hear, but his eyes were locked on Atyra. "If those creatures weren't Kimra, the prophets would have warned us. You, though, have little faith. Worse, you convinced others to defy the prophets."

"Could it be the prophets spoke through us?" Atyra asked, aware of the peril in challenging Loran's authority and making him look foolish to all. She knew she had no other alternative, yet she now feared Loran's wrath. She would accept any punishment he meted, but she worried for the eleven others who had followed her. They were her responsibility because she was their leader. She suddenly knew how Drea felt when her decisions could imperil others.

"The prophets don't speak through females," Loran said. "You continually defy the prophets and make a mockery of the rules the prophets demand we abide."

Atyra saw Loran looking at her sword. Having a weapon of war was forbidden. It was another rule of the New Order she had broken. "I am solely to blame, Loran. If I offended the prophets, do with me as you wish, but in the name of the prophets, spare the others."

"Very well," Loran said, after a moment of thought.

Atyra felt a chill run through her as she saw the hint of a smile on Loran's face.

"Atyra, in the name of the prophets, you are hereby banished. Leave within the hour…and take your child with you."

Atyra knew Loran's decision was final. No begging for mercy would convince Loran to change his mind. His words pierced her heart. She hadn't known what punishment to expect, but she had never considered she would be banished. She despaired that she had failed her clan. She had failed Drea. Mya would never see the new Shamra homeland. The vision of a descendant of Mya's leading Shamra against oppressors would remain unfulfilled.

SHAMRA DIVIDED

Atyra packed her few belongings. From the false bottom of the wagon, she took a copy of the holy book Drea had given her. It wasn't the rewritten version of the clerics, but the original text that held the true history of the Shamra. Just as possession of her sword had been forbidden under the New Order, so, too, was ownership of this rendering of the holy book.

Bashra visited Atyra briefly. "Why couldn't I see through the mist?" Bashra asked.

"Only those who were pregnant could."

"I would have followed you into battle even if I thought they were Kimra," Bashra said. "Why didn't you tell me?"

Atyra didn't believe Bashra. She was no longer a warrior. She had been tamed. But Bashra was her clan's only remaining hope. "I knew my arrogance would be punished. Lon and Tergon have grown sympathetic to the New Order. If you were banished with me, in a generation or two, our clan would be forgotten. Our sacrifices at Monument Gate and in the battles that followed would be rewritten. It's up to you to keep our heritage alive in the new homeland. Your staying behind showed your loyalty to the New Order to everyone."

Cid also came by. She gave Atyra a bag of food. "I should have stood by you. We all should have," she said.

"And been expelled along with me?" Atyra said, shaking her head. "Of all I leave, I will miss you the most. You have the heart of a warrior." She took off a necklace she wore around her neck and gave it to Cid. All members of the hunter's clan celebrated their first kill of an animal by climbing Stone Mountain and choosing a crystal-like stone that proclaimed their prowess. Atyra's was blood red. She valued it above all her possessions, except for Drea's bandana and sword. "You have earned this," she told Cid.

"Where will you go?" Cid asked, placing the necklace around her neck. "It's a long and perilous trip back to your people."

"You may yet see me again," Atyra said, an idea beginning to take shape in her mind. "And if not, don't ever forget what we accomplished today. Inferior females saved our people. Tell your children. Be proud of your heroism."

Loran appeared after an hour had passed. Only then did Atyra see Lon. She thought he had abandoned her, but as Atyra got on her horse, Lon spoke in her defense.

"Loran, please reconsider," Lon said. "After all, she did save us."

"Ye of little faith, Lon," Loran said. "You disappoint me. Atyra may well have carried out the will of the prophets, but she glorified herself. Why didn't she come to you, her husband, with what she had seen? The prophets saw fit to speak through her, yet she turned her back on our rules and sought her own glory. If she stays, she will contaminate others. The prophets have spoken. She is to leave."

"But what of my child who grows within her?" Lon asked.

It was then that Atyra knew Lon only cared for her unborn child. He wasn't pleading for her.

"A child with the blood of betrayal coursing through it will be an abomination, just like the other," Loran said, pointing toward Mya. "The prophets have spoken. Your marriage is dissolved. Choose an appropriate mate, and you will be blessed with children the prophets will smile upon."

Atyra knew she had underestimated Loran. He had recovered from his initial shock at being saved by a group of pregnant females. He had turned what could have become a divisive setback into a triumph for the New Order. And Atyra had played right into his hand. Accepting sole blame allowed Loran to spare the others. But it was not out of charity. Had the others been banished, there would have been dissent. Some husbands would have insisted on leaving with their mates. By taking sole responsibility, Atyra had given Loran what he needed. Atyra was exiled. Females would think twice before they defied the New Order again. And Lon would find a new mate. Atyra doubted if Lon would ever speak of the heritage of the hunter's clan again.

Without a word to Lon or Loran, Atyra rode off with Mya, her daughter's arms wrapped around her.

♦♦♦♦♦♦♦♦♦♦

Two months later, just a week before giving birth, Atyra entered what she knew would be the new Shamra homeland.

After she had been expelled by Loran, Atyra had traveled west for less than an hour. Heading west would have meant admitting defeat, even if she made it back to Drea and her clan, and Atyra wasn't about to give up without a fight. It wasn't the nature of her clan to turn tail the first time they faced what appeared to be an insurmountable obstacle. After an hour, she and Mya made camp for the night. Atyra stayed up most of the night, fearful the creatures she'd encountered earlier that day might attack a solitary traveler.

Before daylight, her plan had crystalized. With Mya, she went through the forest, heading east, passing the Shamra encampment without being seen.

During the night, she had conjured her image of Drea, and now her resolve was more determined than ever. She believed in Drea's vision of the future. Drea's Gift of Sight was not to be taken lightly. Drea had vividly described a land of lush fields that looked nothing like the old Shamra homeland. How could Atyra doubt Drea? And if Drea said she saw a descendant of Mya's leading a Shamra army, Atyra didn't doubt her friend for a moment. Drea's vision guided Atyra for two treacherous yet exhilarating months. Atyra would locate the new Shamra homeland before her people arrived. She would find a way to convince Loran that the prophets had forgiven her or at least offered her a second chance. Lon, she knew, was lost to her, but theirs had been a union of necessity, not of love. It would actually be a relief not having Lon hovering at night. He never pretended to love Mya. Atyra would never have to guard her words in her own home again.

Atyra knew Loran led the Shamra due east. Even when they came to a raging river they couldn't cross or mountains that couldn't be scaled, Loran made a detour, then followed stars that the prophets had provided him as signposts. So Atyra headed east.

As she feared, three days into her journey, she encountered the Tweeble she had foiled. When not traveling or hunting, she spent her time teaching Mya to use a slingshot and a knife for self-defense. Mya was too young to shoot a bow and arrow, but children of the hunter's clan learned at an early age the art of self-defense. Mya also accompanied Atyra as she hunted. Mya was rapidly learning how to track. Soon she would be able to kill a small animal.

When they could, Atyra and Mya slept in the forest. Atyra would urinate in a circle, marking territory as hers, just as many animals did. Her scent seemed enough to keep animals from attacking them while she slept.

On the plains, before going to sleep, Atyra constructed devices to warn her of intruders. Long before a combatant was near, crudely fashioned bells tied to strings would alert Atyra to any danger.

Atyra spotted the creatures of the mist well before they knew they had been seen. They were following her, waiting for the best time to strike, knowing that alone she was vulnerable. They must have returned to their homeland, for they had fresh horses.

Atyra knew she and Mya were in terrible peril. The Tweeble knew the terrain; Atyra did not. She was far outnumbered, even if the creatures were smaller than she was. And she might not only have to fight them, but protect Mya as well. Atyra knew she couldn't wait for an attack. These creatures were cunning. Something ahead would distract Atyra, or there would possibly be a canyon she'd have to pass through, which would make her an easy target. So Atyra took the initiative.

Making camp in a wooded area, Atyra dug a shallow trench for Mya to sleep in. She covered the hole with a blanket of leaves. Under the cover of darkness, she slipped out of the woods and rode west for a quarter of a mile, as if retracing her route. She turned north, then east, and came upon the creatures' camp from behind. She counted two dozen sitting by a fire, eating the remains of a slaughtered animal. With her knife, she slit the throats of two guards before they could sound an alarm. Then, back on her horse, she charged into the camp, heading straight for their leader. He rose, but before he could unsheathe his sword, Atyra had swung hers. The creature's head fell into the fire. Her sword dispatched three more of the creatures as the rest scattered. She turned to rush at several others who had bolted toward the woods, but something fell from a tree and landed on her back. It must have been a third sentry she didn't spot. She reached behind her to pull the creature off her right when a stone hit the creature in the head, and the creature fell to the ground. Turning her horse, Atyra saw Mya behind a tree, reloading her slingshot. Filled with fear for Mya's safety, Atyra jumped from her horse and, with one swipe of her sword, killed two of the creatures who rushed at her with spears. Another crumpled to the ground, felled by a rock from Mya's slingshot.

Atyra turned toward one of the creatures who stood by the fire. It looked at Atyra and at its fallen comrades, then put down its sword and raised its hands. It let out a shrill whistle, and the thirteen remaining creatures emerged from the trees with their hands raised. Atyra herded them all together. Mya came out of hiding, picked up one of the wooden swords, and stood by Atyra.

"Are you their leader?" Atyra asked the one who had signaled the others.

"Our leader has fallen," it said. "I command now. Why did you attack us? We weren't—"

"You've been tracking us. A solitary traveler with a child. You were just waiting for the right moment to strike."

"We should have been invisible to you," it said, sounding bewildered.

"You were easy to spot," Atyra said.

"No, we made no attempt to hide from you. You still shouldn't have seen us."

Atyra understood. "When will you learn your Mist of Illusion has no power over me?"

"It has never failed us before," the creature said, as much to itself as to Atyra.

"It failed you twice with our people. I will spare you and the others only if you give your solemn vow to give me, and those of my people who follow, safe passage through this land."

"Done," the creature said.

"And I'd like a horse for my daughter. Give her one, and you may all keep your weapons."

The creature signaled, and a horse was brought to Mya.

"Honor your word," Atyra said, holding the tip of her sword at the leader's throat. "You can bring one hundred reinforcements and you will surely slay me. But the cost will be high. There is far less dangerous prey than me and my people. Let us be, and we won't tell others how to pierce your Mist of Illusion."

"You have nothing more to fear from us," the leader said.

Mya grabbed two pieces of meat that the creatures had dropped by the fire. She offered one to Atyra and chewed on the other.

The leader smiled. "You are a ferocious fighter," it said to Atyra. "But we had you beaten until the child appeared. That one so young can slay us so easily is even more frightening than you with your sword."

Atyra sat Mya on one of the dwarf horses, and the two rode back toward the forest where Atyra had left their supplies.

"I should be angry that you didn't heed my instructions to remain hidden," Atyra said to Mya.

Chewing the meat from the bone she had taken, Mya shrugged.

"Like your mother and your aunt, you are reckless and bold." Atyra smiled. "You've proven yourself a warrior this night."

While Mya slept, Atyra cleaned one of the bones Mya had taken from the fire. She cut off a small piece, colored it with red dye, and slipped a string through it. When Mya awoke, she put it around the child's neck. "There is no Stone Mountain for you to climb, so we make due with what we have. Next time I won't leave you behind. You *will* learn to follow instructions. We fight as one, just as your mother and aunt, and later your aunt and I, did. Understand?"

Mya nodded.

The next seven weeks were full of joy and wonder for Atyra and Mya. A week after the battle with the Tweeble, Mya began to talk. Sometimes Atyra thought the child would never cease. She asked Atyra questions, and each answer elicited another question from Mya. Mya even began to talk in her sleep. Atyra thought she was most definitely a product of her clan and her family. She was also a delight, and Atyra came to love her more with each passing day.

Atyra passed through three other inhabited countries. Her story was always the same. She had been part of an advance scouting party for her people, traveling in peace. They were to spread the word that those who followed several weeks behind meant no harm. The others in her scouting party, Atyra said, had succumbed to the hazards of uncharted territory. One had eaten poisonous fruit. Another had been swept to his death crossing a raging river. A fever had taken a third. Soon Atyra almost believed what she said. Her people wanted nothing more than to pass peacefully on their search for a new homeland.

Atyra and Mya were treated with courtesy and friendship by all. Mya played with the children wherever they stopped. She was never rough with them and allowed others to defeat her in athletic contests. Atyra knew Mya could have often prevailed. While only a child, Mya was not only a warrior but a diplomat. A natural leader, Atyra thought. It saddened Atyra a bit to know that if accepted in the new Shamra homeland, Mya would not be allowed to use her many talents. A submissive female, she'd have to become.

Wherever they stopped, Atyra and Mya left with gifts of food, seeds, blankets, and medicine in exchange for the goodwill they showed. They also left with the promise that the Shamra who followed would be allowed to pass unmolested.

When Atyra finally came to the new Shamra homeland, she recognized it immediately. It wasn't anything like Drea had described. Much of the land was desert. But far to the east, just before swamps, was a river bordered by trees. Atyra immediately saw its potential. Her people's new home. It was as if this land spoke to her; it welcomed her, had even seemed to have been waiting for her.

Knowing she must appease Loran in order to remain when the Shamra arrived, Atyra, with Mya's help, built a large hut for Loran and his assembly to meet. She knew it would be demolished and a far grander one built by craftsmen, but it was the gesture that would have meaning for Loran and the others. Or so she hoped. She despaired, at times, that Loran might use the words of the prophets in some way against her. His disdain for her was genuine. It was also personal. And deep within, she knew he also feared her. He had to know there was no way she'd ever abide by the rules of the New Order, especially after her victory over the Tweeble. And Mya was so much like Atyra that she would also be viewed as a threat to Loran. Still, Atyra had to make an attempt. Drea's vision of the future made Atyra work at times to the point of exhaustion.

She built a small hut for herself and Mya a quarter of a mile away from the assembly hall. For irrigation, she dug a trench from the river. A small stream ran past her hut. She planted seeds she had been given on her travels, then feverish lay down in her hut. She knew it was time to deliver her baby.

Three weeks later, Atyra was tending to her crops when riders approached from the west. The Shamra had arrived. Atyra had been surprised at how quickly the seeds she had planted had sprouted and blossomed. It was as if the earth wanted to prove itself worthy so the Shamra would cease their wandering.

Atyra had expected Loran and was prepared for his bluster. Instead she was greeted by Lon and a female she assumed was his mate, along with Cid, Cheron, who was a cleric from the religious clan, and a craftsman and a farmer she recognized but didn't know by name.

Lon greeted Atyra stiffly and introduced his wife Nyla.

"I see you're with child," Atyra said. She was glad for Lon. He deserved happiness even if he had turned his back on his clan.

"Yes, a son," Nyla said. "I can feel it in my bones," she added.

"And your child?" Lon asked, as if he were merely curious.

"Dedra is with Mya," Atyra said, and pointed toward the river.

"A daughter," Lon said. He smiled and seemed to relax for the first time.

Atyra held her tongue. She knew Lon was relieved. Atyra thought he'd become a coarse and shallow male. Instead of ridiculing Lon, she spoke to the others, telling them what she had done to prepare for their arrival.

"We've been digging trenches to divert water from the river for farms. The soil may look coarse and barren, but it's full of nutrients. Look at the crops that spring from its womb," she said, pointing to the grain and vegetables and trees of fruits that surrounded her.

"This is where you plan to live?" Cheron, the cleric, said, not unkindly.

Atyra knew she had to choose her words carefully. Since her arrival, each night she had dreamed of the vision of the future Drea had revealed. She knew it may have been her imagination, but she felt as if she now shared Drea's vision. She saw this land as it would look two hundred years in the future. She saw the Shamra warrior Drea called Dara in the swamps wearing a red bandana with black polka dots. She knew the destiny of the Shamra lay with this Dara. If she and Mya were banished, there would be no one to fight those who would enslave the Shamra in that future. She had prepared words nightly to convince Loran to allow her to remain. Now she had to satisfy Cheron.

"The prophets don't speak to me, Cheron," Atyra said. "I am a female and aware of my shortcomings. Yet when I entered this land, it was like a hand stopped me. I knew this was to be the new Shamra homeland. I don't claim the land for myself, but for all Shamra."

"And you plan to live among us," Cheron said.

"I know I failed the prophets and deserved to be banished," Atyra said, intentionally not making eye contact with Cheron. "I know, too, I had to persevere to atone for my sins. I have been humbled in the two months I traveled alone with only my daughter. I came to understand I was vain and self-centered. I ask only for a chance to prove myself and show Loran and the rest I have learned from my mistakes. I am a Shamra first and always."

Atyra pointed to the hut she had constructed for the assembly, then at the one she occupied. "This hut I have built for myself, but if it is the will of the prophets, I will give all this up and start anew where I am told. I am no longer the Atyra who was exiled."

"Loran has taken ill," Cheron said. "I speak now for the priests, at least until he recovers. I do sense a change in you. Maybe your expulsion was for the best. You no longer think only of yourself. Your travels were noted as we made our way through unfamiliar territory. You have been a good ambassador for our people. The prophets demand absolute adherence to their words as spoken to the priests. The prophets tested you. The prophets accept your acts of contrition. Your banishment has ended, my child. You are welcome to rejoin us and live among us."

"Thank you, Cheron," Atyra said. "I won't fail the prophets again."

"We go now to get our people," Cheron said, and turned to leave.

"Atyra doesn't look well," Cid said. "May I stay and care for her while you get the others?"

Cheron nodded and rode off with the others. When they were out of sight, Cid dismounted and embraced Atyra in a bear-hug.

"It wasn't easy to swallow your pride," Cid said with a mischievous smile.

"You question my sincerity?" Atyra asked, but she, too, smiled.

"Cheron makes light of your deeds," Cid said. "He doesn't want to admit a female, one who was banished, no less, paved the way for our safety. He knows, though. We *all* know. Wherever we passed, we were greeted with open arms. The first time, Loran was suspicious. He was told of a female Shamra and her daughter, the only remaining members of an advance party, who had stayed with them for a week. Wherever we went, we no longer had to trade seeds, grain, cattle... *anything* for good hospitality. We were actually given seeds and other essentials to use when we found the new homeland you had spoken of. Loran was furious, but what could he do? In a different time, tales of your heroism would be told by all and celebrated. Still, we are aware and grateful."

"What's wrong with Loran?" Atyra asked.

"He was bitten by a snake just two days from here. He's failing. It looks like Cheron will lead the priests."

"Is that a good thing?" Atyra asked. She really didn't know much about Cheron.

"All priests are pretty much the same," Cid said. "But Cheron is more tolerant than most. He won't praise you, but he believes you are contrite and welcomes you back. I can't say Loran would have done the same. And Cheron has a far better disposition than Loran." She paused a moment. "Have you really changed? Will you abide by the New Order?"

Before Atyra could answer, Mya came running up, followed by Dedra. Both wore colorful bandanas. Atyra took her bandana from her stomach pouch and wrapped it around her head. "It's in the hands of the prophets," she said with a smile.

CHAPTER 9

~ *The Present* ~

"I owe my very existence to Atyra," Dara said when Briana finished the story. "She was as brave as Drea."

"Perhaps more so." Briana said forlornly. "She and Drea were like you and Pilla. They weren't related, but were closer than sisters."

"And separated for the good of the clan, just as Pilla gave her life so I wouldn't be captured trying to rescue her," Dara said.

Briana suddenly stiffened and put a finger to her lips. Dara understood and went silent. Off in the distance, they heard the sound of horses making their way through the forest. Briana took out a tapered metal cylinder with glass at either end.

"What is that?" Dara asked.

Briana looked at Dara. "Your Shamra must be really primitive," she said, then put the glass to her eye and, after several moments, grunted. She gave the cylinder to Dara.

Dara put it to her eye. She saw six Galvan on horseback within yards of them and gasped. "We can't escape them. They're almost on top of us."

Briana let out a giggle, then put her hand to her mouth. "I'm sorry. This," she said, holding the metal rod, "makes things far away look closer. They're still half-a-mile away, but closing quickly."

"You said the Galvan didn't hunt," Dara said.

"Look at them closely," Briana said. "Especially their faces."

Dara took the eyepiece and peered through it. "They're all expressionless," Dara said.

"And..."

"Their eyes," Dara said excitedly. "Their eyes are black. The Galvan have yellow eyes."

"They're no longer Galvan," Briana said, and saw the confusion on Dara's face. "Something has taken control of them. Taken them over. They have the body of a Galvan, but it's like a camouflage. And they're after you. Come, we must hide the Fangala. Cover the blood with dirt; then we hide and hope they don't detect our scent."

"We should wipe the blood of the Fangala over us," Dara said. "It will mask our scent."

Briana looked at Dara oddly.

"I haven't hunted nearly as much as you, and I don't claim to be a great warrior," Dara said. "But, in our fight for freedom and in my travels, I've learned much. There were any number of times I stared death in the eye. I don't have your experience, but I am no novice."

They both covered themselves with the blood of the Fangala and hid. Ten minutes later, Briana gestured with her hand, and the two scurried deeper into the forest. They hid behind some boulders. If necessary, they could escape to the left, the right, or retreat deeper into the forest.

"You've seen them before?" Dara said.

"Atyra and Drea did," Briana said. "Not as Galvan, but in other bodies possessed by some other entity. Let me tell you about Chaos."

Chapter 10

~ Chaos Reigns ~

196 years ago

Atyra sat with Bashra and Cid, watching their children play. They were far from prying eyes, but Atyra was still vigilant. The consequences if they were seen were ominous. Four years had passed since Atyra had first laid eyes on the new Shamra homeland. A warrior at heart, Atyra couldn't say she was truly happy, but here in the fields, she wouldn't deny she was at least content.

Swamps and a river surrounded by coarse gray soil had appeared anything but hospitable the day she had reached this land with Mya. But the earth had exceeded all expectations. Trenches the Shamra dug brought water to the nutrient-rich soil, and fields of wheat, trees of fruit, and vines of vegetables flourished. Building a country from scratch had been no easy chore, but the Shamra were an industrious people and their hard work had paid off.

Still, the hunter in Atyra often grew restless. She farmed, but was no farmer. When she could take no more, she would venture with her daughters into the forbidden swamps to hunt. Atyra saw creatures she had never cast eyes on in the old Shamra homeland she had left. Mya, at four, was particularly adept with a slingshot. Around her neck, Mya still wore her necklace with the bone from a dead animal dyed red, symbolic of her first kill four years earlier. Dedra, six months younger, preferred a bow and arrow, forbidden to females under the New Order of the Shamra priests.

Only in the swamps did Atyra feel truly alive. Only in the swamps could Atyra release her pent-up aggression and follow her true nature. After a kill, Atyra and her daughters would eat the fresh meat in the swamps, since hunting was still forbidden under the New Order. Still, Atyra refused to waste any part of the animal. It had been the way of her clan, and her main responsibility was to teach Mya and Dedra the heritage and traditions of their clan, which they would, in turn, pass down to their children.

Mya's slingshot, which had to be hidden in their hut, was made from bones and innards of an animal Atyra had killed, as was Dedra's bow and arrow. Uneaten meat was dried and hidden in a cave that Atyra marked with her urine to ward off scavengers. The hide of an animal became a coat and blankets used when Atyra and her children camped in the swamps. Scales from other creatures were fashioned into weapons, also hidden in the cave. If the Shamra were attacked, Atyra was determined not to be defenseless.

The fields her children now played in were not the swamps, but even here, hidden from other Shamra, Mya and Dedra didn't have to follow the rules set by the priests. And both Bashra and Cid were good company. Only in the past year had Bashra ventured into the fields with her two children. Kyle, a year older than Mya, competed against her. He could outrace Mya, but she was more skilled with her slingshot than he. He accepted defeat gracefully. Atyra teased Bashra that her other son, Kril, had a crush on her daughter.

"He could do worse," Bashra said, laughing. "Far worse."

Cid now had ten children, five males and five females. Like Atyra, she continued to defy the New Order by allowing her daughters to learn self-defense and compete against males. She still wore the blood-red crystal on the necklace Atyra had given her four years earlier.

Cid was far more like those of Atyra's clan than Bashra was. She had a restless spirit and a streak of recklessness not seen among Shamra females. There was no one Atyra trusted more. Looking at Cid, Atyra thought it was good to have someone to confide in. Atyra hadn't had such a confidant since she had left Drea.

"Time I get back before I'm missed," Bashra said, calling to her children and not making eye contact with either Atyra or Cid. Her husband Tergon, while a member of the hunter's clan, followed the rules of the New Order to the letter. He had recently been accepted as a member of the Assembly, a dozen Shamra who advised the priests on matters of importance to all Shamra. But it was the priests, interpreting the words of the prophets, who had the final say. If Bashra was caught in the fields with her children, breaking more rules than she could count, Tergon would be cast out from the Assembly.

Atyra nodded. She understood. It was a fine line Bashra walked. Atyra had no mate. Unlike Bashra, Atyra could speak her mind in the privacy of her own home without consequences. She answered to no one. The trade-off was not being able to share her bed with another.

As Atyra rose to leave, the fields before her disappeared. She found herself standing on a rock with members of her clan. A waterfall raged in the distance. Her clan was in battle. Many were wounded and bleeding. They parted, and Atyra recognized Ramorra. There were tears in her eyes as she cradled a fallen warrior. Ramorra lifted her dead comrade. It was Drea.

Atyra collapsed.

Opening her eyes, Atyra saw Cid and Bashra standing over her, worry etched on their faces. Mya ran up and put her bandana, dripping with water, on her mother's head. Atyra looked at Mya and Dedra. "Drea's dead." Without another word, she passed out again.

Atyra woke in her hut. She thought she was alone, but sensed a presence. She felt feverish and lightheaded. "Mya?" she called weakly.

"Will I do?" another voice answered.

Atyra turned her head, closing her eyes a moment as the room spun around her. She opened her eyes to Drea. When Atyra felt utterly alone, she would conjure an image of Drea to talk to. She thought this was the imaginary Drea before her now. Drea seemed to read her thoughts.

"I'm not a figment of your imagination," Drea said.

The image of Drea dead, cradled in Ramorra's arms, returned to Atyra. "You're dead," Atyra said.

"Yes, but it was a glorious death," Drea said. She told Atyra of trying to help the Weetok, who had been enslaved by the Kimra, just as the Shamra had. "I envied you, Atyra, the adventures and peril you'd encounter on your journey. I don't know if it was folly for me to lead our clan against the Kimra, but I hadn't felt so alive since you and I fought the Kimra side by side. We lost many warriors the day I was killed, but I think the spirit of our clan was ignited by the battle."

"It was worth dying for?" Atyra asked.

"For me, yes. But as you can see, I'm not truly dead," Drea said.

"I conjured you," Atyra said.

Drea shook her head. "I'm not the Drea of your imagination. I'm the Drea who sent you off four years ago. It had to be done, but it's still my biggest regret."

"But if you're dead now—?" Atyra began.

"I merely passed from one existence to another. I live through those who remember me," Drea said. "I can walk into the future. I can be summoned when needed. There are no set rules. You didn't summon me, but here I am. I wasn't sure you'd made it to this new Shamra homeland, or that there even was a new country where our people settled, until I'd passed over."

"Was there any doubt? Your Gift of Sight—"

"Not until I died," Drea said.

"Wasn't I destined to make it here so Mya's descendant could free the Shamra hundreds of years from now?" Atyra asked.

"I thought so. But when I died, I was given the choice to return to my body and live. Had I done so, the future would have been altered. So maybe you weren't destined to get here safely."

"What do you mean you *could* have come back? I saw you dead," Atyra said.

"I died. My legacy is what keeps me alive. Summoned, like I told you, in times of need. But I could have re-entered my body and lived. Don't ask me how. I have no idea. I chose not to."

"You chose death," Atyra said.

"It's not death. I'm here, aren't I? And in times of peril, I *will* be summoned," Drea said. "For what, I don't know. I have glimpses into the future, but it's not carved in stone. My new life isn't mapped out for me. It's what makes it so precious." Drea paused a moment. "You've done wonders with Mya," Drea said.

"She and Dedra, my daughter, are my life. They've kept me from despairing. Yes, our journey was filled with adventure, but frankly, I'm bored. I've *been* bored for years. If not for my daughters, I would return to our clan in a heartbeat. I named Dedra—"

"After me," Drea said. "I know. I have a daughter. Anis. Named for you."

"Do any of Dedra's descendants—?"

Drea shook her head. "You don't want to know. The Gift of Sight can sometimes be a curse. I know far too much. Sometimes it's a burden. But there's much that's still a mystery to me. You know I always loved to venture into the unknown. It drives me now. To answer your question, Drea's descendants play an important role in Shamra history. That's all I can tell you. At least they do in the future I've seen. Remember, though—"

"Yes, it's just one possible future," Atyra said.

"My appearing to you now can alter that future," Drea said, and shrugged. "I had to take the chance. I had to say goodbye." Drea bent and kissed Atyra's forehead. "I've got to go. I just wanted you to know how proud I am of you. You were in my thoughts daily when I lived. You're with me daily now."

"Is that you, Mom?" Mya called out, entering the hut.

Atyra turned to look at her daughter. As usual, Mya's bandana had slipped down her forehead. "This is Mya," Atyra said, and turned to Drea, but there was no one there.

"Who were you talking to?" Mya asked.

Atyra wondered if Drea had been an apparition she'd conjured in a fevered state. "What's this?" Mya asked, holding a yellow bandana with black polka dots.

"She *was* here," Atyra said aloud, but was talking to herself. Atyra had given the bandana to Drea as a gift before she had left with Mya.

"Are you okay?" Mya asked.

"I will be," Atyra said. "Tell me about Drea, Jana, and Nyvia while I rest my eyes."

Mya smiled and told Atyra tales of the hunter's clan they had left behind in the old homeland. Tales she promised Atyra she would tell *her* children so one day Dara, who Drea spoke of, would know her heritage.

Later that night, with both Mya and Dedra beside her, Atyra felt it time to reveal the one secret she had kept from Mya. Drea's death had made Atyra consider her own mortality. Over one hundred Shamra had died on the journey to the new Shamra homeland four years earlier. And life on this land was filled with hazards. A fever had killed two dozen Shamra the first year. Accidents had also taken their toll. Atyra knew she courted danger whenever she ventured into the swamps. That, of course, was part of the swamps' allure. Her death could be right around the corner. Mya must know everything; though Atyra feared she might lose the child with the truth she had to reveal.

"I've told you all about our clan," Atyra began. "No matter what the priests here say, you are to hold your heads high. You are different from other Shamra females. You are the equal of any male."

Dedra stifled a yawn with her hand, and Atyra laughed. "I know, it's the same old story. But tonight there's something more I must share with you. It's difficult, so I babble on, repeating what you know by heart." Atyra looked at Mya. "I didn't know when the time would be right, so I kept putting it off. I love you, Mya, like my own daughter, but in truth, you are not my flesh and blood."

Dedra was no longer yawning, and Mya's brow was furrowed with concern.

"Nyvia, your great grandmother, was leader of our clan. Then Sera, your grandmother, led us. She had two children, Jana and Drea, just as I've told you. Sera and Jana died fighting the Kimra. Jana had an infant child. Drea asked me to take that child to the new Shamra homeland so the blood of her family would endure here. You're that child, Mya. Jana's daughter. The blood of Nyvia, Sera, Jana, and Drea courses through you. I've been selfish, Mya, putting off telling you—"

Mya hugged Atyra. "*You're* my mother," she said.

Atyra knew Mya could sometimes be stubborn. She had to make her understand. "I love you like a mother, but Jana's your mother."

Mya shook her head, still clutching Atyra. "I am of Nyvia, Sera, Jana, and Drea. I understand. But *you're* my mother. You'll always be my mother. You raised me. I know no other. I *want* no other mother."

"But you do understand the blood of Jana runs through you?" Atyra said. "Your descendant will one day lead our people."

Mya nodded.

"What does that make me?" Dedra said, frowning.

"What I was to Drea," Atyra said. "Someone Mya can confide her deepest fears and secrets to, and the other way around. You are the only one who will stand up to Mya when she is hardheaded. Drea and I were as close as sisters. *Closer* than Jana and Drea."

Mya put her arm around Dedra's shoulder. She looked at Atyra, and smiled. "Just as I am closer to you than I am to Jana, a mother I never knew."

Atyra laughed and hugged both her children. Mya *did* understand. And Mya was right. Just as Atyra and Drea were as close as sisters, Atyra was the only mother Mya knew. What a fool she'd been to think she might lose Mya. "No more secrets," she said to her daughters.

"Is Lon my father?" Mya asked.

"Jelon was your father. He, too, was killed by the Kimra," Atyra said.

"That's why Lon never loved me," Mya said. "He never wanted to have anything to do with me."

SHAMRA DIVIDED

"A foolish male, Mya," Atyra said, and hugged her daughter even tighter.

◆◆◆◆◆◆◆◆◆◆

The next day, a different fever struck Bashra. Atyra had told Bashra she knew Drea was dead, but she hadn't told her about Drea's visit. Bashra wouldn't understand.

A day after she'd collapsed, Atyra was tending her vegetable garden. Atyra wasn't fond of vegetables, and neither were Mya and Dedra. She craved meat, like all in her clan. And the swamps were teeming with prey. Atyra had a vegetable garden mainly so she wouldn't stand out. If Shamra didn't have a trade, they farmed. Atyra traded her vegetables for other essentials.

"Feeling better?" Bashra asked Atyra, bending to help Atyra pluck some weeds from the garden.

"Much," Atyra said. "I'm sorry if I frightened you."

"You said…you said Drea's dead. What did you mean? Or was it just a fever?" Bashra asked.

Atyra suspected Bashra would have been happy if Atyra lied, but Bashra was of her clan and deserved to know the truth. "Drea died yesterday. I saw her body," Atyra said. She described the aftermath of the battle in which Drea had perished, leaving out Drea's visit the night before. There was only so much someone like Bashra would be willing to allow herself to accept.

"How could you know?" Bashra asked.

"There's magic all around us, Bashra," Atyra said. "The creatures that appeared to us as the Kimra, for example. Surely that can't be explained. Drea is dead. Accept it or not. I can't explain it. I just know it."

"Yet you don't grieve," Bashra said.

"Have you forgotten the ways of our clan so quickly, Bashra?" Atyra asked, trying to keep the irritation out of her voice. "We don't grieve. We celebrate the lives of those who pass over. Of course I'm saddened, but I have so many memories I re-live and treasure, it's like Drea is still with me."

"I envy your strength," Bashra said. "You cling to the past—"

"No, Bashra, I celebrate my heritage," Atyra said, cutting Bashra off. "There's a difference. I have no desire to be accepted as a Shamra female under the New Order. I follow the rules of the New Order out of necessity. But my thoughts are my own. I am of the hunter's clan. It's who I am."

"That's why I envy you. For me, our clan is becoming a dim memory. I do tell my children of our past, but it seems like a lifetime ago."

"You have Tergon demanding conformity," Atyra said. "He's ambitious. I don't condemn you, Bashra. We each have to lead our life the best we can. I'll celebrate Drea's life, not mourn her death, just as if I were by her side when she fell."

"Can you tell me some stories of Drea?" Bashra asked. "It might be good for both of us."

Atyra didn't need prompting. For the next hour, she talked nonstop. She had Bashra laughing at some of their antics as children. How she and Drea had hunted in the forests when they were not much older than Mya and Dedra. How they were sometimes lucky to escape with their lives, yet how exhilarating it had been.

"The two of us were always competing. Here, we were children, and if I saw a boar to chase, Drea wanted to find one bigger. If Drea killed one with her bow and arrow, I had to kill one with a spear because you had to get closer to do so. It was far more risky. If Drea used her slingshot, I'd want to kill one with a knife. It's a wonder we made it out of the forest in one piece. Other than the battles against the Kimra, those were some of the best times we had. We faced death and walked out of the forest triumphant. We were too young to know what fools we were." Atyra laughed. "But if I had it to do all over, I wouldn't change a thing."

She also entranced Bashra with tales of their battle against the Kimra. Bashra was from Ramorra's family. She hadn't seen the worst of the Massacre at Monument Gate. Bashra had remained outside until Drea had climbed the gate and told Ramorra's family to batter it down so those inside wouldn't perish.

"I've forgotten so much," Bashra said, sounding forlorn. "You're right, though. Our people didn't grieve. We celebrated the life of the departed. How could I have forgotten?"

When Bashra left, Atyra was a bit concerned. Bashra had grown silent after her last comment. It was as if she were looking within herself to find something she'd misplaced and sorely missed.

That evening, Tergon came to Atyra's hut with distress, almost panic, etched on his face. "Something's wrong with Bashra," he told Atyra. "She's feverish. She's babbling. Can you come?"

"Shouldn't you get a healer?" Atyra asked. She and Tergon seldom crossed paths. He seemed to intentionally avoid her, which didn't bother her in the least.

"You don't understand. She's…she's babbling about her clan," Tergon said. "She's delirious. She has no idea that she's speaking what's forbidden. I can't take the risk of a healer telling the priests of her ramblings."

"*Our* clan," Atyra corrected Tergon, finding it difficult to keep the bitterness from her voice. "Deny your heritage all you want, but you were born into the hunter's clan. You fought against the Kimra. You laughed at death. But that was ages ago. Now you fear going to a healer because he might repeat what Bashra's saying in her delirium. You should be ashamed of yourself."

"She's asking for you," Tergon said.

Atyra noticed Tergon didn't deny her accusation. Still, if Bashra was asking for her, it was her duty to help her friend rather than argue with Tergon. If Bashra needed medical help, though, Atyra would fetch a healer no matter how much Tergon protested.

When Atyra saw Bashra, she knew no doctor could help her. She told Tergon to leave them alone and sent him out of the hut. Yes, Atyra saw, Bashra had a fever. She was drenched with sweat and complained of cramping in her legs and stomach. But this wasn't any ordinary fever, Atyra knew. Maybe Tergon had forgotten. Maybe he had never seen such a fever, but Atyra had. Bashra's eyes were blood red, as if the inside of her head were on fire. Her white hair had turned orange. Red blotches dotted Bashra's face. They were almost the color of her eyes. Hunter's fever, Atyra knew instantly. Only females of the hunter's clan were afflicted, and only when they were despondent and had gone long periods without hunting. When her country was enslaved by the Kimra, their oppressors allowed the hunter's clan to go into the forest. Half of all meat and half of the hides of animals had to be given to the Kimra. Twice, Atyra recalled, a hunter had escaped, and the entire clan drew the ire of their oppressors. They weren't allowed into the forest for weeks at a time. It was then that the fever struck. Atyra remembered proud Sera groveling before the Kimra, asking permission for the stricken to be allowed to hunt.

"We hunt, or the fever strikes," Sera had told the Kimra who guarded her village. "If they're not allowed to hunt, they'll die. There's no other cure. What good are dead Shamra to the Kimra? With each death, there's less we have to offer."

The Kimra thought Sera mad but accompanied a party of ill females into the forest. They returned cured, with many animals they had slain, all of which Sera offered to the Kimra to show her gratitude.

Now Bashra had the fever. Maybe, Atyra thought, it was the stories she had told Bashra. It must have awakened something long dormant within her. Atyra soaked her bandana in cool water and washed the perspiration from Bashra's face and forehead. Bashra gave off a pungent odor that those of her clan emitted before a hunt or battle—another telltale sign of the fever.

Bashra suddenly opened her eyes and saw Atyra. She grabbed Atyra by the collar of her shirt.

"Hunt," Bashra said. "Hunt. Kill. You. Me. Now!" She repeated it over and over. The red splotches on her face pulsed with a life of their own, like drums beating out a rhythm as she spoke.

"Not in the dark, Bashra," Atyra said. "It's too dangerous even for me, and I'm familiar with the swamps. Tomorrow. I promise."

Her words seemed to soothe Bashra. She let go of Atyra and fell into a fitful sleep.

"What is it?" Tergon asked when Atyra came out of the hut.

"You don't want to know," Atyra said. "Tomorrow I must take Bashra into the swamps—"

"Tergon cut her off, "It's forbidden."

"No one will know. If she doesn't go, she'll die. If you don't believe me, go fetch a healer."

"No!" Tergon almost shouted. "No healer."

"Then she goes with me to the swamps or dies. Your choice, Tergon," Atyra said.

"Save her, Atyra, but I don't want to know anything of what you plan. Do you understand?" Tergon asked.

"Perfectly," Atyra said, her voice bitter. "I'll bring Mya and Dedra to Cid's and then return. I'll stay with Bashra for the night. We have no further need of you. When we return, she'll be fine, and you won't have to worry that Bashra will stain your reputation. I won't be long," Atyra said, turned, and left. Tergon sickened her right now.

In her hut, before she could rouse Mya and Dedra, she felt a presence. She turned and saw Drea, who looked worried.

"Don't go with Bashra into the swamps," Drea said. "Don't let Bashra go into the swamps."

"Why are you here, Drea?" Atyra said. "I didn't summon you. Aren't there rules?"

"I told you there are no hard-and-fast rules. You need me. I'm here," Drea said.

"What happens if Bashra goes into the swamps?" Atyra asked.

"Chaos will reign," Drea said.

"What's that supposed to mean?" Atyra asked, irritated with her friend. They had never kept secrets from one another. Atyra knew Drea was holding back. Why?

"There's only so much I can tell you," Drea said. "Actually, there's only so much I know."

"Then there *are* rules," Atyra said.

"You're impossible," Drea said.

"No, I'm Atyra. The same Atyra you knew, loved, and trusted because I asked questions that had no easy answers. I'm doing the same now, only you're shutting me out."

"I'm acting on instinct, Atyra," Drea said. "I've only been at this for a few days. Just like with leading the clan, it's something I'll grow into. Something within tells me there's only so much I can tell you now. And I can't foretell the future. There are many possible futures. All I can tell you is that if you keep Bashra out of the swamps, Chaos passes you over."

Atyra heard a noise behind her. She turned, and Mya was staring wide-eyed. Atyra turned, and Drea was gone.

"Was that Aunt Drea?" Mya asked.

"You saw her?" Atyra asked in return.

Mya nodded.

"Yes, it was Drea."

"You said she died, but I saw her here…and…"

"And what?" Atyra asked.

"And…and then she was gone. How…" Mya began, then shook her head.

No secrets, Atyra thought, and quickly told Mya about Drea's Gift of Sight, walking through the waterfall, and her appearing when summoned in times of need. "Do you understand?" Atyra asked.

Mya shook her head. "But I believe. I heard her. I saw her. I saw her vanish."

"We'll talk more later; I promise," Atyra said. "Bashra's sick, and I must help her. I'll take you and Dedra to Cid's. Then I must go to Bashra."

On her way from Cid's hut to Bashra's, Atyra thought of Drea's warning. What should she do? What *could* she do? If Bashra didn't go into the swamps to hunt, she would die. If she did, according to Drea, this Chaos would appear. No, she corrected herself. Drea had said, *Chaos will reign*.

At Bashra's hut, Atyra found Tergon lying on the earthen floor. Bashra was gone. She roused Tergon. He opened his eyes and groaned.

"Where's Bashra?" Atyra asked. She saw panic in Tergon's eyes as he looked at the empty bed.

"Someone hit me from behind when I came in. It's all I remember."

Atyra helped Tergon outside. "One of the horses is gone," Tergon said. "Where did Bashra go?"

"I'll find her," Atyra said. "Back into the hut with you." She gave Tergon a drink of water and some herbs. "If your headache's not gone tomorrow, go see the healer. Leave Bashra to me."

Atyra went to her hut for weapons and her horse. Mya was sitting on Atyra's bed.

"Why are you here?" Atyra asked.

"Drea said not to go into the swamps. There's nothing you can do for Bashra," Mya said.

"You saw Drea? Spoke to her?" Atyra asked.

Mya nodded. "There's nothing you can do for Bashra," Mya repeated. "Go into the swamps, and Dedra and I lose you. Do as Drea says. Trust her like you always did."

Atyra smiled weakly. *Chaos reigns*, Atyra thought. She'd have to be prepared. Instinctively she knew only she could defeat Chaos. She looked at Mya. Well, maybe with a little help from Mya, she thought. Mya looked far older than her four years, just as Drea had looked far more than fifteen after she took over leadership of the clan. You and me, she thought, looking at her daughter. Mya, as if understanding, reached out and grasped her mother's hand.

♦♦♦♦♦♦♦♦♦♦

The next day Enron returned, and with his arrival, Tergon seemed to forget Bashra was gone.

Enron had been a priest who, along with Loran, believed in strict interpretation of the New Order. He and twelve of his most ardent followers had been lost in the wilderness during a fierce sandstorm that had struck as the Shamra journeyed to their new homeland. He had been given up for dead. He and Loran, leader of the religious clan, shared similar beliefs. Loran had been bitten by a snake two days before the Shamra had reached their new home. Loran hadn't died, but after four years, he was little more than a vegetable. He couldn't speak, couldn't write, couldn't communicate in any way. Word was that he could hear but was trapped within his own body. Atyra wouldn't say it aloud, but she wondered what sin Loran had committed that had so angered the prophets. She could list many.

Cheron had led the Shamra the first two years in their new homeland until he succumbed to a fever. Now Hoban led the clerics. He was considered far more benevolent than either Loran or Cheron. Until Hoban, all priests stayed behind the doors of an enormous temple constructed by those who had been of the craftsmen clan. From a balcony, one of the priests would lead the Shamra in prayer at sunup and sunset. Hoban had been the first to mingle among the people. He visited the sick, praying for their recovery. He went to the houses of new parents, blessing the birth of every new child. Rather than simply reading from the holy books, Hoban told stories that gave life to the prophets.

"Hoban has strayed from the path of the prophets," Enron said the very day he returned. "He glorifies himself. *He* likes to be worshiped, as if he himself were a prophet."

Enron refused to enter the lavish temple of the priests, saying it hadn't been sanctified. He couldn't feel the presence of the prophets at the temple. Instead, he built a simple hut with his own hands and preached to those who listened. His first day back, a dozen listened to Enron tell how the prophets had guided him through the storm and led him to the new Shamra homeland. Each day, the number of his followers grew. A week after his return, he condemned Hoban before one hundred supporters.

"The words of the prophets demand strict adherence," Enron told his growing number of disciples. They nodded their agreement. All were male. Enron wouldn't allow females to attend his gatherings. A female's role, so said Enron, was to raise Shamra children and tend to Shamra homes and hard-working husbands. "The prophets speak as one. Hoban commits blasphemy trying to give a face and history to the prophets. There is but one voice of the prophets, and it has no face, no body. Saying otherwise is heresy."

Up until then, Enron had only preached. He hadn't called for any action against Hoban and the other priests that he condemned. For his part, Hoban ignored Enron. He had welcomed Enron upon his return. He wouldn't speak ill of his fellow cleric. He spoke from the balcony of the temple, praying Enron would see that Hoban and the priests did indeed speak for the prophets.

Tergon and Lon had become two of Enron's most devoted disciples.

"The prophets have been angered, and we will soon feel their wrath," Enron said. "Tomorrow the prophets speak."

"Praised be the prophets," Lon and Tergon said, kneeling next to Enron. They had pledged their lives to safeguard Enron and carry out his wishes to restore the New Order to Shamra society.

The next day, torrential rains fell. Day and night, without cease, it rained. Crops were destroyed. Heavy winds that accompanied the rain swept Shamra huts into the air like pieces of parchment.

Hoban called for prayer. Enron issued no orders, saying the rain and wind was just the beginning. "The prophets are not finished with their wayward children yet. We who have sinned will feel their fury."

After three days of continuous rain, the river that was the lifeblood of the country overflowed its banks. The village that housed Hoban and the priests flowed with raging water one day and mud the next. Hoban ordered all Shamra to leave the village to ensure their safety. Only he and the priests remained in the temple, on the upper floors, where the water had not yet risen. Only Hoban himself ventured out to calm Shamra who were beginning to panic.

"The worst is yet to come," Enron told his followers, who now numbered in the hundreds.

It seemed Enron was prophetic. Disease spread among the cattle, and hundreds had to be slaughtered. With the rain unabated, the diseased cattle couldn't even be burned. They had to be buried. Their bodies sometimes washed up, as if they had risen from their graves, and were swept from village to village by the flowing waters.

This was followed by severe temperature fluctuations. One hour the heat was all but unbearable. The falling rain hissed as it struck the ground, and the whole country was enveloped in a soupy fog. An hour later, the weather changed within a period of minutes. The cold was intolerable; the falling rain felt like needles on any unfortunate Shamra who was caught outside.

On the sixth day, lightning lit the skies. The bolts of lightning were like spears hitting the huts, engulfing all within in a fire from which there was no escape.

When the rain began and threatened to destroy fields of grain, fruits, and vegetables, Atyra, along with Mya and Dedra, went to Cid's to help. Atyra herself had little to lose, but with ten children to feed, Cid and her husband couldn't afford the destruction of their crops.

Atyra had heard of Enron's rabble-rousing but at first took little notice. Life under Enron would have been hardly different for her than with Hoban leading the clerics. And during the first days of the storms, Enron's following, while enthusiastic, was still small.

When the rain didn't stop, when Cid's cattle began to sicken and die, and finally when lightning destroyed a farmhouse next to Cid's, Atyra recalled Drea's words. *Chaos reigns.* Could this be what Drea meant?

Amidst the storms, as if defying them, Enron and his growing number of followers rode from village to village venting his venom toward Hoban. Atyra took Mya to get a look at the cleric. How would she know if Enron was sent by this Chaos Drea had spoken of? A priest was, well, a priest. Atyra and Mya hid behind an overturned wagon as Enron and his entourage of fifty rode in. From a distance, Enron looked very much like Loran, her old nemesis. He was slight of build, his face chalky from spending much of the day indoors at prayer, and he was bald like all clerics.

It was only when Enron's horse passed and he turned toward where Atyra and Mya hid that they got a good look at his face.

"It's Bashra," Mya whispered, her voice shaking.

"Hush," Atyra said. But Atyra saw Mya was right. She didn't see the cleric, but saw Bashra. But looking into Bashra's eyes, Atyra knew this wasn't really Bashra. Bashra's eyes were a deep brown; the eyes that looked her way were black and soul-less. As Atyra looked on, Bashra's face dissolved, and Atyra peered into eyes without a face. The black pupils began to rotate like a whirlpool in a lake, attempting to suck her in. With difficulty, she turned, then put her hands over Mya's eyes. Atyra knew *this* was Chaos. Somehow, like the creatures who had used a Mist of Illusion on the Shamra, Chaos cloaked himself as Enron. For a reason she couldn't comprehend, Atyra and Mya saw Bashra behind the facade, but it wasn't the Bashra they had known. Chaos's eyes must have mesmerized those who looked upon him. Chaos was going to use his growing number of followers to tear the Shamra apart. That was what Chaos was all about, after all. She didn't need Drea to draw her a picture.

Atyra looked at Lon and Tergon. Their eyes were blank, devoid of expression.

"Like the walking dead," Mya said, echoing Atyra's thoughts.

Atyra nodded.

When the group passed the wagon, Enron stopped. He looked directly at Atyra, though she was hidden. He bent to say something to Lon.

"Leave now," Atyra whispered to Mya.

As Enron talked to Lon, Atyra and Mya slipped away. From behind a building, Atyra saw Lon and Tergon knock over the wagon where they had hidden. They began ripping the wood of the wagon apart, as if they would find what they were looking for between the boards. Atyra felt a chill run through her. She had been taught from her earliest recollections that there was no such thing as a warrior without fear. Fear brought vigilance. It was harnessing fear that a warrior required. For the first time in her life, Atyra felt raw fear she didn't know if she could contain. Chaos was like nothing she had ever encountered. Still, Atyra couldn't deny that the challenge Chaos posed made her blood boil. While she'd fled now, she knew she would confront Chaos. Containing her fear, she now felt anticipation and could smell the odor of the hunt wafting from her body.

Atyra and Mya ran back to Cid's to get Dedra.

"We can't stay here, Cid," Atyra told her friend. "I can't explain now, but we could put your family in danger."

"I'm not afraid of this creature you speak of or the crowd of Shamra who follow him," Cid said. "You're welcome to stay. I'll stand with you if they come. You're family."

"Which is why we can't stay. Fear Enron and whatever he is. Don't provoke him or the others. If I need your help, I'll ask," Atyra said.

"Promise?" Cid asked. "I know how stubborn you can be."

Atyra smiled. "Me, stubborn?" she said, and they both forced a hollow laugh. "Look, Cid, every Shamra is in peril. I am not so arrogant as to fight this beast and his followers alone. Just don't expose yourself needlessly. I've got to figure out how he can be defeated. Then you'll be the first I come to for help. Promise."

Drea was waiting for Atyra when she got to her hut. She had Atyra's sword and the copy of the original holy book in her hand.

"Enron senses you pose a threat," Drea said. There were no pleasantries. There was no playful or combative banter between Drea and Atyra. Both seemed aware time was at a premium. Atyra felt as she had when she and Drea had fought side by side against the Kimra at Monument Gate. Two warriors with one mission. "Enron will send his followers to find these and brand you a heretic. I know where you can hide these in the swamps," Drea said.

"How can I fight them without weapons?" Atyra asked.

"Not with this sword, Atyra," Drea said.

Atyra nodded. She had used the sword against the creatures with the Mist of Illusion. While she had saved her people, possession of the sword had been used against her anyway. Drea was right. Weapons, she would need, but not the sword.

"Tell me what you know of this Chaos," Atyra said. "It wears many faces. Beneath the priest is Bashra, and beneath Bashra are eyes without a face. Eyes of pure evil that can mesmerize others." She paused. "Drea, between us, rules were always meant to be broken. And we did break them. So tell me who this Chaos is so I can defeat him."

"Come," Drea said. "I'll explain as we go." As they ran toward the swamps, Drea told Atyra and Mya what she knew. "Chaos has been around since the first living creatures. Chaos appears, then disappears for as many as twenty-five years. Maybe it's satisfied with the havoc it has caused. Maybe it needs time to regenerate. I truly don't know. Chaos has awakened, and not just here. Other countries are now at its mercy. Just like here, Chaos masks itself and attempts to make people turn on one another. If a culture can be destroyed, Chaos is victorious. Even if a culture survives but is in shambles for years, Chaos is satisfied."

"Why did I see Bashra in Chaos?" Atyra asked.

"It used Bashra as its vessel. The Bashra you know is dead. Weeks from now, when Chaos has fled, she will be found in the swamps. Chaos is like a parasite. It needs a host to latch on to. That's why I warned you to stay away from the swamps and keep Bashra from entering. I was mistaken. Chaos would have found some other host to feed upon if Bashra had stayed out of the swamps."

"It seems to have Lon and Tergon in its grip," Atyra said. "Their eyes are vacant. Are they dead too?"

"They live, but they're under its spell. It has the power to brainwash with the eyes that tried to trap you. In its grasp, your thoughts are no longer your own. Because Lon and Tergon were members of the hunter's clan, Chaos sought them out. It's their warrior instincts Chaos desires. They will fight to the death for the one they know as Enron. They will lead others. It's the nature of our clan to lead and for other Shamra to follow."

"What does Chaos want with us?" Atyra asked. She had just one other question. It was the most important, but she wanted to know as much about her enemy as possible.

"I know you don't believe, Atyra, but our people need the prophets. They need some higher power to guide them in times of disaster, like now. Chaos's goal is to discredit the prophets, to make the people doubt their most fundamental beliefs. Once that occurs, strife will tear our people apart. Just as Enron has many supporters, Hoban and the other priests have just as many ardent adherents who will oppose Enron. There can be no compromise. Shamra will fight one another—something they have never done before. Whatever the outcome, Chaos will prevail. Just as you believed in me as head of our clan, and now believe in what I've become, so, too, do our people need to believe in the prophets."

Atyra finally asked the most important question. "Then what do we do?"

"Turn the tables on Chaos," Drea said.

They had come to a cave Atyra had never seen in her travels in the swamps. Small crystals on the floor of the cave lit their way. A small number of transparent crystals hung from the ceiling.

"I have seen this cave in the future. Dara's time," Drea said. "It looks far different. Bury your sword and holy book in the center. They will be protected."

"Will Dara use my sword?" Atyra asked.

"The future remains to be written, Atyra. The sword will be here if she needs it. And don't make light of the importance of the original version of the holy book," Drea said.

"What are you not telling me?" Atyra asked.

"There will be no Dara if Chaos can't be dealt with here and now," Drea said.

"So how do we turn the tables on Chaos. It sounds wonderful."

Drea left the cave and soon returned with a creature. "I believe you've met," Drea said.

Atyra and Mya stared wide-eyed at the leader of the Tweeble. The creature standing before her now had replaced the leader she had killed. It was half her height and covered from head to toe with fur. It wore a bandage around its head that covered one of its eyes.

"You brought it here," Atyra said, anger welling within her.

"Through the waterfall," Drea said. "The same way I'll return him. He has no idea where we are."

"Do you have a name?" Atyra asked, her anger abated.

"Ishry," he said.

"Why would you help us?" Atyra asked with suspicion.

"For several reasons," Ishry said. "You and your daughter," he said, looking at Mya, "spared us and let us keep our weapons. You said you wouldn't tell others how you pierced our Mist of Illusion. You kept your word." He paused. "And for revenge. The monster your friend calls Chaos visited my people," Ishry said, his hand touching the bandage over his eye.

"What happened?" Atyra asked.

"We *thought* we'd found easy prey. This Chaos had cloaked a ferocious army to make them appear no threat. Then it removed *our* Mist of Illusion. Not only was our war-party almost completely wiped out, they attacked one of our villages, killing everyone, even children. As if that weren't enough, Chaos restored the Mist of Illusion to some of us and not others. It caused...well, chaos among our people. I lost my eye in a battle."

"How did you get rid of Chaos?" Atyra asked.

"We didn't. It tired of us and left. It will be generations before we have recovered."

"And you can help us?" Atyra asked.

"Yes, with pleasure," Ishry said. "With the Mist of Illusion, I can make the one you call Enron appear to be the Kimra your people fear. That might make them think twice about following his commands."

"Sit, Ishry, and let's plan our attack," Atyra said. "Unmasking Enron might not be enough. I want Chaos destroyed."

"It may not be possible," Drea said.

"We'll try. It certainly won't take kindly to being foiled," Atyra said.

The plan they came up with was simple. Enron would be unmasked, and Atyra would draw it toward the swamps. Atyra would pass through the swamp so that a tree with its branches filed to spikes could be launched by Mya, Dedra, and Ishry to behead Chaos.

While the others built the weapon, Mya tracked Enron. Atyra and Ishry then went to the village where Enron was speaking. Over one hundred of his supporters were with him as he spewed venom toward Hoban and the wayward priests who had failed the prophets.

"You see all around you the results of angering the prophets," Enron said, as heavy rain pelted the crowd. "It's time—"

There was a gasp before Enron could continue. Enron looked at Lon and Tergon. They cowered in fear. Others began running away in panic.

"It's the Kimra," one yelled.

"The Kimra," screamed another.

"Enron is a Kimra," shouted a third.

Only then did Enron seem to understand. As terrified Shamra bolted in every direction, Atyra rode up on her horse. She kept a safe distance between herself and Enron.

"You've been unmasked for the sham you are. By a female, no less," Atyra said. She then headed for the swamps. She heard a howl of anger as loud as a thunderclap. She turned and saw Chaos pursuing her. Almost at the edge of the swamps, Atyra's horse slipped on the rain-slicked grass and went down. Atyra lay on the ground dazed.

Enron rode up and glared at Atyra. He withdrew a sword from the priest's robe he wore.

"You think you have defeated me," Enron bellowed, his voice so loud Atyra's head ached. "A minor setback." Enron whipped his hand in front of his face, and he was Bashra. He drew his hand across his face again, and Atyra saw only the black eyes whose whirlpool threatened to suck her consciousness in and turn her into what Lon and Tergon had become. Chaos laughed. Lying on the ground, Atyra tried to avert her eyes. She saw Dedra rush toward Chaos.

"No, Dedra!" Atyra yelled.

Dedra had a spear in her hand and ignored her mother. Chaos looked at Atyra, then at Dedra, and laughed. "First your daughter, then you," he said.

As Dedra approached, Chaos slashed at her with its sword. Atyra leaped to her feet and lunged at Dedra. The sword went through Atyra's back and exited her chest. Atyra fell, knowing she was mortally wounded. Barely conscious, she saw Mya creeping forward in the tall grass. With her slingshot, Mya unleashed a rock that hit Chaos in his right eye. The eye exploded, and bright light poured out like molten lava as Chaos bellowed in pain. Before Mya could reload, Chaos rode toward the swamps. Ishry, who had returned, launched the tree trunk, which hit Chaos squarely in the head, knocking Chaos off his horse.

At that instant, the rain stopped. The howling wind ceased. The sun, not seen for a week, parted the clouds. Atyra closed her eyes and...

♦♦♦♦♦♦♦♦♦♦

...found herself at the foot of a waterfall. Atyra stared at her body, which lay on the grass where she had fallen. She looked at Drea.

"I didn't know," Drea said. "There are many futures—"

"There's no need to explain," Atyra said. "I died saving my daughter. Is there a more glorious death?" she said, smiling at Drea. "Dedra risked her life to save me. A mother couldn't ask for more." Atyra said proudly. "What of Chaos?" she asked.

They saw Ishry standing where Chaos had fallen.

"He's gone," Drea said. "The robes he wore are all that remain."

"Is he dead?"

"I doubt it," Drea said. "And he's but one of many."

"So it was all for nothing," Atyra said, crestfallen.

"Not at all," Drea said. "The chaos he created here will take years to undo, but it would have been far worse if you hadn't interceded. I really can't foretell the future, but I still see Dara. The future I saw is unaltered by the events that took place. Once again, you've preserved the future."

Atyra watched as Mya and Dedra turned Atyra's body, which lay on the ground below, over. Neither cried. I taught them well, she thought, smiling to herself. A Glimmer landed on the Atyra that lay on the ground. Glimmers were beautiful flying insect-like creatures that had been plentiful when the Shamra first arrived in the land. Shamra were voracious eaters of insects, and within a year, only a handful remained. Cheron, who had led the priests at the time, prohibited the further eating of Glimmers. Stories spread that if a Glimmer was caught and then released, a wish would be granted. Atyra didn't believe it for a moment, yet she knew magic did exist. It made a good story for Mya and Dedra, even if there was no proof a wish had ever been granted. Now a Glimmer was perched on Atyra's body. Dedra reached for it and gently grabbed it as it attempted to escape. She held it for a moment, then let it go.

"I wonder what she wished for." Atyra said. Then she looked at Drea. "So what happens next?"

"We go through the waterfall to a new life," Drea said.

"Will I see the future like you? Will I be summoned?"

"I don't know," Drea said.

"You know, you're very selective with your knowledge of the future, Drea. I do believe there can be more than one future. You wouldn't have let me go through with my plan if you knew it would cost me my life. I don't have the Gift of Sight, so how can I see into the future?" Atyra asked.

"You can't," Drea said.

"And will I be summoned?" Atyra asked.

"You've saved the Shamra twice. It's what legends are made of," Drea said.

"If I were among our clan, I'd agree. Here, females can't be heroic," Atyra said. "Other than in Mya's, Dedra's, and Cid's mind, I'll be forgotten not long after I'm buried. For the rest of the Shamra, I am just another female who had grudgingly accepted the New Order. One can't be a heroic female in the New Order. Can you deny that?" Atyra asked

Drea shook her head. "You'll be a hero with your family. You'll see events unfold as they do. And you'll be there for me. Together again, forever."

"It's not like I have a choice, do I?" Atyra said forlornly.

Drea closed her eyes. "As a matter of fact, you do."

"What do you mean?" Atyra asked, taken by surprise by what Drea had said.

"The same choice I had. You can return to your body and live out your life. Don't ask me what kind of life it will be," Drea added quickly. "I don't know, and even if I did, I wouldn't tell you."

Atyra looked down below. "When you were offered the chance, you chose death."

Drea nodded.

"I have my own destiny to fulfill," Atyra said. "There's much I still have to teach Mya and Dedra. I want to make sure there will be a Dara to save our people. I choose to live."

Atyra saw Drea's eyes tearing. "I often wonder if I made the right choice," Drea said. "My daughter is growing up without her mother. It can't be easy for her."

"We even choose different paths for the same reason, Drea," Atyra said. "Without you, Chaos would have reigned here. There may well have been no Dara in the future. You paid a price, but don't question your decision. You never did as leader of our clan. Don't now." She paused, looking at her body below. "Will I see you again?" Atyra asked.

"You'll join me when your time comes. Not as you appear today, but our friendship will never end. Now go to your children."

Drea pointed, and a bridge of stones appeared. Atyra walked unseen into her body, then opened her eyes.

"Mommy!" Dedra said. "I caught a Glimmer. I wished you'd come back."

"Now we know the stories about Glimmers are not just tall tales," Atyra said and smiled. She looked up. She knew only she could see Drea and the waterfall. She nodded toward her friend. She saw Drea wipe a tear from her eye and enter the waterfall.

"It was a glorious battle," Mya said. Her bandana had slipped and almost covered one of her eyes. She and Dedra were bathed in sunlight.

Atyra smelled their pungent odor. "My little warriors," she said. "Now you have your own stories to tell your children. My little ones defeated Chaos."

CHAPTER 11

~ *The Present* ~

"What fools we've been," Briana said when she'd finished her story. "When the Galvan targeted my family, we thought it was a new strategy they had concocted. Our family has been a thorn in their side for two hundred years. Kill our family, and not only are we weakened, but there would be infighting to see who would lead the clan. During this period of…chaos, I guess you'd call it, the Galvan would have the opportunity to strike when we're most vulnerable. But it *wasn't* the Galvan. Chaos is among them. These minions of Chaos want to destroy our family, but for a different reason. Chaos doesn't care if the Galvan slaughter us. Chaos simply wants our clan in disarray. Whether the clan survives or perishes is of no importance. And now Chaos seeks you."

Dara shook her head. "That's ridiculous. It's *you* they want. I'm not a ruler; I've told you over and over again. I learned that when I ruled my homeland for nine months. And I won't be stuck living out my days on Stone Mountain. My destiny...my desire, is to seek adventure."

"Let's test your theory," Briana said. "We've fooled them awhile, but they are making their way here. Come, I know where to go. Where to prove whom they want to claim."

Briana led Dara around a river of mud. As a youth, Dara had seen such a river in the swamps that bordered her homeland. If one tried to cross it, he was literally sucked under. There was no escape. Briana and Dara waited on a dirt slope not far from the river's edge. They could be seen from the other side, but to capture them, the Galvan would have to go around the river, and by then, Dara and Briana would be long gone.

"When you came here five days ago, you showed me a stick. You said it was given to you by..." Briana paused, looking a bit bewildered.

"The Rulan," Dara said. "But I haven't been here—"

"Let's not argue about that now. Do you have the stick with you?"

Dara reached into her stomach pouch and removed it. It was far smaller than the walking stick the Rulan had given Dara for her journey across what seemed a never-ending desert. The stick had saved her life. If she drew a circle around her and then drew an X from one side to the other, she was protected from predators who might desire her for a meal while she slept. She had lost the stick in a windstorm. Later, when she visited the Rulan again, she was given another—the smaller stick she now held.

Meeko, ruler of the Rulan, had explained to her:

"When you told us what happened with the walking stick, we experimented. The size of the stick has no significance. I gave you a walking stick because it would help you

SHAMRA DIVIDED

travel across the desert. But this smaller stick is just as effective protection. You can store it in your stomach pouch."

Dara now held the stick up to Briana.

"Will it protect you from an arrow?" Briana asked.

"Nothing can penetrate it," Dara said. "I can protect the both of us."

"Draw your circle with an X around you," Briana instructed. "I won't need a shield."

"You're that sure?" Dara asked. "What if you're wrong?"

"The river is wide," Briana said. "It would still take an excellent shot to hit me. The Galvan were never great marksmen. Chaos may control their minds, but they still have the limitations of the Galvan. I like my chances."

Dara shook her head. "More obstinate than even I. More arrogant too," she said. "It will be the death of you if you don't change your ways. But you won't heed me, so why waste my breath." Dara drew her protective circle with its X. Ten minutes later, the Galvan appeared. Dara could easily make out their faces. Still blank, without emotion. The two in the lead unsheathed their bows. Two arrows rained upon Dara, both bouncing harmlessly off the invisible protective shell that surrounded her. They reloaded, and the other four were now also armed. Six more arrows. *All* aimed at her. It was as if Briana didn't exist.

Before they could fire again, Briana told Dara to run with her into the forest. She had made her point. Hidden behind trees, they saw one of the Galvan attempt to cross the river. He and his horse were immediately sucked under. The others began the long trek around the river.

"I thought they couldn't be killed," Dara said. Before Briana could answer, the Galvan who had sunk into the mud suddenly surfaced and, with difficulty, made his way to the shore. His horse was lost. Without a horse, he could only look across to where Dara and Briana hid.

"They can be killed...or at least injured, but not by drowning," Briana said. "So they'll flee." She paused. "There's a cave not far from here. We can hide and plan a strategy. We must escape the forest. There's no way we can elude all six."

"You never told me why your clan left the valley for Stone Mountain," Dara said, as they made their way to the cave. "When the Galvan arrived, did you just flee?"

"Does that sound like the warriors Drea led?" Briana asked.

"That's not an explanation."

"You're right," Briana said. "It was among the darkest days of our clan. For the first time since our family ruled, the clan was divided. No, I take that back," Briana said, and paused. "Our *family* was divided, and that made it all the worse."

CHAPTER 12

~ PROBLEM CHILD ~

185 years ago

Anis finally had the wild pig trapped. She had tracked it for over an hour. She *could* have killed it long before, but she wanted to give it a sporting chance. She wanted to back it into a corner to see how it responded. Would it cower and die meekly, or did it have the will to fight to the death? The pig had long, razor-sharp teeth that jutted from its mouth. It certainly wasn't defenseless. To Anis's chagrin, though, the beast seemed to have no desire for confrontation. Run. Hide. Run. Run. Run again. Each time, Anis caught its scent.

Now that it was trapped, Anis saw it stare at her in indecision. Then its eyes hardened. Anis smiled. It wouldn't die without a fight. Anis dropped her spear. She had only her knife. The pig charged, squealing in anger or terror, Anis thought. Or maybe both. Anis held her ground. The pig jumped at her as it drew closer, knocking Anis to the forest floor. Its jaws went for her neck. Anis thrust her right arm sideways into the beast's jaw so it couldn't bite down. With her left hand, she cut the pig's throat. Blood splattered Anis. She drank the rich, warm blood. She thought nothing tasted as good as the blood from a fresh kill. She pushed the creature off her and stood, a look of triumph on her blood-smeared face.

Janis and Dyann, who had been with Anis, approached cautiously. Anis had forbidden them to interfere. The consequences for crossing Anis were ominous. Her temper was renowned. She would just as soon fight Janis or Dyann for defying her as kill the pig, who had finally showed its courage.

"Do you *want* to die?" Dyann asked. At twenty-six, she was eleven years older than the fifteen-year-old Anis. Dyann was the big sister Anis never had. Anis loved and respected Dyann. That didn't mean she always heeded her advice.

"I want to taste death, Dyann," Anis said. "I want to cheat death," she continued, licking the pig's blood from the corners of her lips.

"One day death may prevail," Dyann said.

"It's a risk worth taking," Anis said. "It's been a good while since I've felt so alive."

"You sound just like your mother," Dyann said.

The smile on Anis's face vanished. Her mother Drea had died in battle eleven years earlier, when Anis was just four. Drea had been nineteen at the time. Dyann, who had fought by her side, had been fifteen. From stories others told, Dyann had been as reckless then as Anis was now. Not one to follow orders, she had been chosen to attack with Drea's warriors. Dyann might defy others, but never the head of her clan. Even now, far more mature, Dyann wasn't quite tame. That wild streak was what drew Anis to Dyann. Now Anis shrugged at Dyann's comment.

"You should take that as a compliment," Dyann said.

"My mother abandoned me. I hardly remember her," Anis said.

"Rubbish. The clan recounts her exploits daily. She lives in all of us," Dyann said.

"I know what she *did*, Dyann," Anis said. "I just never got to know *her*. To you and the others who hunted and fought with her, she was flesh and blood. Me, what do I know other than her heroic deeds?"

"She didn't plan to die on the raid against the Kimra," Dyann said "Like you, she thought herself invincible. And like you, the hunt and the need to do battle ran wild in her blood. I was like her once, but our clan is no longer what it was."

"She had a responsibility to me," Anis shouted. She wasn't angry at Dyann, but bitter at her loss. "My mother turned her back on me for the glory of battle. I don't want to speak of her anymore," Anis said. She lifted the dead pig and draped it across her shoulders.

When she entered her village, her cousin Kel, leader of the clan, greeted her. "You're going to empty the forest," he said uneasily. Anis knew Kel was not good at confrontation, especially with her. She had little respect for her cousin and didn't hide her feelings. And if she ever dared challenge Kel for leadership of the clan, they both knew he would die.

"Then I'll journey to another," Anis shot back. When Drea died, Kel became leader of the hunter's clan. He had been but fifteen himself at the time, but he was the eldest of their family. Anis's family had ruled the clan for over a hundred years. Unless challenged, someone from Drea's family would become the new leader upon her death. At four, Anis was too young. Her father, Pror, six years older than Kel, had suggested he lead in Anis's name until she turned fifteen. His claim was dismissed by the rest of the family, who would choose their new leader. Pror didn't share their blood, so he could never rule. Pror took his defeat gracefully. He told Anis when she was older that, while he had been a great warrior, he was uncertain whether he wanted the responsibility of clan leadership.

Kel's only competition came from his younger brother Tobin, who had been eleven. Tobin had fought valiantly against the Kimra. Physically, he was Kel's equal, even though he was four years younger. Where Kel was cautious, Tobin was more like his mother Jana, Drea's sister. The family chose Kel solely because of his age. Before dawn the next day, Tobin had ridden off alone. There had been no goodbyes, and he didn't return.

Kel, Anis would agree, had been an effective if uninspired leader of the clan. The last eleven years had been lived in peace. Most of the clan was satisfied reminiscing about past battles. Kel occasionally hunted in the forest that bordered the Shamra land, but unlike Drea, he had never left the country to feast upon new prey or seek adventure to satisfy the thirst that had driven Drea to venture into the unknown.

Anis took the boar to Ramorra, now a clan elder at thirty-seven. Anis hadn't been raised by her father after Drea's death. It was clan tradition that a female who lost her mother, like Anis did, be raised by other females in the clan. Ramorra and Dyann were Anis's mentors. Janis, Ramorra's youngest daughter, was Anis's closest friend.

"Your bandana is blood-soaked," Ramorra commented as Anis told her of the hunt. "It will reek of the stench of the pig if not washed."

Anis removed the bandana and tasted the still wet boar's blood. "I'll wash it soon, Ramorra," Anis said. She would suck the garment dry before washing it. The yellow bandana with black polka dots had been her mother's. Despite the bitterness she felt toward her mother, she treasured the bandana, along with a necklace she wore with a green stone attached. It was also her mother's, and she had added a second identical stone. Her mother would have been proud of her today, while Ramorra was anxious and Dyann was concerned. It only made Anis resent the loss of her mother more.

While Ramorra gutted the boar, Anis started a fire. Ramorra looked at her with disapproval. She knew what Anis planned. After a particularly challenging or satisfying kill, Anis burned a symbol onto her shoulder or arm to honor the slain animal and to remind herself of the kill.

"You desecrate your body," Ramorra had told her years ago, when Anis marked the kill of a boar. "It's unheard of in our clan."

"So I start a new tradition," Anis had said.

"And if I forbid it? If Kel forbids it?" Ramorra had asked.

Anis had smiled and said nothing and marked the kill on her arm. She now had a dozen.

✦✦✦✦✦✦✦✦✦✦

Two months later, the Galvan came, and life for the Shamra was forever altered.

When a Galvan scouting party arrived, they were greeted hospitably. Regor, their leader, spoke for the group. They had had some contact with the Kimra, so they could converse with Kel, Ramorra, and two others who represented the clan. At the last minute, Anis demanded she be allowed to hear Regor's plea. Kel had reluctantly agreed. It was the first time Anis had taken an interest in anything other than hunting and studying Shamra history and traditions under Ramorra.

The Galvan were hairless green creatures, generally a head taller than the Shamra. They had two arms and two legs like the Shamra. They had claw-like talons for hands. Their faces were tapered, and they had narrow slits for eyes, which were set close together. They had nostrils but no nose. And they breathed through two gill-like incisions on each cheek. As a result, they would speak a sentence or two and then pause to get air. It was sometimes difficult for the Shamra to know when they were finished speaking or if they were simply pausing for breath. It made for awkward silences at times, as Kel didn't want to be rude and interrupt before Regor had finished speaking.

After an offering of gifts from Regor, Regor told the story of his people's wandering. He presented Kel with a dozen horses, including several dwarf ponies that would delight the clan's children.

"We number two hundred," Regor began. "We left our country rather than accept the rule of the majority."

Kel waited for Regor to continue. When he didn't, Kel spoke. "How do your beliefs differ from the majority?"

"We are farmers. We eat grains, fruits, and vegetables, not meat. We believe in self-defense, but those who lead our country demand all males serve four years in the army."

Again Kel waited before speaking. "Does the army of your country raid other lands like the Kimra?"

"No, they have no desire to conquer others," Regor said and paused. This time, he continued. "But a permanent army is seen as a deterrent to those like the Kimra." There was yet another pause; then Regor continued: "Over thirty years ago, the Kimra *did* attack us. They couldn't defeat us. Now our people trade with the Kimra, but our leaders still made military service a requirement. The Kimra remain a threat, and there are others who would enslave us if we aren't vigilant. My people strive for peaceful coexistence. We agreed to one year of military training solely for self-defense, but this was not acceptable to our country's leaders."

"So you left," Anis said, when Regor did not continue. Kel looked at Anis with disapproval. Anis returned his stare. There was no need for words. Anis would not be bullied into silence by Kel. He might be her clan's leader, but she was no longer a child. She feared Kel would be misled. She was determined to learn the truth from these strangers. "And you find our country appealing?" she continued.

Regor looked confused. He had addressed Kel, leader of the Shamra. Now he seemed to wonder if he should also address Anis. Kel seemed to understand, even if he didn't approve of Anis's undermining his authority. "I lead my people, Regor, but Anis or any of the others are free to speak their minds."

"We notice you are few, and most of your country lays barren," Regor said, looking at Anis. "In exchange for use of the land that lays fallow, we can provide you horses and other livestock. You say you are meat-eaters—"

"Hunters," Anis corrected.

"Our forests no longer teem with prey," Kel said, ignoring Anis.

"We have animals. We don't eat them, of course, but their milk feeds our young, and their hides clothe us all. We will trade our animals for permission to share your land. What you do with the animals is of no concern to us."

After another forty-five minutes of discussion, Kel told Regor he would confer with his people and come to a decision by sunrise the next day.

Kel spoke to the Circle of Families that night. One member spoke for each family in the clan. The rest of the clan gathered and listened.

"I see no harm in sharing our land with the Galvan," Kel said, after he'd told the others what he had learned. There would be no vote. Kel, as the clan's leader, had final say. "On the contrary, with the thinning of the forest, what they offer is most attractive."

"You are too trusting, Kel," Anis said. She stood outside the Circle of Families and *should* have remained silent, but refused. There was a murmur among a number of the others when Anis spoke. Kel shot Anis a look of disapproval, but

Anis knew he lacked the courage to demand her to be silent. "You accept their story without proof," Anis continued. "I don't oppose sharing our land, but I have a feeling there is something vital they are hiding."

"And what would you have us do, Anis? How do you propose we learn what you feel is the truth?" Kel asked, issuing a challenge of his own.

"That we...that I and a party you choose go to the Galvan homeland to verify their claim," Anis said.

"I would be offended by such a demand placed on us were the situation reversed."

Others nodded in agreement.

"Then we go without telling them," Anis said. "If they speak the truth, no one need be the wiser."

"We don't deal in deceit," Kel said. "*My* instincts tell me the Galvan will be good neighbors. We will accept their offer."

"Have it your way," Anis said. She was tired of arguing. She was disappointed in her clan. Rather than be wary, they had grown slothful. She realized she had erred in not enlisting the support of others before contesting Kel's authority. She had spoken on impulse. She hadn't planned to break clan tradition. This battle was lost, but maybe the seed of doubt had been planted. "Just remember you were warned," she added, turned, and left the gathering.

Later, Ramorra and Dyann entered Anis's hut.

"All of a sudden you are interested in clan affairs?" Ramorra said. "You never were before."

"The Galvan are a threat to our way of life. To our very existence. Mark my words, Ramorra," Anis said.

"That's a bit harsh," Ramorra said. "But I don't believe your request was without merit."

"You feel something's wrong?" Anis asked.

"I have always been the voice of caution," Ramorra said.

"Then talk to Kel," Anis said.

"His decision is made, and knowing Kel, it is final," Ramorra said. "He leads our clan. You were wrong to humiliate him before the others."

"Someone had to speak," Anis said.

"Not at the Circle. You should have met with Kel in private *before* the clan met," Ramorra said. "You might have achieved something. You've always been impetuous, Anis. You saw tonight that no good comes of being so headstrong."

Anis shrugged. "It wouldn't have made any difference if I'd spoken to him. His mind was made up."

"Then so be it," Ramorra said. "I have taught you about the traditions of our people. Kel leads. We follow. Your family doesn't air misgivings in front of others."

"Everything shouldn't revolve around tradition," Anis said. "The past is a guide, Ramorra. That doesn't mean it should be followed blindly."

"We must trust Kel's judgment," Ramorra said.

Anis shrugged. "Have it your way," she said, echoing the words she'd spoken to Kel. "I will be a good Shamra... for now. This will not end well for us. And I refuse to remain silent if Regor's promises turn out to be hollow."

✦✦✦✦✦✦✦✦✦

The Galvan came. They were courteous. They were generous. They were peaceful, though Regor had a dozen guards to protect him and his family. And they gave the Shamra horses to ride and animals to slaughter and eat. They also multiplied far more rapidly than the Shamra had anticipated. Females gave birth to four or five offspring at a time and gave birth after only two months. In two months, the two hundred Galvan had increased to four hundred. Regor met with Kel and asked for more land. He suggested the Shamra move closer to the forest, where the land was not as suitable for farming, in exchange for more horses and livestock. Kel agreed and broke the news to the Circle of Families.

"This is just the beginning," Anis said. Her latest outburst drew looks of disapproval from far more than before. She cursed herself. Again, she had been caught off guard. She hadn't forged alliances with others. Angry at herself, she vented her frustration at Kel and the others in the clan. "You would have me be silent in the face of this new threat?" Anis asked. "I refuse. I warned you we hadn't been told the entire truth. We know now for a fact the Galvan reproduce at an alarming rate. They want our land...*all* of our land. They will drive us from what is rightfully ours. Can't you see that?"

"Regor has given his solemn vow this is the last time we will be asked to move," Kel said. "I take him at his word."

"You lead us, Kel," Anis said with sarcasm in her voice. "Maybe to extinction," she added, and left.

Anis was too angry to remain in the village. The rest celebrated, slaughtering animals Regor provided, and gorged themselves. Anis went into the forest alone to hunt.

Deep in the forest, Anis heard the noise of something thrashing, making no attempt to remain hidden. The animals Anis hunted possessed far more stealth. Anis saw a Galvan female emerge from a tangle of bushes with a wild boar in pursuit. The female fell, and the pig leaped at her, its teeth bared. Instinctively, Anis threw her spear and felled the pig. The female stared at Anis. She was breathing deeply from the slits in her cheeks.

"You...you saved my life," the Galvan said between breaths.

"The boar will make a fine meal. You drew it toward me," Anis said. "What are you doing in the forest alone?"

"I got a little lost," she said.

"There's no such thing as being a little lost in these woods. The forest is my home, and yet I sometimes get caught in its web. I've spent many a night here unable to find my way out. You shouldn't be out here alone."

"I wasn't. I always travel with...escorts. It gets tiresome," the female said.

"Guards, you mean," Anis said.

The female nodded.

"Who are you?" Anis asked.

"Cym, daughter of Regor," she said, looking at Anis with pride. "And you?"

Anis appraised the female for a moment before speaking. Cym appeared to be the same age as she. She was no child, but wasn't yet an adult.

"I am Anis."

Cym's eyes widened. "Why do you hate us?" she asked.

"Our people don't hate your people," Anis said. "What makes you—?"

"No, not your people. *You!*"

"You've heard of me?" Anis asked, incredulous.

"My father speaks of you. Your leader..." she paused and shook her head.

"Kel," Anis said.

"Yes, Kel. Kel tells my father you are suspicious of us."

"Kel should keep his mouth shut," Anis said, not aware she had said the words aloud.

"Does he speak the truth?" Cym asked.

Anis nodded. "Yes, I suppose. But I don't hate you. I just don't trust you. There's a difference."

"You don't know us," Cym said.

"I have no great desire, truth be told," Anis said. "Even if I did, your people keep to themselves. It only adds to my distrust."

"Yet you saved my life," Cym said.

"You brought me a meal," Anis answered.

"Say what you want; you saved my life." Cym paused. "Teach me to hunt," she said.

"Why? You don't eat meat. It's wrong to hunt solely for the sake of killing...or do your people think otherwise?" Anis asked.

"I want to learn how to defend myself," Cym said.

"The army in your country is for males only?" Anis asked. The Galvan culture sounded much like the Kimra, where females were submissive to males.

Cym nodded. "Any animals I kill, I offer to you as... payment for my...lessons." Cym paused. "If you get to know me, your fears might be put to rest."

Anis shrugged. Cym had a point, though not the one she mentioned. Study your enemy, Anis had been taught. That was how the Kimra had been defeated. Gaining Cym's trust would allow Anis to gain insight into the Galvan. She might even learn some of the secrets she was certain had been withheld from the Shamra.

Cym proved a quick study. She was excellent with a bow and arrow, sword, spear, and knife, though clumsy with a slingshot. Her talon-like hands were far more pliable than Anis had imagined. The Galvan also had a keen sense of smell, and Cym proved an excellent tracker. She also showed courage equal to any Shamra.

She was guarded with her answers when Anis questioned her about the Galvan homeland. Anis did learn that the Galvan grew to maturity in just four months. Cym was twelve, an adult, but you couldn't tell the difference between her and a Galvan who was a year old unless you saw their backs. Cym lifted her shirt, and Anis saw a series of spots.

"One for each year," Cym said.

"What is your lifespan?" Anis asked.

"My father is twenty, a fully mature male. At twenty-five, he will begin to slow down and relinquish power to one of my brothers. At thirty, he is old. Not many of us live past thirty-five."

"What of the army you hide from my cousin?" Anis asked another day. She knew of no such army, but sensed the Galvan had one. It couldn't hurt to ask.

SHAMRA DIVIDED

"We only seek to protect ourselves," Cym answered.

"From whom?"

Cym shrugged.

"How large is your army?" Anis asked.

"I thought you knew. You have played me for a fool. Here I thought we were friends, and you use me to betray my people," Cym said, her voice filled with chagrin.

"*You* are not my enemy, Cym," Anis said. "You are honorable. If all the Galvan were like you, we could coexist in harmony. But your people harbor secrets. I fear what I don't know will lead to our downfall. Do you deny telling me half-truths? Sometimes you speak freely. Other times you seem to weigh each word you utter. You're evasive. I wonder why."

"I appreciate all you've taught me," Cym said stiffly. "And I consider you a friend. But my lessons must end today. I have learned to protect myself." Cym turned to go.

"Am I wrong to be wary of your people?" Anis asked. "Answer truthfully. Tell me I am mistaken."

"You have nothing to fear from me," Cym said. "You never will."

"That's not what I asked," Anis answered. "I don't hate your people, Cym. The Galvan are not my enemy. But you have not put my fears to rest, as you desired. I am a warrior, Cym, and I'd rather fight to the death than give up my freedom. Relay that message to your father."

Cym turned and left. Anis never saw her in the forest again.

✦✦✦✦✦✦✦✦✦✦

Four months after Regor had asked the Shamra to move for the last time, he came to Kel again. The Galvan needed yet more land. They now numbered close to a thousand.

Anis was better prepared for a confrontation at the Circle of Families. She had learned from the last two meetings that she needed allies. Without mentioning Cym, she told

Ramorra she had learned the Galvan had an army and reached maturity in four months.

"What do you propose?" Ramorra asked, sounding weary.

"We fight for what we have, meager as it is, or soon we'll be driven from our land," Anis replied.

"We're badly outnumbered," Ramorra countered.

Anis knew this was how Ramorra taught Anis and how she weighed her actions. She would question Anis until satisfactory answers were given or a plan was abandoned.

"So was my grandmother and mother at Monument Gate," Anis reminded Ramorra. "And the Galvan army will only be larger and more powerful the next time we are told to move."

"It's suicidal," Ramorra said. "Remember your grandmother Sera and your Aunt Jana perished at Monument Gate, as did many of our warriors."

"Noble deaths, you've told me often enough," Anis said. "Will you support me? Will you enlist the help of others?"

"It will divide the clan," Ramorra said, as if not wanting to commit herself.

Anis said nothing.

"I will consider your request," Ramorra said. "You might consider other options."

Anis received the backing of Dyann and Janis, though Dyann feared the consequences of challenging Kel.

Later that afternoon, Tobin returned from his eleven-year odyssey. As he rode up, Anis recognized him immediately.

"Cousin Tobin!" Anis shouted, and hugged him after he dismounted.

"Anis?" he asked. "It can't be. The Anis I knew was this high," Tobin said, reaching down to Anis's knee.

"It's been eleven years!" Anis said and laughed. "Where have you been? Why have you returned? You must tell me of your adventures." Anis stopped talking. She didn't think Tobin was listening any longer. She saw his face cloud. She turned and saw Kel approach. Kel, too, looked wary. Then Tobin smiled, and the brothers hugged. Anis thought it was a bit strained. Still, they had welcomed one another.

"Welcome back, Brother," Kel said. "Do you plan to stay?"

"Would you have me leave?" Tobin responded.

"Hardly," Kel said. "It's just...well, you've been gone for so long. We've had no word of you."

"And now I've returned home," Tobin said. He turned to Anis. "How is Ramorra? And Dyann? And your father, Pror?" he asked.

"Come," Anis said, taking his hand. "I'll take you to them."

"We'll talk later, Kel," Tobin said. "We have much catching up to do."

Before they got to Ramorra's hut, Tobin stopped Anis. "You and I must talk," Tobin said. "I know of the Galvan. It's why I've returned. Tell me about their arrival and what they've done since," he said.

Anis didn't need prompting. She told Tobin everything, including her own misgivings.

"You are like your mother," Tobin said.

"So Dyann tells me," Anis said, without enthusiasm. "I am *not* my mother. She wouldn't have challenged Kel's authority."

"I don't know about that, but it's besides the point," Tobin said. "You don't let Kel lead you by the nose. And you understand the Galvan far better than Kel. In my travels, I encountered the Galvan. Regor lied to you. He and his people did not leave his country willingly. The Galvan reproduce far too quickly. Many of their young die soon after birth, which controls their growth. But lately, more of the young have survived. There was a civil war in Regor's country. His supporters were defeated. They were exiled. They have lulled Kel with offers of gifts in exchange for land. Now they are too many for us to defeat."

"So we flee our homeland?" Anis asked, disappointed.

Tobin smiled. "You are courageous, Anis, like your mother, but Drea was no fool, and neither are you. There is another option."

"Go on," Anis said when Tobin paused. Tobin pointed to Stone Mountain. "You're kidding," Anis said.

"It's just as habitable as the land Kel has been forced to accept," Tobin said. "Better still, it's defensible. I climbed the mountains often as a child. Other than the woods, there was no greater adventure until your mother led us to other lands."

Tobin kneeled and, with a stick, drew a sketch of the mountains. "There are dozens of caves in which we can live. We can booby-trap others in case the lower levels are breeched. And from the lowest levels, there are passages that lead far from the mountain," he said, drawing with his finger a path to where one of the tunnels led. "There's nothing in the original holy book about these tunnels, but someone used them, maybe a race that lived here before we arrived. From these tunnels, we can leave the mountains unseen to hunt in the woods." He looked at Anis. "I won't lie to you, Cousin. Life won't be easy. It gets far colder in the mountains than we are used to. We won't have the freedom of movement we have now. But once we've set up defenses, we can't be driven out, no matter how many soldiers the Galvan send."

"Can you convince Kel this is where we must go?" Anis asked.

"You asked why I returned, Anis," Tobin said, without immediately answering her question. "You never asked why I left. Yes, I was bitter when Kel was chosen to lead our clan solely because he was the eldest. But there was more. The conflict you had with Kel, I anticipated long before I left. Kel was always cautious. When your mother led the attack to free the Weetok, Kel was opposed. He said nothing to Drea. That wasn't his way. But he complained endlessly to me."

"He turned out to be prophetic," Anis said, still unable to put aside the bitterness she felt toward her mother.

"It's the battle not the outcome that stirs our blood, Anis," Tobin said. "You've never been in battle, so you can't know. Kel wasn't prophetic. If the Weetok leaders hadn't been discovered, Drea's plan may well have succeeded. Not to attack even with the odds against us, *that* would have been a betrayal of all we stood for. You've heard of the story of Monument Gate. It was a massacre. But that defeat led to ultimate victory. We're warriors, Anis. A frontal assault against the Galvan would be both suicidal and foolhardy. Stone Mountain allows us to retain our dignity and freedom. Kel cares only about survival. Our bodies live, but our spirits wither. It's far worse than physical death. Kel's no fool. By now he knows each *last* request will lead to another. He will agree to the Galvan demands until we are forced from our land."

"So what do you suggest?" Anis asked.

"Confront him tonight, as you did before," Tobin said.

"Look what good it did me," Anis answered.

"You have an alternative this time," Tobin said. "Like you said before, enlist the support of Ramorra and others you trust. There are still some males who will follow me." He outlined his plan to Anis.

That night at the Circle of Families, Kel explained the latest Galvan demands. "I admit," he said, looking at Anis, "that my judgment was clouded at the outset. Looking back, we shouldn't have moved when their population first increased. I take full responsibility. But their numbers have swollen so quickly we no longer have the option of refusal. They outnumber us close to ten to one. We have no choice but to comply." He looked at Anis, as if he knew she would object.

Anis rose. She saw Kel smile grimly. "Have your say, Anis," he said, fatigue in his voice.

"There's always a choice," she started, speaking to all gathered, not just Kel. "We know where this ends. With us being driven from *our* land. *Our homeland*. I find that unacceptable. What concerns me most is the duplicity of the Galvan. Did you know their young reach maturity in four months?" she asked. She didn't wait for an answer. "Or that there is a Galvan army?" Now there was some murmuring among the clan. "And Tobin," she said, looking at her cousin, who sat to her left, "says the reason Regor said they left their homeland is a sham. They didn't leave of their own accord. They were expelled after a civil war because of overpopulation. Why would they deceive us, Kel? I'll tell you," she said, not waiting for Kel to respond. "To lull us into a false sense of complacency so we would agree to their requests. Now that they have multiplied and greatly outnumber us, they don't have to ask. They demand. We capitulate. Until now, it *seems* we've had no choice but to comply or face extinction."

"You have an alternative?" Kel asked. "March our army in and expel them?" he said, echoing Anis's earlier sentiments.

"No, Kel. I would gladly give up my life for freedom, but I'm neither suicidal nor a foolish child. They now have an army that far outnumbers us," Anis said. "Tomorrow, at sun-up, I leave for Stone Mountain. It is defensible, where this land is not. It shall be the new Shamra homeland, where we can stand and fight like the warriors we are. I ask all who oppose this policy of appeasement and surrender to join me. I go whether it be alone or with all of you."

Kel now rose, anger etched on his face. "I forbid it. We act as one, as it has always been. I've allowed you to defy clan tradition and speak, even though you're not in the Circle, but now you have gone too far."

"Desperate times call for desperate measures, Kel," Anis said, meeting his eyes. "I only speak in defiance of clan rules because we face annihilation. I am not challenging your leadership. I'm simply stating my intentions and inviting others to join me to defend our homeland."

"And what do we tell the Galvan when they see you on Stone Mountain? They will claim it as theirs," Kel said.

"You tell them we go only to explore, just as you and your brother did as children," Anis said.

"We lie to them?" Kel asked.

"They initiated the deception," Anis snapped back. "They are artists at deceit. We simply return the favor. Later, you can tell the Galvan that those who follow me have deceived you...if you refuse to join us. That will keep you in their good graces," she said bitterly. "Meanwhile, it will take only a short time for us to fortify our mountain defenses."

"Is this why you returned, Tobin?" Kel asked. "To fill Anis's head with foolish notions. You were jealous when I became clan leader. *You fled*. Now you return to tear the clan apart."

"This is *my* decision, Kel," Anis said, when Tobin remained silent. "Long before Tobin returned, I opposed your policy of yielding to every Galvan demand."

"Dividing our clan will only lead to ruin," Kel said.

"Moving whenever the Galvan demand has already done that," Anis answered. "I leave tomorrow at dawn. I hope you will be there to lead us, Kel," Anis said, turned, and left.

The next morning, twenty-six Shamra had gathered to join Anis—nineteen other females and seven males.

Stone Mountain was everything Tobin said and more. After checking out the many caves and the underground passageways that led out of the mountain, Anis took Ramorra aside. "I want to make Stone Mountain impregnable. I want caves booby-trapped so that if we have to abandon them, any Galvan who enter will be destroyed. I want to know the most effective positions to make the mountain impenetrable with the small number of warriors we have. I want weapons—"

"You want to make the impossible a reality," Ramorra said.

"Yes, and I want you to do it," Anis said.

"You won't like me saying this, but you sound just like your mother," Ramorra said.

"I've heard it so often lately, in a complimentary way, I no longer wish to debate it." Anis sighed. "I don't resent it. How am I like Drea?"

"Your mother knew I was no great warrior. What made her an extraordinary leader was inspiring others...*and* making each of us feel vital in carrying out her plans. She knew my strength lay in organizing. She led. She had a grand scheme. My strength lay in the details. Putting together all the pieces. You have a plan. You have warriors who will follow you without question. I will make Stone Mountain the fortress you desire."

In two weeks, Ramorra had succeeded.

"There is much more that needs to be done," Ramorra told Anis, after showing her what had been accomplished. "But our twenty-seven can defend Stone Mountain against an army of hundreds." Ramorra was most proud of her use of the tar pits she had discovered in several of the caves. Arrows bearing burning tar could rain down on the enemy. Balls of hot tar could be dropped or launched against an advancing army.

"It's incredible. *You're* incredible," Anis said, giving Ramorra a hug. "You've done wonders, just as you did for my mother."

A day later, Kel came to meet with Anis. Anis had her own council of advisors, all of whom were present when she met with Kel. Tobin and Dyann had already led groups of warriors through the underground passages to the forest for food. They were on the council. Ramorra was her senior advisor.

SHAMRA DIVIDED

And Janis spoke for the young who had grown impatient. Some wanted Anis to take the initiative and attack the Galvan before the enemy became too strong. Anis listened. She had once suggested such an attack, but now wasn't the time. So Anis sent Janis and the young warriors out with Tobin and Dyann to hunt. It got them off the mountain, and they were cheered when they returned with fresh meat.

Now they sat in a circle and listened to Kel.

"The Galvan can no longer be deceived into believing you are merely exploring the mountain. They claim it as theirs. They want you off the mountain by noon tomorrow."

"And if we refuse?" Anis asked.

"They will drive you from the mountain," Kel said.

"Do you still believe in their good intentions?" Tobin asked. Unlike the Circle of Families, Anis allowed, even encouraged, her advisors to speak. She was their leader. Her word was final. But Anis didn't want to stifle dissent or discussion.

"It no longer matters," Kel said. "We are at their mercy."

"Come join us, Kel," Anis said. "Bring the rest of our people with you. We can defend this mountain. We can make it our home."

"If I could, I would," Kel said, and sighed. "The Galvan no longer make their objectives secret. They claim the entire country for themselves. We are their guests," he said bitterly. "Regor sent me to speak to you because he knew I wouldn't abandon our people. He has surrounded our village with his army and has warriors in the village itself. There's no way we can escape."

"Give me six warriors, Anis," Tobin said. We will travel through the forest, surprise the Galvan, and bring our people here," Tobin said. He didn't mention the underground passageways, Anis noticed. The gulf between the brothers was as wide now as ever.

"You can do that?" Kel asked.

"What do you advise, Ramorra?" Anis asked, not answering Kel's question.

"It can be done," Ramorra said. "But the Galvan must not be killed. Any of our people who get caught would be punished, possibly put to death. We cannot afford to lose even one warrior."

Anis nodded. "Janis, you and Tobin choose who will go. Heed Ramorra's words. No Galvan are to be killed unless absolutely necessary in self-defense. Am I clear?" she asked, looking at Janis and Tobin.

Both nodded.

Anis looked at Kel. He seemed older and smaller than ever. His eyes were a sickly gray, as if he had finally acknowledged defeat. "Before you go, map out the Galvan forces in our village," she said, then paused. "Tell Regor Stone Mountain is ours. We refuse to relinquish it. Have our people ready at midnight. They must leave behind everything except weapons and the clothes on their backs. They are to follow Tobin without question. Tomorrow we shall face the Galvan as one."

At midnight, Anis and Ramorra stood together halfway up the mountain, where they could see the entire countryside.

"I wish I were with them," Anis said. "A leader should set an example."

Ramorra looked at Anis and smiled.

"Something my mother would have uttered, right?" Anis said.

"Almost word for word," Ramorra said as she nodded. "But a leader must also choose her battles, Anis. You will have ample opportunity to set an example for our people. It's just as important to show faith in others. If you believe in them, they will lay down their lives for you. Let them have the glory tonight."

Still, Anis paced like a caged animal.

SHAMRA DIVIDED

Ten minutes later, the stillness was shattered by yells that could be heard across the windless landscape. Ten minutes after that, fires erupted in what had been the clan's village. Anis looked at

Ramorra, who seemed to read her mind.

"Patience," Ramorra said. "Going out now serves no purpose."

"You know me too well," Anis said.

An hour later, Tobin returned with his rescue party and nine Shamra. Kel wasn't among them. Blood dripped from Tobin's arm.

"What happened?" Anis asked.

Tobin and Janis stood before her. The others in the party had taken the nine who had been rescued to get medical attention.

"There were dozens of Galvan in the forest, far more than Kel mentioned," Tobin said angrily.

"And?" Anis asked.

"I was spotted," Tobin said. "I had to kill one of the Galvan before he sounded the alarm."

Anis winced.

"I had to kill others as well," Tobin said.

"How many?" Anis asked, trying to control her anger.

"Three, four," Tobin said quietly. "Once we entered the village, the Galvan were alerted. We could only rescue nine in all. Two others were killed by the Galvan as they fled."

"And you killed three of the Galvan in the village?" Janis asked, her voice shaking.

"It was unavoidable," Tobin said.

"And Kel?" Anis asked.

"His hut was surrounded by guards. I feared he would be killed if we stormed the hut," Tobin said.

"The fires?" Anis asked.

"Set by the Galvan after we left," Tobin said.

"A disaster," Anis said.

"We freed nine of our people," Tobin said. "How can you call that a disaster? Only a partial success, to be sure, but we didn't fail."

"By your own count, seven or eight Galvan were slain. There will be repercussions," Anis said.

"If you thought no blood would be spilled to keep our freedom, you are naive," Tobin said, his eyes blazing.

"I am no fool, Tobin," Anis said. "Blood will flow. I'm prepared for casualties. What I fear is reprisal against Kel and the others. They're defenseless. That's what I meant."

"They had ample chances to join us. They chose their destiny," Tobin said. "I'm going to look after my wound," he said, and left.

"Was the killing necessary, Janis?" Anis asked. She didn't know why she was uneasy with Tobin's account. She decided it just didn't feel right.

"We were spread out. There *were* more Galvan than we expected," Janis answered.

"That doesn't answer my question," Anis said.

"Those killed in the village couldn't be avoided. Kill or be killed," Janis said.

"And those in the forest?"

"The rest of the party and I were able to subdue the Galvan with our slingshots. They will have headaches—"

"Yet Tobin had to kill three or four," Anis said. "Was it unavoidable?"

"We were spread out," Janis said.

"Go, tend to the others," Anis said, frustrated by Janis's evasiveness. If nothing else, Janis was loyal to Tobin, for which Anis couldn't fault her. When she left, Anis turned to Ramorra. "I should have accompanied them."

"We don't dwell on the past," Ramorra said. "Get your rest. The Galvan will storm our defenses at daybreak."

Anis nodded but stood alone for another hour, watching the fires from the Shamra huts burn then smolder. "I should have accompanied them," she said aloud.

Shamra Divided

Daylight brought the Galvan in force, with Regor in the lead. He approached the base of the mountain. In the distance, Anis saw Kel and thirty-five Shamra who had remained in the village.

"Who leads you?" Regor called out.

"I, Anis, descended from Nyvia and Sera, and I'm the daughter of Drea."

"You are the cause of the suffering your people will endure," Regor said.

"The blame is yours and yours alone," Anis said. "You deceived us from the day you set foot on our soil. We accepted you, and all the time you planned to expel us, just as you were exiled from your homeland. You forgot, though, we are warriors. You attack us at your own peril."

"You killed eight of our people last night," Regor said. "You will surrender those who attacked our unarmed guards. You will leave this mountain and return to your village," Regor said.

"And if we refuse?" Anis asked.

"We will execute the Shamra traitors who have facilitated the deception," Regor said, pointing at Kel and the others. "And we will storm the mountain and make it ours. You gain nothing and lose everything by your intransigence."

Anis felt lightheaded for a moment. Regor, she knew, was not bluffing. He would butcher Kel and the others before the eyes of those who protected the mountain. Surrendering, though, was not an option.

"Have you learned nothing about us, Regor?" Anis asked. "Slaughter innocent members of our clan, and face our wrath. You may defeat us, but the land will be stained with blood. Galvan blood. Give us this mountain, and the rest of the country is yours. It's not much we ask."

"Silly child," Regor said sadly. "The mountain will be ours by noon. You will be the last to perish. You will see the destruction of your people." He raised his fist. His soldiers advanced on Stone Mountain. Simultaneously, Galvan soldiers fired arrows at the shackled Shamra they held hostage.

Anis bit her lip and raised her arm. Fifteen Shamra warriors rose and fired arrows at the advancing army. Each arrow found its mark. They fired a second, then a third time. Soon the ground was littered with Galvan, dead and wounded. The paths up the mountain were narrow and treacherous. Only one horse or soldier could advance at a time. Anis's warriors picked the Galvan soldiers off one by one. Anis raised her other arm, and Ramorra, Tobin, and nine warriors launched balls of burning tar that landed on Galvan soldiers waiting to scale the mountain. As each bomb landed, hot tar splayed in all directions, burning and maiming a dozen of the Galvan.

Regor was forced to pull his troops back. He raised his arm in a closed fist, and Anis saw a Galvan guard swat a horse that approached the mountain. Kel, with his hands tied behind him, was on the horse. He was strapped to the animal so he wouldn't fall. As Kel became visible to Anis, Regor lowered his fist. Galvan soldiers showered Kel with arrows. More than two dozen struck him.

"No!" Tobin shouted. He stood and glowered at Regor, who simply nodded in return.

The Galvan withdrew, leaving fifty soldiers to encircle the mountain. A barricade, Anis thought. It would do no good with the passages that led out of the mountain.

Tobin grabbed his bow. Anis stopped him from firing. "You'll hit one, and they'll move a bit farther. I know the pain of loss, Tobin, and I promise we'll avenge Kel and the others. This isn't the way."

Tobin yanked his arm from Anis and stormed off.

"Let him go," Ramorra said. "I know Tobin. He'll come back with a plan. Meanwhile, you have to deal with your conflicting emotions."

"What are you talking about?" Anis asked testily.

SHAMRA DIVIDED

"I am no great warrior, but I have been in battle. There is nothing more exhilarating for those in our clan, especially when you've triumphed. And we were victorious. At the same time, you look out at those who were executed—"

"Slaughtered," Anis corrected Ramorra.

"—slaughtered," Ramorra said, "and you feel responsible. You feel guilty for not feeling worse. Your warrior blood boils from the battle. Why don't you feel more remorse for those who were butchered, you ask yourself."

"So I shouldn't feel guilty?" Anis asked.

"The Galvan are cowardly. They hoped the slaughter would devastate us. You can't blame yourself for their failings. Maybe their plan wasn't to drive us from our land but to slay us in our sleep. Forty of us remain, and your responsibility is to them. They look to you for strength. More than ever, you must act as your mother would."

Anis assigned guards to keep watch over the Galvan who surrounded the mountain. She gathered the others, and in the clan tradition, each told stories of the prowess of those who had fallen. Tobin finally joined them and spoke of the wrestling matches he and Kel engaged in as youths. As he finished, the others broke out in song, a tribute to all who had fallen. Anis thought the Galvan must have thought it odd. The Shamra were celebrating the slaughter of friends and relatives. "We have many surprises for you, Regor," Anis said as the others sang.

Ramorra, who must have overheard, looked at Anis and smiled.

Anis and her council met after the next changing of the guards.

"We must strike…tonight," Tobin said, as Anis's advisors gathered. "They have us surrounded, so they think. They can't storm us, but we can strike them. We do the unexpected. They will be totally unprepared for an attack." Tobin pointed to two villages on a map of the country he unfurled. Neither village was far from Stone Mountain. Both, though, were far from Regor's village, where his army was garrisoned.

"A quick strike," Anis said, nodding. "We can't afford any casualties. We kill only males. We are not the barbarians the Galvan are."

"And set fire to their fields," Tobin said. "We strike at their food supply."

Anis nodded. "I will lead one attack," Anis said. "Dyann, you are with me. Tobin, you lead the other attack. Janis, you go with Tobin. Ramorra will be in charge of our defenses. When we strike, the Galvan surrounding us may feel we're vulnerable."

"Tar balls will discourage them," Ramorra said.

That night, at the outskirts of the village Anis was to attack, she sat on her horse next to Dyann and six warriors.

"Your first taste of battle," Dyann said. "There is nothing better. You and I fight side by side."

"I don't need your protection," Anis said.

"You misunderstand, Anis. My first battle...my *only* battle, I fought by your mother's side. It was a privilege. You honor me by letting me fight with you."

"You don't fool me for a moment, Dyann, but have it your way," Anis said.

They rode into the village. Truth be told, there wasn't much to fight. Galvan males with pitchforks, shovels, and axes met them. They were no match for the Shamra swords and bows and arrows. Anis's warriors killed a dozen males, set fire to the fields, and fled. It had taken all of twenty minutes. They appeared like ghosts in the wind, which is what Anis wanted Regor to think.

Anis waited for Tobin's party at the entrance of the underground cavern. Her group had taken no casualties. Minutes later, a jubilant Tobin joined them. His seven warriors looked unusually subdued.

SHAMRA DIVIDED

"What's wrong, Tobin?" Anis asked. She saw none of Tobin's warriors were injured.

"It all went according to plan," Tobin said.

"Not according to *your* plan," Janis told Anis. "Tobin told us to kill *all*. Males, females, and children. Then burn the huts and fields."

Anis was furious, but held her tongue. While not experienced at leading, she knew better than to chastise Tobin in front of the others. "Let's see if the Galvan struck while we were gone," Anis said. Only when Anis saw that the Galvan had followed orders and remained in their positions around the mountain did she confront Tobin in private.

"Why did you defy me?" Anis asked.

"I ask for your forgiveness, Anis," Tobin said. "As we rode toward the village, the image of Kel filled my mind with rage. I saw his horse approach us and arrow upon arrow strike his body even long after he was dead. I wasn't myself."

"We are not the Galvan, Tobin. We don't kill defenseless females and children. The Galvan are like the Kimra. Females don't fight. And butchering children makes us no better than the Galvan. I understand your rage. But I need to know I can trust you to follow my orders."

"I won't disobey you again. You have my word," Tobin said.

"Explain to your warriors you were wrong. That shall be your penance. You ask for *their* forgiveness."

Later that night, Anis and Ramorra stood looking out at their country. It had become a daily ritual.

"Much has changed this day," Ramorra said. "How did it feel to lead your warriors into battle at the village?"

"I would rather have fought soldiers," Anis said.

"Still, a battle is a battle no matter who the enemy," Ramorra said. "Or am I mistaken?"

Anis smiled. "It was glorious…until I found out what Tobin did."

"Keep an eye on Tobin," Ramorra said. "There's something about him. I can't put my finger on it, but he follows his own rules."

"He saw his brother die a horrible death," Anis said in his defense.

"There was no brotherly love between them, Anis," Ramorra said. "Kel's death was an excuse for Tobin to butcher, just as he killed the previous night against your wishes. Send Dyann with him next time to curb his excesses. Janis should accompany you so she can enjoy her triumph."

Anis smiled. "I'm glad you're by my side, Ramorra. Much as I value Dyann's and Janis's company, I have much to learn. You don't fear putting me in my place. Did you do the same for my mother?"

Ramorra laughed. "Hardly. We were rivals when she took over the clan. And Drea had Atyra, who wasn't awed by your mother. Drea didn't come to appreciate my talents until we prepared to help the Weetok. Had she lived, we may have grown closer. After Atyra left, though, there was a void only you could have filled had your mother lived."

"Then it was my mother's loss," Anis said.

Anis and her council met just before dawn. They expected a response from the Galvan. Anis probed for any weaknesses in their defenses. For every question, Ramorra had an answer.

"Tonight we attack more farms," Tobin said. He seems to have recovered from any remorse he felt for his actions earlier that night, Anis thought.

"We must be careful," Ramorra said.

"Now is the time to be bold," Tobin countered. He spread out his map. "We hit them here last night," he said and pointed. "We circle the woods and attack here tonight." He showed them the spot on the map. "Then— "

"Then we destroy Regor's credibility," Ramorra cut in.

All eyes were on her. Anis saw Tobin look at Ramorra with fury.

"If we kill too many Galvan, Regor loses face, and compromise is impossible. He'll be forced to storm the mountain no matter how many soldiers he will lose. We can win a dozen battles and lose the war," Ramorra said, her eyes on Tobin.

"What do you suggest, Ramorra?" Anis asked.

"We made our point last night. We avenged Kel and the others. We're not trapped on the mountain. So we sit tight. The blockade can't succeed. They'll storm the mountain, but only to keep us on edge and to spot weaknesses in our defenses. Without a single casualty on our side, their number of dead will increase. By simply defending the mountain, in time Regor will tire of his mounting losses. Their population, remember, continues to grow. He'll have greater problems than a few Shamra on a mountain. Time is on our side, *if* we don't humiliate Regor."

"That's absurd," Tobin said. "Ramorra sounds like Kel. Do nothing. Look where that got him." Tobin's voice kept rising as he spoke, his eyes glued on Ramorra.

"No attack tonight," Anis said before Tobin could continue. "We're all under a lot of stress. Tobin, you're still feeling the anguish and rage from Kel's death. This is no time to make hasty decisions. We fortify our positions. We see how the Galvan respond. Difficult as it may be, we must be patient. I'm talking days, Tobin, not weeks or months."

Tobin looked at Anis. He seemed about to say something, thought better of it, and remained silent. He turned his gaze again upon Ramorra. He didn't take his eyes off her for the next fifteen minutes, during which Anis instructed Dyann and Janis to take a group to the caves near the top of the mountain, which hadn't been fully explored.

"Ramorra, keep working on the catapults we discussed. The Galvan will surely have some of their own. We can't afford casualties. We must be able to launch our tar balls farther and cause more destruction than theirs." She turned to Tobin. "We need arrows. Hundreds, thousands. The Galvan will send soldiers to all farms. If we decide to attack, frontal assaults may not be practical. We make arrows now for use later."

Tobin nodded, but remained silent.

"It's been a dizzying day and night," Anis said to the others. "I know I'm emotionally spent. You all know what you have to do. Do it. We meet again tomorrow."

♦♦♦♦♦♦♦♦♦♦♦

Ramorra returned to her quarters in a cave she had chosen. Her hand was shaking. This was one of the few times in her life she felt real fear. She had never been the warrior Drea had been or Anis was now. It wasn't cowardice, though. She had fought even if she hadn't distinguished herself. She was a competent fighter, nothing more. But an army needed more than just soldiers. Drea, and now Anis, saw that her strength lay in implementing grand schemes. They got the glory, but both Drea and Anis appreciated the role she played. Warriors from Ramorra's generation were being replaced by the younger generation. On the other hand, she was valued more now than ever.

This morning she had felt fear, and it had nothing to do with the Galvan. When Tobin had glared at her, for a moment it hadn't been Tobin, but someone...or *something* else. Something about Tobin had disturbed her since just after his return. Now she knew. The eyes that had warned her to be silent that morning were not Tobin's. They weren't Shamra. *He* wasn't Tobin. *He* wasn't Shamra. Yet, she couldn't just tell Anis. What could she say? She had no proof.

A feeling of dread filled Ramorra. Tobin was leading them to ruin. Just as chilling, she sensed Tobin now viewed her as a threat. She didn't fear death, but she longed to die in battle for her people rather than have her throat slit while she slept.

"Where are you when I need you, Drea?" she called, her feeling of helplessness weighing heavy on her.

"I'm here," a voice said.

Ramorra turned and saw Drea standing in front of her with a short fur-like creature by her side. Ramorra rubbed her eyes.

"It's no apparition," Drea said. "You summoned me. Here I am."

"You're dead," Ramorra said, feeling foolish for stating the obvious. "I cradled you in my arms."

"Am I dead to Anis?" Drea asked.

"You live in the stories we repeat almost daily," Ramorra said. "But—"

"Am I dead to Dyann? Am I dead to those of the clan who weren't born when I was killed?"

"Your exploits—" Ramorra began.

"Keep me alive," Drea said. "A different life, to be sure, Ramorra, but as long as I am remembered, I live. And when summoned, I come."

"You should be speaking to Anis," Ramorra said, almost accepting it was truly Drea she was speaking to.

Drea shook her head. "She's still too resentful. If I told her to turn left, she'd go right just to spite me."

"We're in danger, aren't we?" Ramorra said, "And not just from the Galvan."

Drea nodded. "The Galvan pose no real threat, in great part because of you. The danger lies within. Already, half our people have perished. You know who's responsible."

"Tobin?" Ramorra asked.

"He isn't Tobin," Drea said. "You've met Chaos in the form of Tobin. It dropped its guard in anger. You had a glimpse of Chaos before it recovered."

"His eyes," Ramorra said.

Again, Drea nodded.

"What is this Chaos you speak of?" Ramorra asked.

"It's a force out to divide and destroy a people. Remember when we were young. Atyra and I were mischievous, yet we were seldom caught. Think back to the time Nyvia conducted practice for young warriors with bows and arrows. Atyra and I filed the others' arrows the night before the lesson so when you and the others practiced, the arrows flew every which way. Nyvia had a fit. Atyra and I just watched. We set it all in motion, and then there was—"

"Chaos," Ramorra finished for her.

"Nyvia's tirade that day wasn't forgotten by any of us. And she made us run through the forest without shoes, without weapons. Layla later looked at one of the arrows carefully and understood what had occurred. She didn't tell Nyvia but accused *all* of us. We argued. There was even a fight, I recall. Everyone was accused *except* me and Atyra. I was the daughter of our clan's leader, and Atyra, my close friend. So, there was chaos. We were playful, though. The Chaos who resides in Tobin has no sense of humor. He can destroy our clan, where the Galvan can't."

"Can this Chaos be destroyed?" Ramorra asked.

Drea shook her head. "Chaos has been around since the beginning of time."

"So we're doomed," Ramorra said.

"I wouldn't have returned with that message. You can't destroy him, but you can unmask him. He will flee, and then you can contend with the Galvan," Drea said.

"What must I do?" Ramorra asked.

"Toss your fear aside. Do as I tell you. Let my little friend here turn the tables on Chaos. He's done it before." Drea explained.

❖❖❖❖❖❖❖❖❖❖

Tobin entered Ramorra's chamber at midday. He was surprised to see Anis, not Ramorra. "I must talk to Ramorra," Tobin began, irritated at not being able to confront Ramorra.

Then his voice softened. "I have a suggestion to strengthen our defenses that I want to discuss with her."

"I sent her to get something from my chambers," Anis said.

"I'll explain at Council," Tobin said, and left.

Chaos had spent the morning weighing the Ramorra problem. She had been an irritant since his arrival. Anis was young and impressionable. Anis would listen to the one she thought was Tobin, who was eleven years her elder. Anis had, but she had also leaned on Ramorra, which was exasperating. Victory was within his grasp, and only Ramorra stood in his way. He had divided the clan, as he had intended. He had been filled with joy when the Galvan had slaughtered those who had stayed with Kel. Now he was on his way toward dividing the remaining Shamra. Anis had surprised him. She wasn't as malleable as he'd thought. She was quite fearless and self-assured, for one so young. With leadership thrust upon her, she had become cautious. She was no longer defiant and reckless, but weighed her options carefully. And she listened to others, especially Ramorra.

The morning Ramorra had foiled his plan to attack farms, he thought she may have seen through his facade, if only for a moment. Taking up residence in a creature was always a chore. His true nature was a mixture of rage, hatred, betrayal, and guile. While in Tobin, he had to rein his emotions. Had Ramorra kept her mouth shut, further attacks on Galvan villages would have split the Shamra. A fight for leadership would have followed. He would have accomplished what he'd set out to do, then would have slipped away.

It was time to use his powers on Ramorra. This time he would let her peer into *his* eyes, not Tobin's. With his power to mindwash, he would control Ramorra. She would advise Anis to attack Galvan villages and kill all, females and children included.

Now he hurried to Anis's chamber to find Ramorra. Ramorra was sitting on the floor with a bandana in her hand. "Ramorra, we talk," Chaos said. The face of Tobin had dissolved. All that remained were black soul-less eyes that would draw Ramorra's will from her.

The female on the floor looked at Tobin in shock. "Who…*what* are you?" she cried out.

"Chaos," a voice called out from behind.

Chaos turned and faced Ramorra. He spun around. The female on the floor was Anis. Chaos bellowed in rage. He turned toward Ramorra. She had a knife in her hand and threw it at his head, hitting him in the right eye. It exploded into blazing streaks of light. Now it was Chaos who cried out in pain. Bright liquid light dripped from his eye.

Chaos fled as Ramorra took another knife from her belt.

♦♦♦♦♦♦♦♦♦♦

Anis stood up. "What just happened?" she asked, her voice shaking.

Ramorra had agreed not to tell Anis about Drea. She whistled, and the small fur creature entered Anis's chamber. "That wasn't Tobin," Ramorra said. "The real Tobin is dead. What you saw is called Chaos. He meant to divide us so we'd destroy one another."

"And how do you know this?" Anis asked.

"I told you yesterday that I sensed something wrong about Tobin. When he looked at me this morning, the mask of Tobin vanished for a few seconds. Later, this creature visited me. His name is Ishry, and he's fought Chaos before."

Ramorra saw Anis look at Ishry. Ramorra knew what Anis was thinking. The creature didn't seem to possess the ability to humble a monster such as Chaos. He was half the size of a Shamra. His brown fur contained more than a little gray from age. He wore a patch over one eye.

"*You* defeated Tobin?" Anis said to the creature in disbelief.

"Chaos, not Tobin," Ishry said. He explained what Chaos was. "To survive, my people possess the power to mask ourselves, a Mist of Illusion. I cloaked Ramorra to resemble you, and you to appear to be Ramorra. Then, when the one called Tobin entered your chamber, he discarded his mask, though I would have done so for him if he hadn't. You saw him for what he was."

"It's not something I could explain to you, Anis," Ramorra said. "You had to be shown."

"I've seen, and I still don't know if I can trust my eyes," Anis said. "I didn't know you were so good with a knife," she said with a smile.

"It's the only weapon I'm truly proficient with. I found out by accident. When we'd throw a knife at a target on a tree, I surprised everyone, including myself, with my accuracy. It's all in the wrist," Ramorra said with a laugh. "My weapon of choice."

"What do we tell the others?" Anis asked.

"That Tobin went out on his own to avenge Kel," Ramorra said. "He doesn't return. We assume he's perished."

♦♦♦♦♦♦♦♦♦♦

An hour later, Janis approached Anis. "When do we leave?" she asked stiffly.

"What do you mean?" Anis asked in return.

"Tobin says your orders are to attack a farm," Janis said.

A chill went down Anis's spine. "When did Tobin issue these orders?"

"Before midday," Janis said.

Anis breathed a sigh of relief. He had given orders before confronting her. Anis realized he truly was Chaos. "To attack a farm and do what?" Anis asked.

"Kill all. Burn huts and fields," Janis said.

"Females and children, as well as males?" Anis asked. Janis nodded. "Those were *your* orders, Tobin said."

"Do you agree with my plan?" Anis asked.

"It's not my role to question your wisdom," Janis said. Anis could hear the chill in her voice.

"If the decision was yours, would you issue such orders?" Anis asked. "Speak your mind, Janis," Anis said, when her friend hesitated.

"I agree with my mother that if we keep up these attacks, Regor will have no choice but to storm the mountain no matter what the cost."

"Why didn't you tell me of your misgivings to my face?" Anis asked.

"You lead our clan," Janis said.

"You are my best friend, Janis. Have I become such a tyrant that you can no longer question my judgment?" Anis asked. She didn't wait for an answer. "Yes, Janis, I have the final say, but I rely on the advice of my inner circle. Kel's downfall was that he listened to no others. Don't let me fall into that trap."

"What do I tell the others?" Janis asked, sounding confused.

"Stand down. The council will meet and come up with a better plan," Anis said.

When the council met, Ramorra outlined a bold plan. "For now, we no longer attack villages. We strike at the heart of the Galvan. One hour before the changing of the guard that surrounds the mountain, we attack the barracks. Anis leads one group, Dyann a second, and Janis a third. You attack from here, here, and here." Ramorra pointed to a map. "You don't return through the caverns, but straight at the guards surrounding the mountain. When we see you approach, we launch tar balls and shower the guards with arrows. One group leaves the mountain and attacks the guards from the rear, so they are caught between us. With one attack, we'll deal a devastating blow against the Galvan, killing only soldiers."

Ramorra's plan was met with great enthusiasm. Suggestions were offered, and the plan was slightly modified. Anis could see how relieved Janis appeared.

The attack on the barracks surprised the Galvan, as Ramorra had planned. Janis's warriors drove the Galvan horses off. Anis and Dyann set fire to the barracks, driving the soldiers out, many without their weapons. Three-quarters of the guards were killed or injured. The rest fled in panic.

One hut remained guarded by six soldiers with weapons. Anis led the attack. In hand-to-hand battle, all six were slain. Anis bled from a shoulder wound as she dismounted and made her way into the hut.

Anis found Cym inside. She was tending to the wounds of a soldier. There was a sword beside Cym, but she didn't reach for it. Instead, she spread her arms. "I die for the glory of my people," she said quietly, looking at Anis.

"Why are you here?" Anis asked.

"Garn and I are to be married," Cym said, looking at the soldier who lay on a bed of straw. "He fell ill recently. I was visiting him."

"Will he live?" Anis asked.

"What does it matter? You'll kill us..." she started, then paused. "We won't be taken hostage."

"You won't die this day, Cym. Nor will you or your male be taken hostage. We no longer kill innocents. Tell your father we will fight his troops with our last breath, but our war is not with farmers, females, and children. Whether there is peace, is up to him."

Anis turned to go, then looked at Cym again. "I've missed our lessons," she said, and shrugged. She wanted to say more but couldn't find the words.

The journey back was more difficult, but the element of surprise was still on the Shamra's side. The Galvan didn't expect to be attacked from the rear. They had already been pelted with tar balls and arrows from the Shamra defenders. When Anis's force arrived, a group of Shamra attacked from the mountain as planned. After some fierce hand-to-hand fighting, the Galvan commander sounded the retreat.

For the first time, the clan could truly rejoice. The battle had indeed been glorious. Three Shamra had fallen. Another six were wounded, though none seriously. While a fresh set of guards soon surrounded the mountain, they did not venture as close as the others had. And there was no Galvan attack the next day.

During the third week of the blockade, Ramorra summoned Anis in the middle of the night. The Galvan had attacked only once since the Shamra's bold raid and had been driven back easily. Now Ramorra pointed out fires in several Galvan villages.

"Not our doing?" Anis asked with concern.

"No. It must be similar to what happened in the Galvan homeland," Ramorra said. "Their numbers have continued to grow. They've run out of space—"

"Civil war," Anis finished. "None of our concern," she said after a pause.

The next day, Regor approached on horseback with Cym by his side. "Can we speak in private?" he asked.

Regor, Cym, and the male Anis recognized as the soldier Cym planned to marry were led into a cavern where Anis's council met.

"I won't exclude my council," Anis said. "Speak your mind, but any decision will be discussed with my advisors."

Regor nodded. Anis thought he looked weary. "You could have killed my daughter when you attacked our guards," Regor started.

"She gave you our message, didn't she?" Anis asked. Regor nodded. "You could have taken her hostage."

"It's not our way," Anis said.

"Cym has told me of your meetings in the forest. Of your lessons. Of the friendship the two of you shared. She is disappointed at how your people have been treated," Regor said.

"How you deceived us," Anis said.

Regor nodded. "Self-preservation brings with it hard choices. It brings out the best in some, the worst in others."

"What do you propose, Regor?" Anis asked.

"A truce, at least for as long as I lead our people. Civil war has broken out. Whoever is defeated leaves this country."

Anis nodded. "We won't support one side over the other. As far as we're concerned, you would both turn on us given the chance."

"I won't argue with you, Anis. You have ample cause to distrust all Galvan. I have only one request." When Anis said nothing, Regor continued. "Give sanctuary to Cym and her betrothed. To my other daughter and her mate, as well."

Anis looked at Regor, then at Cym. This didn't involve the council. It was personal. "Done, Regor," she said.

That night, Anis and Ramorra looked over the countryside from the mountains. Fires still simmered from villages burned to the ground during the day. The carnage would continue, they later found out from Cym, with as much as a quarter of the population killed before one side admitted defeat.

"If Regor is vanquished, we will battle the Galvan again," Ramorra said.

"I would have it no other way," Anis answered, then paused. "Spoken just like my mother, you're going to say," she said, and smiled at Ramorra.

CHAPTER 13

~ *The Present* ~

"I can't believe Anis challenged the leader of the clan...of our family," Dara said, after Briana finished her tale.

"The first time it ever occurred," Briana said, nodding. "Kel was a weak and ineffectual leader. Our clan has its traditions, I guess you'd call them. Rules to be followed. But if Anis didn't act as she had, the clan would have been destroyed. Adhere rigidly to traditions at your own peril. And truthfully, you were no different, Dara. A female leading males, you resisted an invading army. The Trocs you spoke of might very well rule your homeland today without your defiance. And you admitted you were defenseless against the Shrieks. Who but you would have ventured into the unknown for allies? Would your religious leaders have allowed you to do so if they hadn't been discredited and you had had to go to them for permission?"

Dara shook her head. "I'm not condemning Anis. It's just hard to imagine the courage it took for her to break with clan tradition."

"Courage she inherited from her mother," Briana said.

"And Tobin was taken over by Chaos," Dara said. "As you were telling the story, I thought he was someone I would have liked to meet. Yet it wasn't Tobin at all."

"I believe it was the first time Chaos meddled in our affairs, almost leading us to ruin," Briana said. "And now Chaos is back."

"Before you told me, I didn't see the value of Stone Mountain, but it became the refuge of the clan, its salvation."

"And eventually, our home," Briana said, "as long as we could occasionally escape its confines."

They came to a cave and entered.

"Won't we be trapped here?" Dara asked. "We can hide, but if we're found?"

"Don't take me for a fool, Dara," Briana said with a trace of irritation in her voice. She led Dara deep into the cave. "There are three avenues of escape," Briana said, pointing each one out to Dara. "Too small for a Galvan to enter without difficulty, but room enough for us to escape."

"I apologize," Dara said. "I sometimes speak without thinking."

Briana smiled. "At least you admit when you're wrong. And, truth be told, your observation was a good one. I've been here before, so I knew we wouldn't be trapped." She paused. "The Galvan will split up. It's the only way they'll find us. We can't fight the five on horseback. But we can pick off one at a time. Not all five at once," she added. "If we can rid ourselves of two of them, we have a good chance of making it back to our horses and escaping. Or, if we're not found by dark, we can go for the horses under the cover of night."

"What is your plan if the Galvan find us here?" Dara asked. She listened to Briana, asked a few questions, then nodded in agreement.

SHAMRA DIVIDED

"While we wait, let me tell you about the hunt for Chaos—for the *source* of Chaos. The Galvan are only minions sent by an entity who controls them. The source was found. It was a glorious battle. Atyra returned. She was reunited with Drea." She paused. "You must be tired. The story can wait for later. Why not get some rest, and I'll keep first watch."

"You're a tease, Briana," Dara said with a smile. "After what you just told me, I'm supposed to sleep? I think not. Out with it, and spare no details."

Chapter 14

~ Like Mother, Like Daughter ~

170 years ago

Anis felt a twinge of guilt as her homeland receded in the distance. It wasn't because she was abandoning her people. She had led them for fifteen years. Leadership had passed to her daughter Dahlia. Her firstborn, now fifteen, Dahlia possessed qualities that Anis thought would make her a worthy successor. Dahlia had been groomed for clan leadership since birth. Anis hoped that in time Dahlia wouldn't come to resent the grand adventure she was missing.

Anis thought leaving would be bittersweet, but in truth, her excitement mounted as she rode into the unknown and Stone Mountain receded from view. I shouldn't feel so happy, she thought. I should be full of regret. Yet no doubts gnawed at her. It had been fifteen years since she'd felt so alive. Any guilt she felt was quickly squashed. She was on an adventure. Where it would take her, she had no idea. That she would face danger, she had no doubt, but that made the journey all the sweeter.

She remembered Ramorra's words—*just like your mother*. So be it, Anis thought. She had come to terms with her mother. Drea had sought adventure rather than accept the responsibility of motherhood. Anis had been resentful for years, but she was reminded daily that she possessed many of her mother's attributes, both good and bad. Anis could be headstrong and reckless, like Drea. She led by example and would never ask others to do what she wouldn't do herself, like Drea. She was a warrior and a hunter whose heroic exploits inspired others. And like her mother, she would rather die in battle than of old age. Yes, Anis could understand how the lure of the unknown had possessed her mother.

Anis had decided to leave the Shamra homeland after Ramorra's death. The truce Anis forged fifteen years before remained. A tenuous truce, to be sure, but still, the Shamra and Galvan coexisted.

A month earlier, Janis had come running to the cavern Anis called her home. Anis had been asleep, dreaming. She was falling—or had she leapt?—into a swirling vortex. A black whirlpool attempted to suck her under. A source of evil, of chaos, Anis somehow knew. Yet she seemed to welcome the descent. Just before she landed, a seven-headed snake appeared, and then she had awakened.

Janis's gray eyes told Anis something was amiss. "Ramorra has been bitten by the snake of seven heads," she told Anis. Janis was Ramorra's youngest child, and one of Anis's few close friends.

Anis knew there was but one place on the mountain the snake could be found—a cave at the very top of Stone Mountain, the only area that had remained unexplored since their arrival. Three others had wandered into the cave. None had returned.

SHAMRA DIVIDED

Anis ran to where Ramorra had been brought. Tron, who knew of healing herbs, looked at Anis and shook his head. Words were unnecessary. The snake's venom was deadly. There was no antidote.

Ramorra lay on a bed of straw, her usually tan face ashen. Few Shamra lived past the age of fifty. Ramorra was fifty-two. Anis sat on the ground next to Ramorra and held her hand. It was cold to the touch.

Ramorra opened her eyes and smiled weakly at Anis. Her normally blue eyes had turned a dull gray. She was dying.

"Why?" Anis asked. She was angry with the old woman. Saying more would betray her fury. Ramorra needed comfort now, not scolding.

"Your eyes blaze red, child," Ramorra said. "You think me foolish. You would like to berate me. You never could hide your emotions. Just—"

"Just like my mother," Anis finished for her. "You didn't answer my question. You know the cave is deadly. Why?"

"To fulfill my promise to you. I vowed to make this mountain impregnable—"

"And you have," Anis interrupted. "What you've done for our people is a story that will be repeated as long as there are Shamra on Stone Mountain. Whenever we repel the Galvan, your name will be on the lips of our people."

Ramorra closed her eyes for a moment

"Are you in great pain?" Anis asked. A wave of regret swept over her. She had been so angry at Ramorra she hadn't thought to ask until now.

"Numb. Almost at peace," Ramorra said. "There is no feeling in my legs. As the venom spreads, I'll lose all feeling, but I'm in no great pain. And I have no regrets. Now listen to me. I grow weary. I have no strength to argue with you." She paused and swallowed with difficulty. "We coexist with the Galvan, but our truce is tenuous. Should they attack and somehow overrun our defenses, we need an escape route." Ramorra paused again, as if resting.

"Surely not the cave," Anis said.

"The cave is our final trap," Ramorra rasped. "We escape by going around the cave. There is a path that leads to the bottom of the mountain, but it is hidden. If the Galvan were to actually follow us, we would be overtaken or met at the bottom by another Galvan army. If the Galvan think we've gone into the cave, we gain precious time. I had to see how far I could go before the snakes attacked. They are clever," Ramorra said, and laughed. It sounded like a cackle to Anis. "I saw their eyes peer at me, but they didn't attack until I had traveled a quarter of a mile. Then one struck, and I was lucky to make it out of the cave. The Galvan are aware we set traps throughout the caves. They will venture in cautiously. We will have gained at least an hour's headstart before the snakes attack the Galvan. There will be panic. If we fortify the path and set traps along it, we will be long gone before the Galvan can regroup and locate us."

"So you risked certain death to test your theory?" Anis said.

"Listen, and understand," Ramorra said, trying to speak forcefully. "I am no warrior like you. I am old and infirm like Nyvia was at her end," Ramorra said, referring to Anis's great grandmother. "She was fifty-two when she died. She had given up leadership of the clan. Near the end, she needed two sticks just to walk. Others had to help her out of bed. A cough was her constant companion. Once a warrior and hunter, she could no longer stalk her prey. She just waited to die and dreaded every minute she lived. I chose my path, Anis. I chose the way I'd die." She paused. Her breathing was shallow. "Leave me now. I must rest. We will speak once more." She closed her eyes and slept.

Two hours later, Janis summoned Anis.

"Have you forgiven me?" Ramorra asked, her voice noticeably weaker than the last time Anis had spoken to her.

"Of course," Anis said. "You have the right to choose your death. I was selfish." Anis paused. "I think I saw your death," Anis said.

"But you couldn't," Ramorra said, her breathing labored.

"I know I shouldn't have the Gift of Sight," Anis said. "It skips a generation. My mother had it, so I can't. Yet, just before Janis woke me, I saw the snake of seven heads. And something else," she said, and paused.

"Tell me," Ramorra said weakly.

Anis explained the dream of the black whirlpool that attempted to suck her down.

"Chaos," Ramorra said, just above a whisper.

"Why do you think it's Chaos?" Anis said.

"I don't have the energy," Ramorra said faintly. "My time's approaching. Listen. Don't interrupt. Dahlia's fifteen. You've groomed her to lead our people." Her eyes closed, and she was barely breathing. Anis was about to say something when Ramorra opened her eyes. "It's not in your nature to live on this mountain and die an old woman." She paused with her eyes almost closed. "So tired. Let me rest these weary eyes for a few minutes."

She closed her eyes. Anis sat by her for half an hour. Ramorra was dead.

❖❖❖❖❖❖❖❖❖❖

Riding south, Anis looked at her army of three. Anis didn't have to be told what Ramorra meant by her final words. Anis had been discontented for years. Every few months, she'd lead a group of hunters off Stone Mountain to hunt in a nearby forest. A few hours of pleasure in an otherwise unremarkable existence. Anis didn't want to grow old on Stone Mountain. Now she had a reason to leave. She had seen Chaos in her dream, and then the snake that killed Ramorra.

She had seen Chaos for a reason. She would hunt this creature down for what it had done to her clan.

She took three others with her. Janis, her best friend, needed to get away from where her mother had died. Dahlia would choose someone closer to her own age to be her confidant. Janis would be lost without Anis.

Cym would also accompany Anis. Anis had given sanctuary to Cym, her sister, and their husbands at the start of the Galvan civil war. Life was harsh on Stone Mountain, and after two years, of the four, only Cym survived. While the same age as Anis, the Galvan's lifespan was far shorter than the Shamra's. At thirty, Cym only had a few years to live. She would be of little use in battle, but before Cym died, Anis thought their travels would give added meaning to her life.

The third was Anis's youngest daughter, Reva. A free spirit, Reva was far more like Anis than like Dahlia. She loved to hunt. She fed on danger. She was reckless. She was skilled with a bow and arrow, a slingshot, and a spear. Knowing her sister was being groomed to head the clan freed Reva from the responsibilities of leadership. She laughed far more than Dahlia. Reva reminded Anis of a younger version of herself, without the bitterness. Only half-sisters, Dahlia and Reva had never been particularly close. Anis knew she had to bear her own children to keep her bloodline in succession to rule, but had never had a desire to marry. While Reva had never wanted to lead the clan, Anis feared Dahlia would feel threatened by her younger sister with Anis gone. What if Reva disagreed with Dahlia? Anis recalled the enmity between Kel and Tobin. So while the danger they faced might be life-threatening, there was no question thirteen-year-old Reva would join Anis on her quest.

Anis had no idea how to locate Chaos. She hadn't had anymore dreams. She had been isolated on Stone Mountain for fifteen years. She knew nothing of the world outside her homeland. She decided there was no sense chasing a ghost in the wind. So when Janis asked, "Where do we go?" Anis had a ready answer. "I want to see the land where my mother died. I wonder if the Weetok are still enslaved?"

The decision made, they rode south, stopping, as her mother had twenty-six years before, at several forests to hunt creatures none of them had ever seen before.

After three weeks, they came to the land of the Weetok. Looking down from a hill much like her mother might have twenty-six years before, Anis saw devastation. There were no lush fields of grain and grass, which Ramorra had spoken of. The land looked barren, the grass brown and stubbly. The few farms she saw were in ruins.

Anis pointed off in the distance. "That's their main village Ramorra told us about. We'll find our answers there."

Riding across the field, Anis almost gagged at the scent of decay. The horses sensed something amiss as well. They tossed their heads and quickened their pace, as if to escape some unseen danger.

"There are creatures in the forest following our moves," Cym said.

Anis looked at Cym and smiled. The Galvan were noted for their keen sense of sight and smell. Anis knew Cym had much to offer, though she was old and frail.

"We're riding into a trap," Janis said. "Inside the city, we'll have no means of escape. Just the four of us against—"

"We live to battle, if we must, Janis," Anis said, interrupting her friend. "We ride."

The gates did close behind them once inside the city, but there was no immediate attack. The city itself was dilapidated. Buildings lay in rubble. Statues had been toppled. A stench like that in the fields permeated the air. Suddenly, a dozen heads appeared from the ruins of the buildings before them. Anis caught movement to her left and right. They were surrounded by several dozen short, round, squat creatures. Some were armed with bows and arrows, others with spears, and some with just pitchforks. Yet they didn't attack. Anis saw Janis put her hand on her sword.

"No, Janis. We come in peace. We fight only if attacked," Anis said.

One figure emerged from behind a pillar and approached Anis and her party, sword in hand. He said something in a language Anis couldn't understand.

"Do you speak the language of the Kimra?" Anis asked. Like the Shamra, the Weetok had been enslaved by the Kimra. It was through that language that Drea had been able to communicate with Bain, the leader of the resistance, twenty-six years before.

The figure staring sullenly at Anis was a head shorter than she was. At just over five-feet, the Shamra were far shorter than the Kimra. Anis noted that one of the creatures eyes were blue, the other green. After he spoke, the leader of the Weetok licked his lips. His arms and legs were muscular. A scar ran along one side of his cheek. Anis noted other scars on his muscular arms.

"I speak our oppressor's tongue," the leader said with hostility. "If you are allied with—"

"We are enemies of the Kimra, not allies," Anis said, cutting him off. "My mother died trying to help your people twenty-six years ago. I wanted to see what she gave her life for."

Another male, far older than the one before her now, emerged from the same building with the pillars and hurried down the steps. He wore a black robe.

"You are Shamra?" the older male asked.

"Yes, Anis, daughter of Drea, leader of our clan who—"

"Gave her life to free us," the elderly male said; then he, too, licked his lips. "You wear the bandana of your mother. The young one does too."

"My daughter," Anis said. "A family tradition," she added.

The male said something to the others that Anis didn't understand, and the Weetok visibly relaxed and lowered their weapons. The leader still locked eyes with Anis. He was the last to sheath his sword.

"Pardon our lack of hospitality," the elderly male in the black robe said. "I am called Gwin. You could say I am the spiritual leader of our people." He looked at the leader. "Tillery, here, leads our army. He's obviously suspicious of strangers, especially those who speak the language of the Kimra."

"What happened to your land?" Anis asked. "Have you vanquished the Kimra? Why do you—?"

"So many questions," Gwin said, his green and blue eyes smiling. "Please, let us treat you as the honored guests you are. We don't have much, but break bread with us. Over food and drink, all your questions shall be answered."

Anis saw that Janis looked anxious. Cautious, like her mother, Anis thought. A reluctant warrior, like Ramorra. Like mother, like daughter, just as others said about her and the mother she barely remembered. Cym and Reva, on the other hand, looked from one Weetok to another with curiosity. Other than the Galvan, these were the first intelligent creatures either had seen. They appeared enthralled.

The four of them sat at a table with Gwin, Tillery, and three other male Weetok warriors. The meal consisted of beans, bread, berries, and wine.

"This is not the land my people describe when they talk about the battle to free the Weetok," Anis said, when their plates had been cleared by two females. The Weetok refused to make eye contact with their guests, Anis noted.

"I am one of the few Weetok who remain who witnessed your mother's heroism," Gwin said. "Tillery here was but a child. The night before the uprising your mother planned, Bain was betrayed. He and several others were tortured, but divulged nothing. But others had been recruited, and not all possessed Bain's courage. The Kimra brought all women and children into this city. If we joined the rebellion your mother led, the Kimra threatened to slaughter them all. We had long ago learned not to doubt the brutality of the Kimra. They never made empty threats. I watched in shame on a farm while your mother's troops rode into an ambush. Your mother, with her bandana, slain many Kimra before she was forced to retreat. You feel your mother's death was fruitless. Far from it," Gwin said. "The bravery of your mother and her Shamra warriors were an inspiration. We bided our time, but we vowed to be free. Your mother's death was not in vain."

"How long did you wait?" Anis asked.

"Twenty-two years," Gwin said weakly. "We are farmers, not warriors."

"How did you gain your freedom?"

"We did precious little," Tillery said unexpectedly, his tone bitter. Anis hadn't thought he'd been listening to their conversation. "You think we rose up and defeated an army of trained soldiers?" he asked. "Our resistance numbered a dozen. Sometimes less."

"Do you blame us for what happened to your country?" Anis asked Tillery. "You don't even try to hide your anger. I know what Gwin said, but do you feel it's my mother's fault that somehow this land is in ruins? Or is it because I'm a female and I don't avert my eyes like Weetok females? Kimra females were submissive. You've adopted their culture."

Tillery rose. "I'm ashamed of my people, not angry at your mother and her warriors," he said. "I've heard the stories of your mother. How Shamra warriors, both male and female, fought the Kimra even though they were outnumbered. And now I see the daughter of the great Drea. I assumed the stories were exaggerated. Female warriors. A female *leading* an army. A female in hand-to-hand combat with the Kimra... *killing* Kimra. It's bad enough knowing we never rose against the Kimra, but knowing that the stories are true, it's...it's humiliating. And, yes, we've adopted much of the culture of our oppressors. Our people have lost their identity," Tillery said, looking now at Gwin, and licking his lips. "We were enslaved far longer than you. I sometimes wonder if we ever had our own culture," Tiller said, shaking his head in bewilderment.

"Sit, Tillery, and stop acting like a child," Gwin said.

"What do you mean that you never rose against the Kimra?" Anis asked. "They're gone."

"Tell her, Tillery," Gwin said.

Tillery sat down. "The Kimra fought among themselves," he said weakly. "Kronin led the Kimra against your mother. He was brutal, but he was a true warrior. After the battle—"

"The slaughter, you mean," Anis corrected, her eyes on Tillery.

"—Yes, the slaughter," Tillery said, nodding. "Soon after, he grew tired of...of sitting around doing nothing. He left for the Kimra homeland. He returned four years ago. He found his people here had grown lazy. They weren't vigilant. They took for granted we would do their bidding. Had we had the nerve, well, we might have defeated them. Kronin constantly insulted Tokar, who now led. Bickering led to a fight for dominance. We just took advantage," Tillery said, licked his lips, then went silent.

"And then?" Anis prodded.

"We fueled their bitterness," Gwin said when Tillery refused to continue. "It wasn't until the very end that we fought. Instead, we spread lies. We committed acts of sabotage, then told each side it was the other's doing. We kept those loyal to Kronin and those to Tokar at each other's throats. The Kimra can be barbaric, especially when fighting amongst themselves. Arguments and insults soon led to bloodshed. We let them butcher one another. When we rebelled...actually, when Tillery defied elders such as myself and decided to act whereas we were too scared, only a few dozen Kimra remained. Kronin killed Tokar, then..." Gwin paused. "Tillery, tell Anis what happened," Gwin said.

"She wouldn't believe me," Tillery said in a whisper. "I still don't believe—"

"Tillery killed Kronin," Gwin said, "but he wouldn't die. Instead, he fled," Gwin said.

"Chaos," Anis said excitedly. "Tell me, Tillery. No," she said, "I'll tell you. Gwin said you killed Kronin, right?"

Tillery nodded. "Rushed into the palace and thrust a spear through his heart."

"And he was no longer the Kronin you knew," Anis said.

"How do you know?" Tillery asked.

"What did you see?" Anis asked.

"His face was no longer Kronin's. He had no face at all. Just his eyes, but not *his* eyes—" Tillery said.

"Black eyes, like whirlpools, trying to suck you in," Anis finished for him.

"You've seen him?" Tillery said, sounding astonished.

"It wasn't Kronin," Anis said. "Never was. At least not the Kronin who left years before. It was Chaos. It visited my people. It split us apart. Janis's mother saw through Chaos, and it fled, just like your Kronin fled. It's been fifteen years, and we still haven't fully recovered. When Kronin fled, without a leader, you defeated the remaining Kimra?"

Tillery nodded.

"But what happened to the land?" Anis asked.

"It was as if the Kimra blood that was spilled poisoned the soil," Gwin said. "When Kronin...the one you call Chaos, left, our fields withered and died in a matter of days. Cattle sickened and lay bleeding from their noses and mouths. That stench you smell now was even worse. Even the buildings began to crumble, though many had stood for centuries. Others burst into flames, though no fires had been set. All the land north is...diseased. We can't even attempt to rebuild the farms. Many of us became ill."

"Yet you remain," Anis said.

"A small parcel of land to the south was unaffected," Gwin said. "We were enslaved by the Kimra for close to forty-four years. We have learned patience. We shall somehow reclaim our land to the north. Meanwhile, Tillery trains our males so if attacked, we won't ever again be defenseless."

"Your warriors would swell if you allowed females to fight alongside you," Anis said, looking at Tillery.

Tillery said nothing but nodded slightly.

Later that night, Anis stood by the gate. The moonlight allowed her to see the fields. She replayed in her mind Ramorra's account of the battle that had taken her mother's life. She heard footsteps behind her. It was Gwin.

"Now that you have seen where your mother died, will you return to your home?" Gwin asked.

"This is just the beginning of my journey," Anis said.

"What will you do?"

"Hunt Chaos," Anis said firmly. "Seems it is my destiny."

"And if you are successful?"

"Destroy him…or it. Or die trying."

"How do you find this Chaos?" Gwin asked.

"Chaos visited my land. It was also here. It has been elsewhere. We travel south tomorrow."

"Just your band of four?" Gwin asked.

"What are you suggesting? Your people have a land to reclaim," Anis said.

"And most of us would make terrible soldiers," Gwin added. "Take Tillery. Like you, he is a warrior. He no longer has the desire to farm."

Anis shrugged. "He is free to accompany us," she said.

"He won't ask," Gwin said. "You shame him."

"Because I'm a female war—"

"Bain was his father," Gwin interrupted. "Though Bain was betrayed, Tillery feels responsible for the death of your mother and the many Shamra warriors who perished while we stood idly by."

"You lost your leader," Anis said. "Your women and children were held hostage. Like you said, you were farmers. My mother wouldn't have condemned you. I certainly don't."

"Tillery sees you and feels disgraced," Gwin said. "Would you—?"

"Males and their pride," Anis said. "I will ask Tillery to join us," she said with a smile. "Maybe one from each land visited by Chaos should become *our* army." She paused. "Somehow it feels right."

Three days later, again traveling south, Anis saw two horses approach from the north. As they drew closer, Anis saw one carried a Shamra, but a stranger to her. Anis also recognized the other rider. It was the Tweeble who had helped expose Chaos for Ramorra fifteen years earlier. On closer inspection, Anis could see it wasn't the *same* creature. While the same size, around three-feet tall, this one was younger. And the creature who had aided Ramorra wore an eye patch. This one didn't.

It was the Shamra who most intrigued Anis. She was old. Not as old as Ramorra was, but most definitely in her forties. And she wore a bandana like Anis. Hers was red with black polka dots, while Anis's was yellow with black polka dots, the same colors Drea had worn. Before Anis could say anything, the Shamra spoke.

"You must be Anis, daughter of Drea," she said.

Anis thought the Shamra might be Chaos, having taken the form of one of her people. Anis would choose her words carefully. After all, there were no Shamra other than those at Stone Mountain, and Anis knew each and every one of them. Still, the bandana tugged at a memory.

"You are no Shamra," Anis said. "If you know who I am, you also know I know all Shamra."

"I was told at Stone Mountain you were no fool. On the contrary, like your mother did, I'm told you saved our people. Consider my age. The bandana, much like yours. And the fact that there is at least one Shamra your mother knew but you never met. Puzzle out who I am, or if you'd rather, tell me to be on my way," she said.

A Shamra my mother knew but I never met, Anis thought. There had been stories. But it couldn't be. "Atyra?" Anis asked.

The female nodded.

"My mother is dead—" Anis began.

"Been dead twenty-six years," Atyra said.

"You were told at Stone Mountain," Anis said, nodding.

"I saw her die," Atyra said.

"That's impossible," Anis said, then stopped. She remembered not to divulge too much. She had to know if this really was Atyra. Let *her* talk, her mind screamed.

"True. I wasn't there, but your mother and I shared a unique bond. I helped find a new homeland for the Shamra. Mya, your cousin, is married and has children of her own who are also married. I was in a field when I was nineteen. There, I saw your mother's death. Call it a vision, if you want, but it was as if I were there."

"My mother gave you two gifts before you left. What were they?" Anis asked.

"Three actually," Atyra said with a smile. There was Mya, of course, which you probably don't consider a gift. And two others. A sword made of metal. We weren't allowed to bring weapons with us on our trek to the new homeland, but your mother had a false bottom built on our wagon to conceal the sword. As for the last gift, it was an original version of the holy book so Mya and her descendants could pass our heritage and traditions through generations until Dara's birth." She paused. "Are you satisfied?"

"I'll accept that you're Atyra. Who is your companion? I've seen one like him before. Older, with an eye patch."

"My father, Ishry," the creature said, to Anis's surprise. "I am Enwee of the Tweeble."

"I know you have many questions," Atyra said, "and I'll answer them all, but we've ridden long and hard. I'm not as spry as I was in my youth. Can we make camp, then talk?"

Anis nodded.

Several hours later, after a meal, Anis took Atyra aside. "Now we talk," she said. "I don't know where to begin."

"Ask me why I'm here," Atyra said.

"Okay, why?"

Atyra told Anis of her life in the new homeland. How females had to be submissive. How of the four from their clan who had been chosen to go with the Shamra, only she remained.

"Other than Mya and my own daughter, Dedra, I had but one friend, Cid, from the farmer's clan, but as much of a warrior as any Shamra. I've had many adventures, but they were all in my youth. It hasn't been easy for me, but I've fulfilled my obligation to your mother. Mya, her child, and her grandchildren have all passed on our heritage as Drea had hoped. I didn't want to die an old woman who's dependent on others. I still hunt in the swamps, though it is prohibited. But I wanted more before it is my time. My first thought was to return home. I encountered Enwee, and I now have a mission."

"What did Enwee tell you that made you change your plans?"

"He can explain far better than I. Simply put, his people were visited by Chaos. I met Chaos when I was nineteen."

"How do you know the name?" Anis asked. "The Weetok had Chaos in their midst yet were unaware."

"Your mother told me."

"My mother was dead," Anis snapped, once again suspicious.

"She lives. May live forever, Anis," Atyra said. "You told me you saw Enwee's father, Ishry, fifteen years ago. When I last saw him, he was no youngster. He couldn't have lived another fifteen years. Enwee said he died twenty years ago."

"But I saw him," Anis said.

"With your mother. Dead, but alive in our memories. And summoned in a time of great need."

"Are you saying my mother is with the prophets…or is one of the prophets?" Anis asked. "I can't—"

"I say only that each of us lives in the memories of others. In Drea's case, she lived such an extraordinary life, tales of her deeds have been passed down generation to generation. When our despair is greatest, some call on the prophets for deliverance. In our clan, your mother lives in the hearts of all. She is called upon. Unlike the prophets, she appears. How do *you* know of Chaos?" Atyra asked.

"Ramorra told me," Anis said.

"Then she summoned your mother. She appeared to Ramorra with Ishry."

"Why did she appear to Ramorra and not me?" Anis asked, feeling hurt.

"Did you summon her, even in your darkest hour?" Atyra asked with a smile.

Anis said nothing.

"I was appalled when I arrived back at our homeland and found Stone Mountain was all we possessed. I was told what happened. I met your daughter, Dahlia. There was only one Shamra remaining that I knew. Dyann. She's four years younger than I. She told me of the bitterness you felt when your mother died. You still resent her, though you are less inclined to admit it now than when you were a youth, I was told. Drea wouldn't appear to you until you made peace with her. Until you asked for her help. You never did. Like her, you can be obstinate."

"And you want to confront Chaos?" Anis asked.

"I'm old, but not infirm. I have but one battle left in me. I met Chaos in my youth and forced it to flee. I want to face it again. If I die, it will be a glorious death, which is all those in our clan can hope for."

"How do I know you're not Chaos taking the form of Atyra?" Anis asked.

"Look deep into my eyes, Anis. Chaos can take the shape of others, but it can't totally hide its black soul-less eyes," Atyra said.

Anis gazed into Atyra's eyes long and hard and finally shrugged. "I don't see Chaos. You and Enwee are welcome to join us. I will surely seek your advice, but on this journey, I lead. I don't expect you to question my decisions once uttered. Agreed?"

"My allegiance is to my clan and its leader, Anis," Atyra said. "In private, your mother and I talked and bickered. Her decision, however, was final. You now lead our clan. You won't find me challenging your authority."

Anis stifled a yawn. It had been a long day. "Another day you will tell me about my mother. I've heard about her from Ramorra and Dyann, but you knew her best of all."

"She's in my thoughts daily," Atyra said. "I will tell you of Drea. Maybe you can finally come to terms with her."

"I already have," Anis said. "I've been told by so many how much like Drea I am; I've given up fighting the notion."

"You still harbor bitterness, Anis," Atyra said. "We'll talk. Often."

Several days later, around a campfire, Enwee told the others of his encounter with Chaos. He and Reva had become friendly since his arrival. Reva was known for her practical jokes. She'd loosened the saddle to Enwee's horse so when he climbed aboard, the saddle fell off and Enwee with it. Reva got away with her jokes because none were meant to be cruel. They were received in good humor. Enwee threatened to retaliate, but Anis took him aside and cautioned him.

"She always has the last word, Enwee," Anis said. "Play a joke on her, and you'll be looking over your shoulder for days or weeks. She'll get you when you least expect it."

Anis thought Enwee had a crush on her daughter. And Reva, far younger than the rest, was drawn to the diminutive Enwee because of his quick smile and sense of humor. He did appreciate a good joke, Anis thought, and he took Anis's advice. Enwee told his story to them all, but Anis could see he clearly wanted to impress Reva.

"The Tweeble are a nomadic people," he told them. "We're also a tad lazy," he added with a broad grin. "If we can get what we need without working, far be it for us to resist the opportunity. Our size also makes combat with others less than desirable. We do have our powers, though," he said with a wink. "To a limited extent, we can read the minds of others. More important is the Mist of Illusion. We can make others see what we want. We travel in groups of a dozen, but when we confront our prey, we appear to be an army of hundreds. And we take the form of those our quarry most fears."

Enwee went silent and closed his eyes. A moment later, Janis let out a shout of alarm, stood, and withdrew her sword. "It's the Galvan," she said. "Dozens of them approaching. Don't—"

Reva laughed and grabbed Janis's arm. "It's Enwee's Mist of Illusion. Haven't you been listening?"

Enwee opened his eyes, and the Galvan were gone. Janis's face reddened, and her normally blue eyes were purple, both signs of embarrassment.

"I didn't mean to frighten you, Janis," Enwee said. "I'm told I'm a bit of a showoff. I couldn't resist the demonstration. I'm sorry."

"I...I knew it wasn't really the Galvan," Janis said, but she still sounded anxious. She kept looking into the distance, as if the Galvan would appear again.

"It isn't uncommon for our people to go off alone for days or weeks at a time," Enwee continued. "We have villages, but as I said, we are nomadic. We live to roam. Chaos took the form of one of our people. It went unnoticed. My father, Ishry, took a group of our warriors hunting. For us, hunting is finding travelers, making it appear we are their most dreaded enemy, and demanding food, livestock, or other valuables to save them from carnage. Not terribly noble or heroic, but it's our way."

"How did Chaos split you?" Reva asked. Patience wasn't one of her virtues, Anis knew. She wanted Enwee to get on with his story.

"In time, sweet Reva," Enwee said. He told the same story Ishry had told Anis before she had confronted Chaos: how Chaos had used the Tweeble's Mist of Illusion against them.

"How did you know Chaos was responsible?" Reva asked.

"Several years later, one of your kind came and asked for our help," Enwee said. "Ishry went with this Drea—"

"When was this?" Anis asked Enwee, standing up, her eyes red with anger.

"Hmmm," Enwee said, scratching the fur on his chin. "I was four, so that would make it twenty-six years ago."

"Impossible," Anis said. "Drea was my mother. She was either leading our people to free the Weetok or already dead."

"*Not* dead," Atyra said. "As she explained it to me, she had crossed over from one existence to another. And like I told you before, she could be summoned."

"How could they summon her?" Anis asked. "They didn't even know she existed. She came to them unbidden, but not to me."

"She came to help *me*," Atyra said, and lifted a hand before Anis could speak. "Not just to help me. For Mya. A descendant of Mya's will help free the Shamra several hundred years from now. You know the prophesy. I had met Ishry. He helped defeat Chaos…well, at least helped send him fleeing. In my journey back to our homeland, I stopped to see Ishry. It's not a story for now, but Ishry and I had met once before on our trek to find a new homeland. I found Ishry had died. I told Enwee of Chaos, and the course of my journey changed.

SHAMRA DIVIDED

I did want to visit our homeland, but my quest ends with Chaos…one way or the other. Enwee's Mist of Illusion is a weapon I used once against Chaos, and it could be of use again."

Anis glared at both Atyra and Enwee. "I've had enough stories for one night. I'm going for a walk," she said, and left.

Anis was sitting by a stream when she heard a noise. She turned, her sword unsheathed, and was staring at Atyra.

"Jealous, are we?" Atyra said.

"I've had enough for one night, Atyra. Please go."

"You are your own best company, right?" Atyra said.

Anis said nothing.

"You still harbor so much resentment against your mother, even if you think you've come to terms with her. Your life without her has been hard. But you're not alone. Do you think I've enjoyed the last twenty-six years, hiding my true nature from all but my family? I begged your mother to tell me to remain rather than go find a new Shamra homeland. We were closer than sisters. We were soulmates. That's why I knew the instant she died. Much as we loved one another, she did what was best for our clan and sent me away. You at least lived among our people. You didn't have to live a lie. If anyone should be bitter, it's me."

"And you're not?"

"When I was young, just surviving and living a lie occupied my waking hours. And I had Mya and my own daughter, Dedra. I chose my path, and I don't regret it. But I wonder what would have happened had your mother told me to remain. Wallow in your self-pity, Anis, if you want. It will be your undoing if we meet Chaos." Without another word, Atyra turned and walked off.

"Why couldn't I have someone like you to confide in?" Anis called after her. "Where is *my* Atyra?"

Anis lay on the ground and was soon asleep. When she awoke, there was a blanket draped over her. "Atyra," she said aloud and smiled.

Barry Hoffman

◆◆◆◆◆◆◆◆◆◆

Anis stood with Cym, Enwee, and Tillery outside of what appeared to be a monastery. Several miles back, she had an army, so to speak, awaiting her return. The two years since she'd visited the Weetok and met Atyra and Enwee had been filled with adventure and danger. It had been the most exhilarating period of her life. She could finally understand how her mother had been drawn from the Shamra homeland. Anis had journeyed to dozens of lands and encountered unimaginable civilizations. Anis often thought it was a shame her daughter Dahlia might never share such an experience

Twenty cultures had been visited by Chaos. Of those, sixteen had agreed to join Anis's campaign to locate and destroy the entity. Some even offered to send dozens, even hundreds, of soldiers with Anis, but she declined. She knew a large army would appear to be a threat when they approached potential allies. So she accepted just one from each.

Her band had been attacked by roving bands of outlaws on three occasions. They had lost two in the attacks. Cym had been badly wounded in the last, and Anis feared for her life. Zyr of the Nephyr, a flying creature with a dozen webbed wings and a reptilian body, had applied healing herbs to Cym's wounds. Her fever soon abated, and within days, her wounds had completely healed. It made Anis appreciate even more what each among them had to offer.

During the journey, Anis had leaned heavily on Atyra. She soon understood the bond between Atyra and her mother. Ramorra had advised Anis and cautioned her when she became impulsive. Ramorra had rarely disagreed with Anis and never fervently argued with her. Atyra accepted Anis as their leader but in private fought tooth-and-nail, just as Atyra had with Drea. Once Anis made a decision, however, Atyra never questioned or second-guessed her. On the contrary, in public, Atyra swayed doubters to Anis's viewpoint.

SHAMRA DIVIDED

Atyra also became something of a grandmother to Reva, who had been deprived of one with Drea's death. She told both Reva and Anis of her clan's heritage. Her stories were far more intimate than Ramorra's. Nyvia and Sera were not just names of ancestors who had committed heroic deeds. Atyra told stories that made them come to life. She told both Anis and Reva up-close-and-personal details of her friendship with Drea. Anis found she could confide in Atyra, something she had always found difficult to do with others. And Atyra took Reva hunting alone so the two of them could just chat. Reva began keeping a journal. Sometimes Anis could overhear Reva reading portions to Atyra. It was the one thing Reva withheld from her mother. Oddly, though, Anis didn't mind. Just as she needed Atyra, so did Reva.

Anis almost welcomed the attacks by outlaws. She was, after all, a warrior and found she had the same bloodlust as her ancestors. Both she and Atyra killed a number of outlaws in hand-to-hand combat. Reva killed something other than an animal for the first time. Reva had fought with reckless abandon. As a mother, Anis was concerned for her daughter's safety. She also couldn't be more proud. And Anis noticed how Enwee was never far from Reva during a battle. Reva had taught Enwee how to use a slingshot, and he was deadly with it. Though he was small, his skill proved equal to that of any Shamra. With Enwee watching Reva's back, Anis wasn't distracted or overprotective of her daughter.

Over the course of the two years, Anis discovered the strengths of those who followed her. She learned who among them could best lead. They needed both strength of will and discipline to follow instructions. Tillery was a born leader, but for the first year, he lacked the necessary discipline Anis required. Tillery was also the most distant of their small army. For the first year, he never went out of his way to befriend or assist others.

It was Reva who eventually succeeded in knocking down the wall Tillery hid behind. Tillery slept like a rock. Reva found he wouldn't even wake when lifted. So Reva, with Enwee's help, would move Tillery from his tent to another while he slept. Tillery would wake totally bewildered and disoriented. Reva also scattered Tillery's weapons from tent to tent. In the mornings, he would go mumbling from one tent to another, apologizing as he sought out his arsenal. While others said nothing, fearing a tongue-lashing from Tillery, Reva followed him around making jokes. At first Tillery remained stoic, but even he had to laugh at Reva's jests. Reva also engaged Tillery in target practice and even hand-to-hand combat. While Anis knew Reva was Tillery's equal, Reva often asked Tillery to show her a maneuver she said she found vexing. Tillery would patiently work with Reva. Later, others came to him for advice. It took a good while, but Tillery did become the leader Anis envisioned.

Others, like Janis, were more suited to follow, Anis learned. Anis had no desire for an army solely comprised of leaders. Janis and others did as they were told. Janis, like Ramorra, was a reluctant warrior, but she was no coward.

Still, after two years, Anis had no better idea where to find Chaos than when she had left Stone Mountain. Chaos appeared. Chaos disappeared. But to where? She wondered how long she could keep the spirits of her coalition from flagging. In truth, she would have been more than satisfied to continue her exploration for the rest of her life. But some among them longed to return to their people and the comforts of where they called home.

It was Cym who came to the rescue. Tillery had first thought Cym was a servant of the Shamra. He had never encountered a Galvan, and Cym didn't appear intimidating. Yes, she was a bit taller than Tillery. And her claw-like talons were as good a weapon as a knife. Still, he wondered why Anis brought her along. He knew Cym was old, and she was most definitely the most frail of their number. After a day's riding, she breathed deeply from the two gill-like incisions on each of her cheeks. She spoke in sentence fragments and then paused to catch her breath. It was Reva who told Tillery that Cym was fearless—that frail as she might be, she would fight to the death. Reva told Tillery how Cym and Anis had come to know one another. She recounted a Shamra raid on the barracks of the Galvan army and how Cym told Anis she would have to kill her, as Cym wouldn't be taken hostage.

Whenever they visited a new land, Cym would accompany Anis. Anis would learn about Chaos and seemed content. Cym, though, always probed deeper, sometimes irritating their hosts with her demand for detail. Tillery, who was often present during these encounters, wondered why Cym persisted in asking what seemed like meaningless questions.

One night, Cym came to Anis with a crude map she had made from the skin of an animal. She had drawn lines from each country Chaos had struck.

"Chaos didn't just appear," Cym told Anis. "In almost every case, it made a point of making sure it was seen entering a country. Atyra spoke of a Shamra priest. Gwin of the Weetok said the Kimra, Kronin, made his return a spectacle of sorts. It was you Tobin greeted when he returned from his travels. It was the same with most of the others. And when Chaos fled, it left in the same direction it had entered."

Anis saw the many lines on the map all intersected at one point. She touched it gingerly, as if she might be sucked into the map.

"If Chaos is not a single entity but sends a part of itself to other lands, as we've speculated," Cym continued, "they still come from one source."

"Where your lines intersect," Anis said.

Cym shrugged. "I could be wrong. Probably am. But we haven't been here," she said, placing her finger where she thought Chaos made its home. "We've traveled nearby, but we found no living creatures. The land is inhospitable. It could be intentional. Why should we—*or anyone, for that matter*—explore such an unwelcome wilderness?"

Anis decided to follow Cym's instinct. Even if it led to nothing, the spirits of her troops were buoyed by the possibility Chaos might be found.

They traveled for three weeks. Zyr and two other flying creatures were Anis's advance scouts. As they neared the area where Cym's map showed the lines intersecting, the landscape abruptly changed. The land seemed dead. It wasn't a desert. The earth was coarse and dry. There was no life of any kind. No vegetation. No water. *Uninviting* was the word that sprang to Anis's mind. Who would venture through this land? No one, which made it a perfect camouflage for Chaos.

Zyr was the first to spot a solitary building almost hidden between two hills. Anis and Atyra went to scout on foot after they had made camp. Behind a dune of coarse ground, they saw a building perhaps a half a mile away.

"No matter where you approach, you're totally exposed," Atyra whispered, as if the still air had ears. "There's no sneaking up. No surprise attack."

"We have to get a closer look at that building," Anis said. "Tomorrow we'll take a small party. Lost pilgrims looking for some water."

Atyra nodded.

An hour later, explosions rocked the land surrounding the building. This time everyone came to the dune to see. All were alarmed. Huge flames of fire and ash broke through the surface. There were twenty detonations in half an hour; then all went silent. The ground repaired itself. It almost looked like a mirage. Forty-five minutes later, the explosions began anew. This time there were twenty-seven, and Enwee commented that they seemed to appear at different locations than the first ones. The fireworks continued throughout the evening and into the night. It seemed totally random. At times, an hour would pass. Other times, minutes separated one burst of flames from the next. There were as few as six detonations at one time and as many as forty-three at another. And the locations varied with each. As they had already seen, the ground repaired itself as soon as the eruptions ended. It was obvious that if the explosions began as they traveled toward the building, they would be incinerated.

Anis's temperament altered from depression to agitation. "Close enough to almost touch, yet as impregnable as Stone Mountain," she said to Atyra. She knew her frustration was contagious, so she spoke in a whisper so only Atyra could hear. She knew the others must be thinking similar thoughts. Time to abandon the search and return home, she could imagine them thinking.

Cym remained behind the dune day and night, making notes, saying nothing. Others brought her food and drink. She took short naps only when another was with her to awaken her the moment the blasts began. While an explosion accompanied each eruption, some were soundless.

In camp, there was little talk. Anis saw some of the creatures whispering to one another. How long can I keep them here doing nothing? she wondered.

On the third day, Anis awoke to find Cym sitting by her side. A smile played at Cym's lips, though she looked exhausted.

"Have they stopped?" Anis asked.

"Hardly. *But* they're not random, as we thought," Cym said. "I had a hunch, and I've charted the eruptions since. There's a pattern. I know when and where. I can plot a safe path to the building."

Anis hugged her friend, and Cym grimaced. "Are you okay?" Anis asked.

"I'm old, that's all. I hurt all over, yet I've never felt so alive."

"Rest now," Anis said. "You've earned it."

◆◆◆◆◆◆◆◆◆◆

Anis and three others stood outside the building, which now appeared to be a monastery. With Cym in the lead, they had traveled the perilous half a mile without problems. Behind them, blasts rocked the ground.

There was no door to the monastery. Inside, Anis saw a dozen monks, each dressed in black robes with black hoods that obscured their faces. The floor inside appeared to be made of blood-red marble. Those inside ignored the intruders. Finally, one of the monks came outside. Anis saw it was Tobin, her cousin, who had been possessed by Chaos. She bit her lip so as not to show surprise. The monk offered no greeting.

"This is a religious order. No one is allowed entrance," the monk said, sounding very much like the Tobin who had fled from Stone Mountain fifteen years earlier. He hadn't aged. Anis knew this Tobin was a manifestation of Chaos.

"We ask only for something to drink," Anis said, trying to sound flustered. "We've been traveling for days. We must have gotten lost..." she said, intentionally not finishing.

"We have little for our own needs and none to spare," Tobin said. He pointed the way they had come. "Leave now before the ground belches its fire," he said, turned, and went inside the monastery. Anis noticed his feet didn't touch the marble ground. He didn't track any of the dust from his bare feet inside. Anis tossed a small stone inside when Tobin turned his back. It disappeared into the marble, almost like a pebble thrown into a lake.

Back at camp, Anis asked each one who had been with her what they had seen. She wanted to get their impressions before she spoke.

"Kronin greeted us," Tillery said, his voice filled with venom. "It was all I could do not to plunge my sword in his eye."

Anis looked at Tillery oddly. She had seen Tobin. Tillery saw Kronin. "Enwee?"

"I saw one of my people. I remember that at some point he disappeared. But with the...chaos among our people, it wasn't uncommon."

"Cym?" Anis asked.

"I saw no face. Just two black eyes that seemed to draw me toward the figure. I had to look away."

"The Galvan weren't visited by Chaos," Anis said, saying out loud what she was thinking. "Your people were already in chaos."

"I don't understand," Tillery said. "How could we each see the...monk, I guess, in a different form?"

"It's Chaos, Tillery, as seen by each of us," Anis said. "Only Cym saw its true form because Chaos hasn't appeared to her people."

"We can't go into the monastery," Enwee said. "The monks inside didn't walk on the red ground. They left no footprints. It must be an illusion they created."

Anis nodded. "I threw a stone, and it disappeared. If we enter, we plunge into an abyss."

"What now?" Tillery asked.

What now? Anis had been contemplating the same question on the ride back from the monastery, so she was prepared with an answer. She knew she had to be firm and decisive. Even with Cym having figured out the pattern of the explosions, morale was low. "The monks are minions of Chaos," Anis said. "We've at least confirmed that. We're in the right place. Chaos sends the monks to do its bidding. We have to find the source. We'll have Zyr fly over the monastery and see what he learns."

Zyr listened to Cym's instructions before he flew to the monastery. He had seen that some of the fires from the underground blasts extended for miles. If a proper course wasn't plotted, he could be incinerated in the conflagration.

When Zyr returned, he was full of excitement. Anis gathered her entire army to hear what Zyr had to say. His twelve wings kept flapping when he spoke. Sometimes he rose as he talked. Once Reva pulled him down and shot him a look. It was only then that he realized what he had been doing.

"To the south, behind the main body of the monastery, is a pit of some sort," Zyr said. "I saw monks emerge. They... they weren't fully formed when they appeared. Some had no arms or legs. Their robes hung limp at parts of their bodies. But after they left the pit, they transformed in front of me. They grew limbs."

"Could you see into the pit?" Anis asked.

Zyr shook his head. "A bottomless pit," he said. "Black as a moonless night."

Anis went to plan her attack. Zyr answered questions from the others. Anis was joined by Atyra.

"Zyr will drop me into the pit to confront Chaos while the rest of you lead a frontal assault to keep the monks occupied," Anis said after just a few moments of thought.

Atyra nodded.

"You're not going to try to talk me out of confronting Chaos alone?" Anis asked.

"Only you are capable of defeating Chaos, if it's even possible," Atyra said.

"It means almost certain death," Anis said. "I don't fear it, but it's not like you—"

"If you want me to talk you out of—"

Anis shook her head. "I'm just surprised. I thought you'd disapprove and that I'd have to fight you every step of the way."

"It's your destiny," Atyra said. "Only you saw Chaos in your dreams. That's what led you on this quest. There is no other. I'm aged. I can do battle, but my best days are far behind me. Cym, too. I've come to respect her. Without her, we'd be lost. And were she younger, she would gladly confront Chaos. It's just not to be. And Reva, well, besides being too young, she's our future. The others can help, and many would volunteer to enter the pit, but you're the guiding force. We need you to lead us, but Chaos must be stilled. Let there be no talk of your death. There is a battle to plan."

Anis and Atyra argued over the frontal assault, but Anis wouldn't be swayed, and Atyra finally acquiesced. They returned to the others. There was an expectant silence as Anis went over the plan.

"Zyr will fly me to the pit to confront the Source," Anis said. She no longer referred to it solely as Chaos, though she knew the words were interchangeable. What lay in the pit was the *source* of Chaos. "The rest of you will attack the monastery in two waves. Reva and Tillery will lead the first. Enwee will use his Mist of Illusion to make our numbers seem like a hundred. We know Chaos creates illusions of its own, and it won't take long for the monks to penetrate Enwee's deception. But it will buy us time."

Reva, Tillery, and Enwee nodded. She could see their mounting excitement. The frontal assault, especially by the first group, was a suicide mission if Anis didn't quickly succeed. Yet there was not the slightest reluctance on their part. She had never been so proud.

"Atyra will lead the second wave to reinforce the first," Anis continued. "If I fail, make for the pit, and attempt to collapse it."

Several of the lands they had visited had explosives and had given some to Anis. She didn't know if the pit could be destroyed, but she knew of no other way to destroy the Source if she failed at her task.

"Rest as best as you can," Anis said. "Tomorrow ends two years of wandering. Tomorrow we triumph over Chaos."

Anis accompanied Atyra to her tent. "Will you sleep tonight?" Anis asked.

Atyra shook her head. "Battles such as this are what we live for. I will have an eternity to rest. Tonight I prepare myself for battle."

"I'm glad I got to know you and learn from your wisdom," Anis said. "And you and Reva have grown close. She certainly doesn't act like a fifteen-year-old."

"Like someone else I knew," Atyra said. "Someone forced to act far wiser than her years. It's still not too late—"

"I know," Anis said. "I'll think on it." Then she smiled. "Whatever the outcome, tomorrow will be a glorious day," she said.

"You'll do your family and your clan proud," Atyra said. "No regrets."

Anis went to the hills to watch the explosions. Deadly as they were, she didn't know if she had ever seen anything as beautiful, now that darkness filled the sky. The flames consisted of all the colors of the rainbow. Truly mesmerizing, she thought. After a pause in the evening spectacle, she sighed. Atyra was right. She had one unfinished piece of business. "I need to speak to you, Mother," Anis said aloud. She felt a bit foolish. *Summon my mother*. It sounded so—

"You waited long enough," a voice said, startling Anis.

"Mother?" Anis asked, looking at the figure who sat by her side. Anis thought she looked all of nineteen years old.

"Yes," Drea said. "I understand your confusion. I look as I did when I left this existence. Younger than you. But don't let my looks deceive you. I'm Atyra's age. And you, my daughter, are still bitter."

"Less than before this quest," Anis said. "I can see the lure of the unknown for our kind. The hunts. The battles. It's exhilarating."

"Yes, but I abandoned you," Drea said. "You can't let that go."

Anis shrugged.

"Your journey was of your own choosing," Drea said. "When I left, our people were about to lose their identity. As leader, I had to rally them. The hunt was planned for a month, maybe two."

"But you had to lead our clan against the Kimra to free the Weetok. And, of course, you had to be out front, teasing death," Anis said.

"Like my mother before me," Drea said. "We led by example."

"And Sera almost destroyed our clan," Anis said. "You didn't learn from her mistakes."

"I won't argue with you, Anis. I admit I was no great mother," Drea said. "I acknowledge as much. When you were older, I…" she started, then trailed off. "I'm proud of you, Anis. I've watched all you've done. I cheered when you stood up to Kel, even when others frowned and mumbled their displeasure. Your stand at Stone Mountain saved our clan. And this quest to find Chaos exists only because of your persistence. I've so wanted you to know you've been a magnificent leader."

"But I never embraced you. So you couldn't tell me," Anis said.

"I feel your anger. It's my one regret. You did call on me, though."

"Not to forgive you or hear your praise," Anis snapped. "I'm sorry," she said hurriedly. "I do understand. I just can't—"

"Time's wasting, Anis," Drea said. "Why did you summon me?"

"How do I destroy Chaos?" Anis asked. "My plan is no plan. Dive into a pit with my sword and some explosives—?"

"You'll need neither," Drea interrupted. "You must simply absorb Chaos. Leap into the pit, and become one with Chaos. You are its opposite. You won't die. Not yet, anyway. The two of you will be in mortal conflict for days, weeks, maybe years, with no clear-cut winner."

"Will I prevail?" Anis asked. "You know the future."

"Been talking to Atyra, have you?" Drea said. "But have you really listened to her? There are many futures. When you jump into that pit tomorrow, you create any number of futures that never existed. It's your inner strength against the darkness Chaos embodies. There's no way to know who will be victorious. I envy you the confrontation." Drea paused. "Do you want me to stay with you tonight?"

Atyra shook her head. "I need to be with me, no offense. There's so much I'd like to ask you, but I need to come to terms with myself...to be at my best tomorrow."

"I understand," Drea said.

"Mother...I do love you," Anis said. "I've been told so many times I'm so much like you..." She paused. "I only wish I had really gotten to know you. I lost you. I never had an Atyra. I sometimes feel sorry for myself. So you became an easy target for my resentment." Tears came to her eyes. "I've had a glorious life. I have few regrets. I just never let anyone get close to me like you did with Atyra, and it's clouded my judgment."

"And it's my fault," Drea said, embracing Anis. "I wish I could make it up to you. We *are* very much alike. I'm as stubborn as you are...maybe more so. I should have sought you out years ago."

"You couldn't—"

"Rubbish," Drea said. "Rules can be broken. I have broken more than a few. You have every right to harbor bitterness toward me. There are times I should have been there for you. So much alike. Maybe we're too much alike. Stubborn to a fault. I have always loved you, Anis. Take that with you tomorrow when you confront Chaos. My love and admiration."

Anis let go of her mother and turned as new explosions erupted. She looked back at her mother. She was gone. Drea's words echoed in Anis's ears. *Love and admiration.* She fell asleep on the hill, a smile on her face.

Shamra Divided

◆◆◆◆◆◆◆◆◆

The next morning, silence engulfed Anis's not-so-mighty army as they prepared to do battle. It was one of anticipation, not fear. Janis had returned from a forest with a fresh kill. She, Anis, Atyra, and Reva streaked their long white hair with the red blood of the animal, as was their clan's tradition. Anis, Atyra, and Reva then put on their bandanas. Others followed their own customs, whether it be Tillery's prayer or Zyr's grooming of wings. Atyra took Reva aside.

"I will take your place in the first assault," Atyra said, so none of the others could hear.

"You don't trust me?" Reva said, sounding crestfallen.

"You lead like your mother and grandmother, Reva," Atyra said. "You are relentless and reckless. You have no regard for your own safety and welfare. Your great grandmother, Sera, led the attack on Monument Gate to free our people. She was one of the first to perish."

"A glorious death," Reva said.

"True, yet it would have been foolhardy had she not had someone to assume leadership of the clan. She *thought* she had Jana, but she, too, perished in the battle. The very existence of our clan then lay with your great grandmother or a fifteen-year-old who never thought she'd have to lead. She succeeded, but don't forget she almost had to fight Ramorra. And now the future of the Shamra at Stone Mountain rests with you," Atyra said.

"Not me. With Dahlia," Reva said.

"Your mother may have erred in her decision that Dahlia succeed her," Atyra said.

"It's been our way. Dahlia's the eldest. She's been groomed to take over for Anis since birth."

"From what your mother says, Kel was chosen to lead over Tobin solely because of his age. The clan was almost destroyed by Kel's weakness."

"Do you have the Gift of Sight?" Anis asked. "Have you seen something?"

"Only your family has the gift, though Drea sometimes considered it a curse. I just have my intuition. I spent a week with Dahlia. First impressions are lasting ones for me, Reva. Your sister doesn't inspire others. She doesn't think well on her feet. She's plodding and lacks vision. She's overly cautious and no longer relies on others for advice. She's insulated herself from all but a few. And she's devious and secretive. When your mother was there to guide her, she may have seemed equipped to handle clan leadership. With Anis gone, Dahlia seems lost. She needs you, even if she won't admit it. If you lead the first assault, you will almost surely die, like Sera. Lead the second, and your chances of survival are far better."

"So you die in my place?" Reva said, shaking her head.

"Not necessarily. I fought Chaos before and survived. I was in the thick of it at Monument Gate, by your grandmother's side. We were outnumbered. I could have died there. *My* gift seems to be self-preservation. And if I fall, far better it be in battle than like Ramorra's walking into a cave of snakes, knowing death was certain. And I won't die old and infirm in bed. If this be my last battle, so be it."

"Will my mother agree?"

"She won't know," Atyra said. "She has to clear her mind for what lies ahead. Enwee will use his Mist of Illusion. She'll see you leading the attack from the air when it will be me."

Reva nodded. "I want to die in battle, whether it is today or many years from now. I saw what Ramorra had become… too frail to take up arms, so she walked into a cave of snakes."

"We'll talk, Reva, after the battle, if it is meant to be." Atyra paused. "Reva, I painted a bleak picture of your abilities, but you have learned much during our quest. And, unlike Sera, you are far more intuitive. It won't help against Chaos, but when you return home, you will be equipped to deal with Dahlia. The future of our clan may well rest with you. Drea trusted my judgment. I think you are mature enough to do the same," Atyra said.

Reva nodded. The two embraced; then Atyra went to tell Enwee her plan.

When Zyr flew off with Anis on her back, Atyra and Tillery led the first assault. Enwee's Mist of Illusion made the advancing army seem like a hundred. Behind them, Atyra heard the explosions from underground. She and her warriors would have to hold off the monks for twenty minutes before the blasts subsided and the second wave could reinforce them.

Two dozen monks emerged from the monastery to meet them. They wore the robes and hoods of monks, but Atyra could see they were faceless. Two disembodied black eyes from each stared at Atyra and her army as they approached.

Aim for the eyes, Anis had said. As Tillery had learned, even a blade to the heart couldn't kill the minions of Chaos. "And try to cut off their heads." One civilization they had visited had told of *killing* Chaos when they cut off its head. They no longer considered Chaos a threat and hadn't joined Anis's crusade. But their information proved invaluable.

The monks were armed with swords, though Atyra could see no hands or arms protruding from their robes. Many of the monks attacked the phantom army conjured by Enwee.

One came at Atyra and sidestepped her as she rode by. The monk plunged its sword into Atyra's horse. It went down, sending Atyra sprawling. The monk lunged at Atyra, grazing her shoulder as she rolled away. It rushed at her as if invincible, and Atyra plunged her sword into one of its eyes. The eye burst into flames, liquid light dripping onto the monk's robe as it wailed in pain. Atyra drove her sword into its other eye, and now it was blinded.

Several other monks now advanced toward her. Atyra glanced around and saw her army of a hundred no longer existed. The Mist of Illusion had been penetrated. They were now outnumbered, and the monks attacked each in groups of two or three.

A slash across her arm, and Atyra lost her sword as she grimaced in pain. She had only her knife.

A sudden silence abruptly surrounded them. The ground stopped trembling. The blasts had ceased. Reva led reinforcements into the fray. The monks appeared confused for a moment, thinking Reva's warriors another illusion. Ignoring the advancing warriors on horseback, several of the monks were quickly felled.

Reva rode up, scooped up Atyra's sword, and flipped it to Atyra. Reva jumped from her horse, and the two were fighting back to back.

"Like you and Drea at Monument Gate," Reva yelled.

Then, without warning, the eyes of a monk who had just struck Atyra exploded. A blinding light erupted from its eyes, and it staggered back, striking blindly with its sword.

Atyra saw other monks all around her do the same. They retreated toward the monastery, several tripping over fallen horses and bodies. They were set upon by Atyra and Reva's warriors. Cut off their heads, they had been told. Cut off their heads is what they did. They then rushed toward the monastery and the retreating monks. Atyra remembered the marble floor was only an illusion. If her army entered, they would plunge to their death. "Tell them to stop, Reva," Atyra gasped, hardly able to speak.

Reva yelled a command. They stopped, and the warriors looked to Reva for direction. Suddenly the walls of the monastery collapsed inward. The building sank into the ground, unable to bear the weight of the crumbling walls. All that remained was a pile of rubble and the pit Anis had descended.

SHAMRA DIVIDED

Then there was utter silence. Atyra fell to her knees and saw a figure approach from the ruins of the monastery.

◆◆◆◆◆◆◆◆◆◆

Zyr neared the pit with Anis on his back. They heard the shouts of their warriors attacking the monastery. Anis hoped that diversion would hinder the concentration of the Source. There had been no goodbyes that morning before the battle. She had hugged each, shaken their hand, or whatever was their custom to wish each good luck. She had to bite her lip so as not to become emotional when she and Reva embraced. There was so much she wanted to tell her daughter. But she had to keep her mind clear. The two locked eyes after they hugged. That seemed to say it all. Then she'd hopped on Zyr. There was no looking back.

Zyr hovered over the pit. Anis had no idea how deep it was. Only blackness from below greeted her. She had brought no weapons. If her mother was right, only Anis herself could defeat the Source. *She* was the weapon.

Anis jumped off Zyr into the pit. A chill numbed her as she plunged into the blackness. She thought of Reva. Of Atyra. Of Dahlia. Of—

Free your mind, Anis.

It was her mother, Anis knew. Instinctively, she did as her mother instructed. Soon she could make out a throbbing in the blackness beneath her. I must be approaching the Source, she thought. As she got closer, she saw a whirlpool in the center of the darkness. She feared she'd be sucked within. *Free your mind*, she told herself. Suddenly, she was no longer falling, but was lying atop the whirling mass. She felt the whirlpool's attempt to suck her under, yet she didn't move.

Anis heard a voice within her head. It was the Source. "You cannot defeat Chaos with your puny army. Chaos has been here since the dawn of all living creatures. Chaos is here for all eternity. You'll serve Chaos. Serve Chaos for eternity. Serve Chaos for—"

Anis tuned out the voice. Chaos wouldn't have spoken to her if it could have devoured her. It sought to weaken her resolve with lies. She'd resist. Maybe she couldn't defeat Chaos, but it couldn't free itself of her. As long as she didn't succumb, neither could overcome the other. Stalemate, she thought. Above her, she heard the crumbling of walls. And deep within the mass, she thought she heard a sigh of despair.

♦♦♦♦♦♦♦♦♦♦

Drea stood over Atyra. Atyra had emerged from the monastery when she became aware of the deadlock between the Source and Anis. Atyra had sustained a dozen wounds, maybe more. She lay on her back, her breathing shallow. A smile played at her lips when she saw Drea.

"You'll be joining me soon, old friend," Drea said.

"Not until you tell me the outcome. Anis? The Source?"

"They have joined together. Chaos cannot defeat Anis, yet neither can Anis prevail. There is still chaos within Anis. For now, they are both imprisoned. The Source cannot send out its minions to create further chaos."

"Then why do you sound despondent?" Atyra said.

"There is natural chaos in the world, Atyra," Drea said. "We saw it within our own people when our clan was exiled. Anis will grow no stronger, but Chaos will feed on the natural chaos. In time, it will overwhelm and consume Anis."

"How long?" Drea could see the life ebbing from her friend. Atyra could only speak a few words at a time.

"I've told you of the elastic nature of the future," Drea said. "Already, what Anis has done has created any number of new paths. Anis will hold her own for a few years or for a hundred. She won't age as long as she's in combat with

Chaos. She will not have given her life in vain. Tens of thousands, maybe more, will be spared because of her sacrifice. It will take another to defeat the Source, though."

"The Dara of the future?"

Drea shrugged. "So many paths, Atyra. So many possibilities."

"The others?" Atyra whispered. "Cym?"

"Fought valiantly, but she is dead. But she died in battle, not of old age."

"Reva? She was with me…"

"Flesh wounds. Nothing more. She relished the battle as you and I once did," Drea said.

"Tillery?"

"Badly injured," Drea said. "Reva tends to him now."

"Enwee?"

"Will live to fight another day," Drea said with a smile. "Very much like his father."

"And Janis?" Atyra asked.

"Very much like her mother. Fought on the fringes and came away unscathed." Drea also told Atyra the fates of the others. Over half had survived.

"And you?" Atyra said, her lips trembling as she spoke.

"Me? I no longer fight—"

"You…know…what I mean," Atyra said, and for a few seconds, her eyes flashed the orange of irritation.

"Anis summoned me, Atyra," Drea said. "There wasn't time to wipe away the years of resentment, but she summoned me, old friend."

"A start," Atyra said. "Like mother, like daughter."

CHAPTER 15

~ *The Present* ~

Tears welled in Dara's eyes as Briana finished. "So much senseless death. And for what? Chaos has returned."

"You're wrong on both counts," Briana said, shaking her head. "Haven't you been listening to the stories I've told you? Or does what I say go in one ear and out the other?" She didn't wait for Dara to answer. "If nothing else, Dara, you must understand what drives our clan...what drives *you* as a member of our clan. We're hunters and warriors. Better to perish in battle than die of old age. Nyvia dreaded the last years of her life. Old and infirm, she was unable to fight one last battle. Atyra had wondrous adventures, but adventure ended in her twenties. For close to twenty-five years, she lived the life of a good Shamra under the New Order to make sure Mya and Dedra passed on our heritage to their children and that those children would do the same when they gave birth. Only then did Atyra return. She wanted to confront Chaos. She wanted to die in battle."

"She got her wish," Dara said bitterly.

"She fought valiantly. She died a hero...and at peace with herself. She crossed over on her terms. What more could one ask for?"

"And Anis?" Dara asked. "She gave her life in her confrontation with the Source of Chaos. Well, Chaos is back."

"She fought on even terms with Chaos for two hundred years. Not a bad legacy," Briana said. With each year, Chaos grew stronger, feeding on the natural chaos that exists in the world. Yet it took far longer for Chaos to overwhelm Anis than anyone ever thought possible. Imagine the strength it took for Anis not to despair and surrender while each day Chaos grew more powerful."

"She is more of a hero to you than even Drea," Dara said. "Now that you know that Chaos is responsible for the deaths of your brothers and sisters, why not summon Anis? Even though she ultimately failed, she might have something valuable to offer."

"I fight my own battles," Briana said. "One summonses when one despairs. It's usually a sign of weakness and desperation."

Dara didn't continue to argue with Briana but wondered if there was something left unsaid. According to these Shamra, upon death, one simply crossed over to another existence. But Anis hadn't died in the traditional sense. She'd battled Chaos to a standoff for two centuries. Dara understood that Chaos had finally prevailed, but what had happened to Anis?

Dara was interrupted from her thoughts by a noise outside. One of the Galvan on horseback. Briana had been right. They'd split up. The Galvan entered the cave, holding his horse by its reins. Dara and Briana stepped out of a corner so they could be seen. The Galvan grunted, and Dara and Briana ran. The cave narrowed, but being short and sleek, Dara and Briana easily navigated to the first exit. Turning, as Briana climbed out, Dara saw the Galvan crawling slowly after them. She had to stifle a laugh.

Once out of the cave, Briana and Dara plugged the hole with several large boulders, then made their way to the front entrance of the cave. They had gathered brush, twigs, and branches, which they'd brought into the cave and hidden behind rocks. Briana set them on fire. The cave was soon filled with smoke. Briana and Dara waited outside—Briana behind a tree close to the cave, Dara standing atop the cave's entrance.

Five minutes later, the Galvan, on horseback, rushed out, coughing from the smoke. Briana stepped out from behind the tree, her sword in hand. The Galvan halted and glared at her. Dara jumped onto his back, took her knife as Briana had instructed, and struck the Galvan in his eye. Bright light poured from the wound as he bellowed in pain. Dara jumped off the Galvan, who fled into the forest, still howling in agony.

"Like a true warrior," Briana said, smiling.

Dara blushed. She had never felt so exhilarated. She had killed creatures she'd hunted. With her resistance fighters, she'd even killed a Shriek. But defeating a part of Chaos by her own hand was incredibly satisfying. She knew she hadn't killed him, but for the first time, she felt like a true Shamra warrior. She had been tested and now proved she belonged to her clan. "What now?" Dara asked, knowing she sounded excited.

"We don't get carried away," Briana said. "I know how you feel. I experienced what you did, though it was a true Galvan I killed, not a minion of Chaos. It's intoxicating. It can also make you less vigilant so you feel invincible. You're not."

Dara nodded. Still, she was already replaying in her mind what she'd done.

"We follow his tracks, backtrack from where he came. The other Galvan will approach from different directions. When one of the others learns what's happened, it will pursue us. We'll be ready for it."

They traveled less than half a mile. Briana was looking for something. Dara remained silent. "There," Briana said. "Those two trees on either side of the trail." She explained to Dara how she planned to fell a second Galvan. They gathered vines, and Briana quickly wove them together. It reminded Dara of Pilla trying to teach Dara how to knit. Dara had been all thumbs. And she'd told Pilla that she would never use what she was being taught. Dara knew she should have listened to her friend, who had chastised her: "You never know when something will come in handy."

When Briana was done with her weaving, she tied the vines to the two trees. Dara hid behind one, Briana behind the other. They didn't have to wait long. Minutes later, one of the Galvan was galloping toward where Briana and Dara hid. Their trail was easy to follow. He had assumed correctly that this was how Dara and Briana would try to escape. As he approached the two trees, Briana nodded, and she and Dara pulled on the vine. The vines rose, and before the Galvan could stop, he crashed into the taut vine and toppled backward off his horse. Briana was immediately on top of him. With her sword, she sliced off his head. It was the only way she knew to kill a servant of Chaos.

Leaving the dead Galvan behind, Dara and Briana no longer followed the trail but headed into the woods, skirting the river of mud. They came to a group of stunted trees that provided cover equal to that of the cave.

"We rest here until dark," Briana said. "Then we make our way back to the horses and escape."

They nibbled on berries, Dara's mind on the Fangala meat they had been forced to abandon.

"There is one more story to be told," Briana said, as if to break the eerie silence. "Reva's return to Stone Mountain and the treachery of her sister. And why we and the Galvan can never achieve a lasting peace. Interested? You could sleep—"

"Sleep is overrated," Dara interrupted, knowing Briana was again teasing her. "There is too much living to do to make sleeping a priority. I want to hear it all," Dara said. "I *need* to so I can understand who I truly am."

Chapter 16

~ Black Dahlia ~

168 years ago

Reva waited in the cavern Dahlia used to see visitors. As leader of the clan, Dahlia had her own private chambers and a second one to meet with advisors and visitors. All other Shamra had just their sleeping quarters. Reva had just returned from an often wondrous, sometimes terrifying, two-and-a-half year journey. Her older sister had summoned her soon after her return. And now Dahlia made her wait. Reva understood. There could be only one leader of the clan. Dahlia wanted Reva to understand they were not equals. Dahlia led. Reva would follow. Strange, Reva thought. They hadn't seen one another for such a long time, yet Dahlia already felt the need to assert her authority.

Though not yet sixteen, Reva was not the child who had left Stone Mountain. In many ways, she was far more experienced than her older sister. She was also intelligent enough not to provoke Dahlia. At least not until many gnawing questions were answered. While she waited, her mind drifted to Enwee. As they had approached Stone Mountain, and before leaving for his homeland, Enwee had taken Reva aside.

"I have grown quite fond of you, as I'm sure you know," Enwee started. "May I speak frankly?"

"So serious and formal, Enwee," Reva had said. Then, seeing the look on his face, she lost her smile. "You have always spoken your mind. Why change now?"

Enwee smiled. "You are not the reckless, carefree youth I encountered when we first met. Yet you are still young and impulsive. Your adventures will be the talk of all the Shamra when you return. It could lead to your demise."

"I should be silent then?" Reva asked. "What I've learned—"

"Your sister will be jealous and resentful," Enwee interrupted. "Speak of all you encountered, and she'll be even more bitter. Confide only in those you trust completely. Even with those, weigh your words carefully."

Reva nodded.

Enwee's smile was broader now. "You will heed my advice while you bide your time. But I know you, little one. You will be a thorn in your sister's side if you disagree with her. It's your nature, inherited from your mother, and I would never suggest you change. Practice patience and caution, though. Rein your temper, and pick your battles with care. I worry for you."

Dahlia entered, startling Reva. There was no embrace between the two sisters. While never particularly close, the two had never had any sibling rivalry. It was Dahlia's destiny, as eldest, to assume leadership of the Shamra. Reva had never aspired to clan leader, so there had been no animosity between the two. Now, however, Reva felt a chill in the air.

"So, little sister, you have returned. You will enthrall us with tales of your adventures," Dahlia said tartly.

"To tell the truth, our travels were mundane. Certainly not glamorous. Hunting animals and creatures in forests was at first exhilarating, but the novelty soon wore off. My stories would bore you," Reva said, choosing her words warily. Reva saw Dahlia relax slightly.

"Why have you returned?" Dahlia asked.

"This is my home. I'm here to serve you in whatever capacity you require." Reva said.

"Where's Mother?" Dahlia asked.

"Her journey is not complete," Reva said, offering no details.

"What of Cym?" Dahlia asked.

"Killed by outlaws," Reva lied. She wouldn't mention the battle with Chaos and its minions. Cym had died nobly in battle. Reva smiled inwardly. Enwee would have been proud of her replies.

Dahlia fell silent, as if she had lost interest.

"What happened to our forest while I was gone?" Reva asked. She had hunted in the forest bordering their land with her mother when she was young. She was shocked and angered to see most of it cleared, inhabited by the Galvan.

"It hasn't been *our* forest for almost nineteen years. Stone Mountain is our home," Dahlia said.

"But—"

"But nothing, Sister," Dahlia shot back. "Know your place. It is not I who abandoned our people to seek the world outside. I don't answer to you. We make due in a hostile environment. We've never been able to deal from strength with the Galvan once they began outnumbering us. Nothing has changed." Dahlia paused. "I have work to do. We'll talk again later."

Reva knew she was being dismissed. *Curb your tongue,* she could imagine Enwee cautioning her. She obeyed his silent command. She was distressed, but before saying anything rash, she'd have to find out what had transpired since she'd left. She sought out Dyann.

When she entered Dyann's cavern, the old warrior's face brightened. She embraced Reva, then stepped back and scrutinized her.

"I heard you'd returned," Dyann said. Dyann peppered Reva with some of the same questions Dahlia had asked. Reva's answers were equally evasive. She didn't know where Dyann's loyalty lay. When Anis had left Stone Mountain, it was thought Dahlia would lean heavily on Dyann for advice. The bond between the two might be strong. Yet it was Dyann who, with Anis, had taken Reva on hunts. Dyann had been Reva's tutor in hand-to-hand combat. As a young warrior, Dyann was known equally for her bravery and her recklessness. She would rather fight with a sword and smell the breath of her opponent than use a bow and arrow.

Dyann faked a yawn when Reva answered a question without elaborating. "You don't fool me, Reva," Dyann said, grabbing Reva's arm. "These scars tell a different story. The slight limp when you entered. Don't think I didn't notice. And the grimace just now when I grabbed your arm. Does your shoulder ache? What manner of wounds does your clothing hide? Janis has been equally as evasive. Her loyalty rests with you. She almost ran from me when I began questioning her," Dyann said with a laugh.

Reva said nothing, but her eyes turned purple from embarrassment.

Dyann put a finger to her thin lips. "You are far wiser than your years. Am I friend or foe? Will I report your every word to your sister? I know your thoughts without you uttering a word. I admire your caution. You were schooled well during your tedious journey," Dyann said with a smile.

"You advise Dahlia, don't you?" Reva asked.

SHAMRA DIVIDED

Dyann sighed. "Dahlia seeks her own counsel. She has no inner circle," Dyann said, sounding forlorn. "I am far too aggressive for your sister. Dahlia stopped listening to me long ago. Actually, I am looked upon with disfavor by your sister. I am a reminder of the Shamra past. Like your mother, I would rather die in battle than live a virtual prisoner."

"I hear your words— " Reva began.

"Actions speak louder than words," Dyann finished for her. "How do you know you can trust me? Will I keep your secrets? When I have proven my loyalty, you can reward me with details of your battles."

"I have questions myself," Reva said.

"I imagine you do," Dyann said. "Come, let us go outside. You'll understand why Dahlia wants nothing to do with me."

Dyann took Reva to the southern exposure of Stone Mountain, where they could see the land of the Galvan and what remained of the forest where Reva had hunted as a child.

"You want to know what happened?" Dyann said.

Reva nodded.

"A few months after you left, Kalin became leader of the Galvan after his father died from a fever," Dyann said.

Reva shrugged. "I never heard of Kalin."

"He was young. There was opposition. He had to prove himself or face insurrection. He's reckless and hot-blooded like you," Dyann said, "but without your wisdom or compassion. We made easy targets, so he ordered a number of attacks on us so that he could gain support. All the attacks failed, but by making us the enemy, he gained his support. It was a short-term solution to his problems and lacked vision. His soldiers took heavy losses. Later, he ordered the forests cleared as the Galvan population grew."

"That's a violation of the truce we had with Regor," Reva said.

Dyann shrugged. "Reva, the truce died with Regor. You know his followers were defeated and forced into exile. Kalin didn't recognize any truce. He told us so when Dahlia demanded a meeting with him. And he said that even if there were a truce, it gave us Stone Mountain and nothing more. One couldn't quarrel with his logic."

"The entire country was once ours," Reva said stubbornly.

"And Kel let it slip away," Dyann snapped. "Your mother couldn't recover what had been lost. Our country is Stone Mountain."

"Dahlia did nothing?" Reva asked, knowing she couldn't counter Dyann's argument. "We're hunters, after all."

Dyann shook her head. "Kalin has only scorn for us. He berated Dahlia in front of Nedir and me. He all but challenged us to stop him. He said we were pathetic. We'd given up everything and, like cowards, were holed up on a pile of rocks. Dahlia was humiliated. Soon after, she stopped seeking our counsel. She had lost face in front of us."

"What did you advise?" Reva asked coldly.

"Hit-and-run attacks to ferment dissent," Dyann said. "Nedir had mapped out the entire Galvan country. She came up with random attacks that would surely have caused unrest among the Galvan."

Nedir was Cym's daughter, her mother a Galvan, her father a Shamra—the only one of her kind. She had her mother's gifts, Reva could see. "And Dahlia ignored your recommendation," Reva said.

"What I proposed was too bold. *Irresponsible*, your sister said. There would have been loss of life. That was unacceptable to Dahlia," Dyann said. "She also feared a full-scale attack by Kalin."

"Which would have been easily repelled," Reva said.

"Your family rules our clan," Dyann said. "I disagreed with Dahlia. I argued against appeasement, but in the end, she is our leader. And the more I argued, the more distant she became."

"So Kalin became bolder, and now most of the forest is gone," Reva said, shaking her head.

"It's worse than that," Dyann said.

"What could be worse?" Reva asked. She wondered if her sister had been so cold toward her because of her humiliation. Dahlia knew Anis would never have condoned her actions.

"We went to other forests, through the many caverns at the base of the mountain. We needed meat," Dyann said.

"We should have attacked their farms and taken the meat we were denied," Reva interjected angrily.

"Dahlia feared retribution," Dyann said, then smiled. "You're as hot-tempered as your mother. Do you want to argue, or should I tell you what must shame Dahlia most?"

Reva chuckled. "I thought I'd learned to contain my temper. Go on."

"Nine of our hunters have been captured by the Galvan. Kalin has forced them into slave labor," Dyann said, and pointed into the distance. "During the day, we can see them working. It may be intentional on Kalin's part. We see them fall from exhaustion. See them beaten if they don't rise—"

"Enough," Reva interrupted, her eyes red with anger. "I get the picture. I'll speak with Dahlia."

"It will do no good," Dyann said. "I've tried. So has Nedir. She's as close to a friend as Dahlia has. Your sister won't budge."

"That's why she greeted me as she did," Reva said. "She was cold and aloof. She let me know in no uncertain terms I was welcome *only* if I knew my place. She knew what my reaction would be."

"What will you do?" Dyann asked.

"You fear I will act impulsively," Reva said with a tired smile. "Maybe challenge Dahlia for clan leadership. Maybe defy her this day and free those who are enslaved."

"The thought has crossed my mind," Dyann said. "You are far more like your mother than Dahlia is. Anis acted, *then* worried about the consequences. At least she did so when she was your age. So, what will be your response?"

"You remember the Weetok?" Reva asked. She knew Dyann had fought side by side with her grandmother, Drea, to free the Weetok from the Kimra over twenty-eight years earlier.

"Of course. Drea died in the battle. How could I forget?" Dyann asked.

"On our journey, we went to the land of the Weetok," Reva said. "The Kimra are gone, but that's a story for another day. One of their kind, Tillery, accompanied us. Talk about a temper. He put me to shame," Reva said with a smile, remembering her friend. "But when he got angry, before he let his temper get the best of him, he'd kick a stone ten times. It gave him time to think, to consider the ramifications of his words or actions. He taught me patience."

Reva took off her yellow bandana with black polka dots. She ran her hand through her thick white hair that fell well past her shoulders, as if she were grooming it. Then she retied the bandana around her head. "I don't kick stones like Tillery. This…ritual, I guess you could call it, is how I control my temper. I'm a stranger to many of my own people, Dyann. I admit it. Let them get to know me again. Let me find allies. With or without Dahlia's blessing, I will free those who are enslaved. Not today, but soon." Reva looked at Dyann. "Will you join me in battle?"

"I'd be honored," Dyann said with a broad smile.

"Will Nedir help us plan a raid?" Reva asked.

"Slave labor baffles and troubles Nedir," Dyann said, without answering Reva's question. "It's not the way of her people…neither the Shamra nor the Galvan part of her. Speak to her about her mother. I *know* you must have stories. Nedir will do what is right."

"We shall restore glory and dignity to our people," Reva said.

"Without humiliating Dahlia," Dyann said. "You don't want our people split. It led to disaster when the clan had to choose between Kel and Anis. It couldn't be helped then, but we're best served when we learn from the past."

Reva nodded. "All credit shall go to Dahlia. I have no desire to challenge my sister. But I will not continue to cower before Kalin. He will become bolder if we don't respond. He must know we are formidable foes."

A week later, eight Shamra gathered in Dyann's cramped cavern. Besides Dyann and Reva, there was Janis. Nedir had been recruited as well as four young Shamra who silently opposed Dahlia's appeasement.

"We go tonight," Reva told the others. "Nedir has shown us how we can surprise the Galvan." She pointed to a route on the map, which was drawn on the skin of an animal. "We free our people. We take no casualties. That is essential. Dahlia won't approve, but if we all return, what can she say? So follow my lead without question…or remain behind. No heroics tonight. There will be plenty of time to show the Galvan we won't be bullied." Reva looked at Nedir. "You will stay behind, Nedir. You have been invaluable, but I don't want Dahlia to know you are associated with us. You may still be able to convince her our path is the right one. If you go on the raid, you become her enemy."

Nedir nodded her acceptance. Reva knew she wasn't happy, but she would not challenge Reva's leadership. Odd, Reva thought, how Nedir was far more like a Shamra warrior than Dahlia was. On her journey, Reva had allied herself with sixteen different creatures, all from vastly divergent cultures. She had learned not to look at how different each was from the other, but at the many traits they shared in common. Nedir had the facial structure and body of a Shamra, but like the Galvan, she was hairless, had narrow slits for eyes, and had two gill-like incisions on each cheek through which she breathed. Inside, she was a Shamra. She had been loyal to Dahlia, though, like Dyann, she disagreed with many of her decisions. And now she aligned herself with Reva. Though she wanted to help free the Shamra slaves, she would do as she was told without complaint.

Reva and her band arrived undetected at what was left of the forest. Nedir's mother, Cym, had drawn a map during their journey to locate Chaos. It seemed like a harmless pastime to combat the boredom of endless days of travel. That map, though, had led the group to Chaos. Nedir's skills were equal to those of her mother. It was almost as if Nedir could see each road, each farm, and each guardpost in her mind and had committed it in writing. Without Nedir's map, this journey would have been far more treacherous.

A hut not far from the forest's edge housed the enslaved Shamra, according to Nedir. Reva saw two guards. She lifted her slingshot to point out one of the guards to Dyann. In unison, Reva and Dyann fired at the Galvan guards, felling them both.

Reva led her party to the hut, told Darcy to stand guard, and entered. Her knees buckled at the sight that greeted her. The Shamra lay on the bare ground with no bedding and no blankets. They were deathly thin, with sores from infection and welts from beatings. Their hair had been cut almost to the scalp. What little clothes they wore were in tatters. Their eyes were a dull gray, indicating sadness and defeat. A stench of sickness filled the air.

Reva was furious. She had seen slaves in some of the lands she and her mother had visited. But none were treated as brutally as her people here. Slaves Reva had encountered had been enemies of those who kept them. Often they had been captured in battle. Yet they were treated with dignity and respect.

Kalin, on the other hand, didn't care whether the captured Shamra lived or died. Worse, he considered the Shamra to be no better than animals. He would work them until they perished. Reva silently vowed Kalin would pay dearly for his contempt and arrogance.

Reva's warriors helped seven of the captives out of the hut. They had brought extra horses for them to travel back to Stone Mountain. Two others were close to death. Their eyes were almost white, a sign the end was near. They wouldn't survive the trip to Stone Mountain.

Reva bent next to one of them, then closed her eyes when she recognized him. Tobor was in his twenties. He looked twice his age. He looked at Reva.

"I…I know you," Tobor said, his voice little more than a whisper. Reva had to put her ear close to his mouth to make out his words. "But you…you were gone."

"It's me, Reva. Yes, I was gone, but I have returned. I will carry you to Stone Mountain myself if you can't ride."

Tobor closed his eyes. "I'm dying," he said. "I refused to do…to do their bidding." With shaking hands, he ripped his shirt from his body. He was covered with welts and sores. The sores were infected. Reva saw bugs feasting on his raw skin. "I want to die with honor. I…I want to make…to make a difference."

"What do you want of me?" Reva asked, though she knew full well what he'd ask of her.

"Corina…my mate. She…she refuses to eat. We die together…here. Cut our throats…with the knife of…of the Galvan. Our deaths will not…will not be in vain."

Reva shook her head.

"You must," Tobor said, and began coughing. Blood dripped from his lips. "We will die. Let us die with dignity."

Reva stood. She felt unsteady. The stench was unbearable. She willed herself to move her feet. She went outside to get the knife of one of the Galvan guards. Dyann was waiting for her.

"What of the two who remain?" Dyann said. "I can carry one."

"Go, Dyann," Reva said. "I will join you shortly."

"But—"

"Do as I say, Dyann," Reva said, and went to get the knife.

She caught up with the others halfway to Stone Mountain. The going was slow with those who had been freed unable to ride without help.

Dyann looked at Reva, her lips trembling, but she didn't speak.

"Tobor and Corina are with the prophets," Reva said. "They died with dignity. They commanded me. I obeyed."

Dyann nodded.

Word spread quickly on Stone Mountain that seven of their clan had been freed. Dozens of Shamra offered congratulations to Reva and her warriors. Spirits were high. Dahlia entered Dyann's quarters, and a hush fell over the room.

"Everyone out except Reva," Dahlia said. All complied.

"How dare you go behind my back," Dahlia said, her voice rising, her eyes red with fury. "You could all have been captured, killed, or yourselves enslaved."

"Have you visited those we freed?" Reva asked quietly, refusing to get into a shouting match with her sister.

"I'm more concerned—"

"Two-and-a-half years I traveled and visited many lands," Reva interrupted. "Never have I witnessed what I saw tonight. No Shamra should live under such conditions. It's barbaric. Two were so ill we had to leave them. Kalin knows no honor. Go see our people, and tell me I was wrong."

"You make yourself sound so heroic, Sister, but *I* must deal with the repercussions of *your* actions tonight," Dahlia said. "You have humiliated Kalin. Only the prophets know what he'll do."

"What can he do, Dahlia?" Reva asked.

"The Galvan number in the thousands. We are less than one hundred. If Kalin wishes, he can overrun Stone Mountain. We are not impregnable if Kalin is willing to make the sacrifice necessary to destroy us," Dahlia said.

"Then we die in glory," Reva said.

Dahlia slapped Reva's face. Reva didn't respond. Dahlia slapped her a second, then a third time. Reva grabbed her sister's hand before she could deliver a fourth blow. She was far stronger than Dahlia. She had fought outlaws, been trained by warriors from many lands, and survived the minions of Chaos. She could challenge Dahlia and easily slay her in battle. Yet she still held hope her sister would see the error of her ways and find her courage. She looked into Dahlia's eyes and saw animosity and fear.

"What happened to you, Dahlia?" Reva asked. "You were so strong."

"You have gone through life without having to face the consequences of your actions," Dahlia said bitterly, wrenching her hand free. "My life was charted for me. I was to lead our people. You…you hunted with Mother and led a carefree existence. Then the two of you left to seek adventure. *I* had to face Kalin alone. And I alone am responsible for the safety of our people. I would love to do battle with Kalin, but it would be suicidal. That's where you and I part company. *I* have to consider what's in the best interests of all our people, even if it means swallowing my pride. You return and want to decide when and how we are all to die. Mother chose *me* to lead because she knew I could make hard choices. Say what you will, but she wouldn't want us all to die in a blaze of glory. Rebelling is easy, Sister. Survival takes far more effort and courage. You have overstayed your welcome—"

"I won't leave," Reva interrupted.

"Then you will do as I say, or challenge me for leadership," Dahlia replied.

Reva shook her head. "Mother never challenged Kel, though, like you, he showed weakness when strength was demanded."

"She escaped to Stone Mountain," Dahlia said bitterly. "Where will you and your rabble flee to?"

"This is our home," Reva said. "Tell Kalin we are renegades, if you wish. Tell him you can't control us and we have isolated ourselves from the rest of the clan. I will not recruit others to help in our attacks, and I won't accept volunteers. But I will not sit idly by, imprisoned in our own fortress."

"The blood of our people shall be on your hands," Dahlia said.

"Better to be die honorably in battle than be enslaved like those we freed," Reva said.

"Remember your words when Kalin retaliates. Remember your arrogance when Shamra blood is spilled. I'll want you...I'll *demand* that you look into the eyes of the families of those who die and speak of the nobility of a glorious death." Dahlia seemed ready to continue, then shook her head and left.

Kalin sent a message the next day demanding Dahlia surrender, by nightfall, those who had killed two Galvan soldiers. "Defy us, and our reprisal will be swift and merciless."

Dahlia showed the message to Reva without saying a word.

"Tell him I will surrender if he returns unharmed the two we had to leave behind," Reva said.

"You would give your life for them?" Dahlia asked.

"Kalin is a crass savage. I'll bet my life he's butchered those we left behind in a blind rage."

"And if he has? Without your surrender, he has sworn vengeance," Dahlia said.

"There is nothing he can do, Dahlia," Reva said. "He knows a frontal attack will be too costly. Call his bluff."

"You don't know Kalin," Dahlia said.

"But I do. He's a bully. Stand up to him, and he'll cave in," Reva said.

Dahlia shook her head and left. She later sent word to Reva that Kalin said her terms were unacceptable. There would be no exchange.

Reva met with Dyann soon after. "Our people are scared," Dyann said. "Many fear we will be overrun, slaughtered, or taken hostage and enslaved."

"Should I surrender? Ask for volunteers to accompany me?" Reva asked.

"Of course not," Dyann said. "I'm only telling you what I've heard. Hothead that you are, you didn't allow me to finish."

Reva shrugged. She tugged at her bandana. Patience, she scolded herself.

"Those we freed would gladly join us if they had the strength. They are our staunchest allies. We have restored pride to many of our clan. Allegiances are split. *That* is what I was trying to tell you."

"I will not lead an insurrection against Dahlia," Reva said. "She is our leader. We are renegades Dahlia cannot control. Kalin has opposition of his own. He can understand Dahlia's quandary. Tonight we take the offensive. We show Kalin that Dahlia cannot control us. We show Kalin's opponents that we will not succumb."

"We can recruit another dozen, just by what you did last night," Dyann said.

Reva shook her head. "We'll have to do with our eight for now. I promised Dahlia I wouldn't recruit others. It gives her leverage with Kalin. We are renegades without the backing of the majority of the clan." She paused. "Actually, I'll need just five, though it will appear there are dozens," Reva said.

"I don't understand," Dyann said.

Reva unbuttoned the top two buttons on her shirt. "Remember how I grimaced when you grabbed my arm my first day back?" she said. She saw Dyann's eyes widen when she saw Reva's wound. Though healed, a thick scar began just below her shoulder and continued below where she had unbuttoned her top. What should have been deeply tanned skin around the scar remained purple, as if she'd been pelted by a score of rocks. "On our way back home, we were attacked by outlaws. I suffered what could have been a mortal wound. I'm told I lost a considerable amount of blood. I lost consciousness and didn't awaken for three days. Enwee gave me a blood transfusion. His blood."

"Who is this Enwee?" Dyann asked.

"The one who accompanied Atyra when she stopped at Stone Mountain."

"So this Enwee gave you a transfusion. What good does it do us?" Dyann asked. "From what I recall, he was a most unremarkable creature. Furry and half our size. Not very threatening."

"Looks can be deceiving, Dyann, and deception is Enwee's specialty. *His power*," Reva said. Before Dyann could respond, two dozen Shamra warriors appeared out of nowhere. After a few seconds, they vanished. Dyann looked stunned. "Enwee possesses a Mist of Illusion. It's how his people combat far stronger enemies. They can cloak themselves to appear in any form they desire. A dozen can appear to be an army of a hundred."

"This Enwee will help us?" Dyann asked.

"He already has," Reva said. "His blood courses through me. I possess the Mist of Illusion. What you saw, I created. I have only limited use, however. I can create an army for twenty minutes, no more. I need at least a week to recover before I can use the power again."

"What do you propose?" Dyann asked.

"A massive attack with phantom warriors," Reva said. "Actually, two attacks. I take two others to the Galvan armory. It will appear dozens are attacking. At the same time, you lead three to a farm and return with meat for our people. A hit-and-run attack so, if possible, we suffer no casualties. I have discussed my plan with Nedir. She'll plot our course but will remain behind, as before. An attack two nights in a row will be unexpected and demoralizing. We then wait until I can again conjure my army and continue our raids."

"Won't the raids force Kalin's hand?" Dyann asked.

Reva knew Dahlia would have balked at Dyann's question. Reva was glad Dyann felt no need to hide her fear. Reva needed her plans probed for any weakness. She led her small band of warriors, but she didn't presume to know all the answers. This question, though, she had already considered. "Kalin faces discord within his own people. We will not kill indiscriminately. Only soldiers and those who fight back. We will not butcher the defenseless. We will not brutalize like Kalin. We don't give Kalin the opportunity to unify his forces. At the same time, maybe Dahlia can broker a truce. Kalin might find it in his best interest. Successful raids will allow her to deal from strength."

For a month, Reva led raids against the Galvan. While Kalin threatened massive retribution, there was only one half-hearted attack on Stone Mountain by one hundred Galvan soldiers, who were easily repelled. It seemed the bully didn't respond well to those who refused to cower.

More Shamra, including three of those who had been enslaved and had now regained their health, volunteered to join Reva's warriors. Reva expressed her appreciation but declined. "Dahlia is our leader," Reva told them. "When she commands you to join us, we'll welcome you with open arms. For now, just be content with the knowledge the Galvan fear us. They may even respect us."

Reva knew the Galvan were terrified of what they referred to as Shamra ghost warriors. Reva heard rumors Galvan farmers thought Reva's soldiers were Shamra who had returned from the dead to reclaim their land. And how could the dead be killed?

Reva recalled the first raid. She attacked the armory with two warriors and two dozen Shamra conjured with her Mist of Illusion. Galvan soldiers fired arrows at her phantom fighters, who refused to die. The Galvan fled in terror.

Each assault further fueled the Galvan's fears. Farmers ran at the sight of the advancing warriors. The attacks were random and at least a week apart. Only soldiers who resisted felt the blade of Reva's sword and the arrows of the few real warriors who accompanied her. Food was the real target. That, and the paralysis of the Galvan. As the Galvan suffered few casualties, Kalin had little support for any massive retaliation.

Reva thought it odd that Dahlia hadn't rebuked her, hadn't demanded a cessation of the attacks. On the contrary, Dahlia never summoned Reva. It was puzzling. No, Reva corrected herself, it was more than that. It was troubling. She wondered what her sister was planning. It gnawed at her, but she kept her fears to herself.

Dyann approached Reva as she was writing in her journal. Since her return, she had decided to record all that had occurred on her two-and-a-half year odyssey. Each attack on the Galvan could result in her death. There had to be some record of the heroism and camaraderie forged among creatures so different from one another. Each time she ventured off Stone Mountain, she entrusted her journal to Nedir. It was only to be read if she perished. She closed the journal at the sight of Dyann.

"Haven't I earned your trust?" Dyann asked. Reva could hear the disappointment in her voice. "When will you tell me of your adventures?"

"Not while Dahlia may be plotting against me. I mean no disrespect, Dyann. I want to tell all our people what I witnessed, but not while there is so much divisiveness."

"Tell me a tale, Reva. A tidbit," Dyann asked. "You don't know this, but I wanted to travel with Anis. She asked me to look after Dahlia. But Dahlia had no use for my vision of a strong Shamra who would rather perish in battle than live in humiliation. I don't mean to sound bitter, but a part of me feels cheated. I should have been with you. So, just one story. I'm not greedy."

Reva nodded. "Once Anis told me she wished she had asked you to join us. I think she was envious of you. You had fought side by side with her mother to free the Weetok. I don't know if she ever came to grips with feeling abandoned, but she became a selfless leader during our journey. Okay, so a tale. About the Weetok—"

"Cowards," Dyann said. Reva realized Dyann's bitterness toward the Weetok ran deep. The Shamra had agreed to help the Weetok overthrow the Kimra who enslaved them. When the Shamra attacked, not a single Weetok joined the battle.

"Hardly," Reva said. "Hasty judgments cloud the mind to the truth. One of the many lessons I learned." She explained why the Weetok hadn't come to Drea's aid twenty-eight years before. "That was the first land we ventured to. We wanted to see where my grandmother perished. The land you saw no longer existed. It was as if the land had died," Reva said, describing the devastation. "The Kimra were gone. They had fought among themselves, and few were left when the Weetok finally rebelled. Most Weetok were farmers, and their task after the Kimra were vanquished was monumental. One warrior, Tillery, requested to join us. He's the one with the temper I told you about. He, along with many others, sort of adopted me. I was by far the youngest. I could fight as well as any in our group, but I had much to learn. Enwee, Tillery, and Atyra, they took me under their wings, but I learned from all who allied with us."

Reva removed her bandana and showed it to Dyann. "There was one final battle. Cym and Atyra perished heroically, as did many who rode with us. A drop of blood from each is on my bandana in their honor." She held out her arm. "Many of the wounds I suffered were from that day. Tillery was badly wounded as well. I grieved for him daily as we made our way home. He was feverish and unconscious most of the time. He was all gruff and ill-tempered on the outside but like a protective older brother within."

Dyann's eyes had turned deep blue with anticipation. She asked no questions, and Reva continued.

"Tillery's arm became infected. Enwee said it would have to be amputated or he would die. I now led them. It was to be my decision. I tell you, Dyann, I changed my mind each time I made my final decision. Tillery certainly wanted to live, but not as a cripple. He'd been a warrior most of his life. Would that life have any meaning with only one arm? What would Tillery want? It should have been his decision to make, but he'd slipped into a coma. In the end, I was selfish. I couldn't let him die. His fever abated somewhat after the amputation—"

"*You* didn't cut off his arm, did you?" Dyann asked.

Reva laughed. "I could slay an enemy in hand-to-hand combat without giving it a thought, but I could never cut off Tillery's arm. Janis did."

"Janis! She had the courage?" Dyann exclaimed.

Reva shrugged. "Janis is very much like her mother," Reva said. "While of little use in battle, she still has much to offer. Janis learned which herbs and roots were best for healing, and unlike me, she wasn't squeamish. Odd, I could cut off the head of an enemy, but when it came to Tillery, I got all queasy. Janis cut off Tillery's arm, staunched the bleeding, and kept him alive until we reached his homeland."

"So he recovered," Dyann said, sounding relieved.

"More than recovered. Gwin, the Weetok spiritual leader, was also a healer. He tended to Tillery and applied a foul-smelling poultice when his fever broke." Reva paused. "Tillery's arm grew back."

"That's impossible," Dyann said.

Reva laughed. "Maybe for us. I traveled with an incredible group of creatures. Some could fly. One could burrow underground and travel a mile without breathing. You come to accept the…the impossible. The Weetok can regenerate limbs. Even eyes. Until I saw Tillery grow a new arm, I hadn't noticed, but no Weetok are crippled and none are blind." Reva paused. "So, are you satisfied?"

Dyann scrunched her small, narrow nose. "More curious than ever, but thank you."

At that moment, Dahlia entered. "Be gone, Dyann," she commanded.

Dyann looked at Reva, who nodded.

"Sit," Reva said.

Dahlia ignored her and remained standing. "You have made your point with your phantom warriors," Dahlia said.

"You remember," Reva said.

"I'm no fool," Dahlia said. "We were both present when Mother told us about the creature who could create illusions. And one visited Atyra after you left. I won't ask how you did it, but you can create the illusion of an army. Ghost warriors. Do you think you can fool Kalin much longer with your parlor tricks?"

"What do you suggest?" Reva asked, genuinely curious.

"You've had limited success," Dahlia said. "The morale of our people has been strengthened. The Galvan don't yet know what to make of you and your phantom army. We can forge a truce from strength."

"To get something, we have to offer something in return," Reva said. "You're going to ask me to surrender. Sacrifice myself for the good of our people."

"Do you think so little of me, Sister?" Dahlia asked. "I don't seek your death at the hands of the Galvan. I wouldn't permit it."

"What, then?" Reva asked. She wondered if Dahlia spoke the truth. Reva's surrender and death would make her a martyr to all Shamra. Dahlia's authority would be weakened. On the other hand, they were sisters, and though relations between them were strained, maybe Dahlia truly didn't desire Reva's death.

"Kalin will be satisfied if you, Janis, and Dyann leave, never to return. You can seek further adventures or settle with some you traveled with," Dahlia said. "Kalin gets to save face. We have a lasting truce. You leave a hero."

"It is not my decision alone to make," Reva said. "Janis and Dyann must consent."

"They'll follow your wishes," Dahlia said tartly. "I need your answer by nightfall," Dahlia said, then left.

Reva met with her warriors and relayed to them Dahlia's proposal. She was greeted by silence until Nedir spoke.

"It's a farce, Reva," Nedir said, then paused to breathe through the incisions in her cheeks. Just like Cym, Nedir could only say so much before taking in air. The condition worsened when she was tense or agitated. "I resented not being allowed to accompany you on raids." She paused again. "You know I'm the equal to all of you as a warrior. You risked your lives while I remained here in safety." Another pause. "Yet, the more successful your raids, the more Dahlia trusted me. Your decision was a wise one, Reva." This time she paused to smile at Reva. "Dahlia has been meeting secretly with Kalin's representatives. I just found out. Yesterday she met with Kalin himself. Dahlia told a half-truth. You, Janis, and Dyann are to go into exile." A pause. "When you're gone, Dahlia will offer the other four aligned with you to Kalin as a sign of good faith. There will be no more slave labor, just swift executions."

"Dahlia would stoop so low?" Reva asked.

"You wield too much influence," Nedir said. "Dahlia wants no opposition. Darcy or Allegra would rebel against appeasement. Get rid of you all, and Dahlia solidifies her position."

"Stubborn pride," Reva said. She shrugged. "We fight on."

♦♦♦♦♦♦♦♦♦♦♦

Dahlia stood contentedly outside by a wall overlooking one of the many hidden entrances into Stone Mountain. She had summoned Nedir and was awaiting her arrival. Ever since she had been rebuffed by her sister, she had stewed. Reva had led two new raids. Kalin was growing desperate. He warned Dahlia that Stone Mountain would be stormed and the Shamra annihilated no matter what the cost if Reva wasn't stopped. Tonight the threat would end. Dahlia wanted to share her victory with Nedir, her only true ally.

When Reva and two of her band left that night, Dahlia sent a messenger to Kalin. Reva always returned to the same cavern in Stone Mountain from which she left. With dozens of entrances, Dahlia had to know which Reva would use. Her predictability was one of her few weaknesses. She would pay dearly. When Dahlia saw Reva's horses in the distance returning from the raid, she asked Nedir to join her. Now the two stood looking down at where Reva would appear.

"You know, Nedir, my sister really should have listened to me," Dahlia said.

"Why is that?" Nedir asked.

Dahlia smiled. "I wouldn't have had to tell Kalin about the ghost warriors. How Reva's phantom fighters' horses didn't make tracks. How easy it would be to pick out the real warriors. Look, Nedir," Dahlia said as Reva drew closer. "Seems they've been wounded. And they return with no meat."

Dahlia saw the look of astonishment on Nedir's face. Nedir was about to speak, but Dahlia continued. She was aware other Shamra had gathered above and below. Watching Reva return victorious was something that they all looked forward to.

"And if Reva had only listened to me, I wouldn't have had the entrance she left from sealed," Dahlia said.

"She'll be slaughtered," Nedir said.

"A glorious death, Nedir. That's what a Shamra warrior craves," Dahlia said. "Watch, and see."

They watched as Reva, Dyann, and Allegra rode up to the entrance. They saw Reva's look of surprise at seeing the entrance impassable. Then a dozen Galvan attacked. They were Kalin's own guards, his most elite soldiers, who dressed in black. The three Shamra fought valiantly, but there was no way they could defeat all twelve. They heard murmurings and cries of anguish from the Shamra who watched.

"Let them help Reva," Nedir said. "It's what our people want."

"I lead. They follow. It's time our people learned," Dahlia said.

"I won't let you do it," Nedir said. "I'll fight by Reva's side. You can watch me die with your sister. Die gloriously." Nedir turned to leave.

Dahlia knew if Nedir joined Reva, others would follow. Why is everyone turning on me? she wondered. She'd given her life to them. She had saved the Shamra from extinction. How was she repaid? Her most trusted ally was betraying her. No, she wouldn't allow it.

Nedir must have heard Dahlia's approach just before she reached her. Nedir turned slightly, and Dahlia's knife struck Nedir in the shoulder, not her back. Nedir fell and rolled on her back, crying out in pain. Dahlia straddled Nedir and plunged her knife toward Nedir's heart. Nedir grabbed Dahlia's hand and the two fought. Nedir used her head to butt

SHAMRA DIVIDED

Dahlia's. She saw Dahlia wince and roll off her. Dahlia lay still on her stomach. Nedir turned her over. Dahlia had fallen on her own knife.

Nedir rose and yelled for the Shamra to go to Reva's aid.

♦♦♦♦♦♦♦♦♦♦♦

Reva knew something was wrong when the Galvan soldiers didn't attack her ghost warriors when she led Dyann and Allegra into the farm. Instead, when they attacked, they came after her, Dyann, and Allegra. They fought off the soldiers, but outnumbered, Reva called off the attack.

It also puzzled her when they weren't pursued as they fled. The Galvan had at last tasted Shamra blood yet let them escape. Before they reached Stone Mountain, Reva's Mist of Illusion dissipated. The ghost warriors disappeared. No problem, Reva thought, as they weren't being followed.

When Reva saw the mouth to the cave she'd left was sealed with boulders and tree trunks, she knew something was amiss. Knew she had been betrayed. Knew it was Dahlia. Before she could react, Kalin's elite guards were upon them. Pinned against the wall of Stone Mountain, Reva knew there would be no escape.

Dyann and Allegra looked at her. Reva saw the faces of dozens of Shamra peering at them from above.

"We fight to the death," Reva said. "We show our people we are no cowards. We each take two or three of the enemy with us before we fall."

Reva unsheathed her sword and charged at one of her attackers, her sword slicing through his armor and finding his heart. She felt a presence behind her. As she turned, a sword tore at her arm. As the soldier struck her again in her shoulder, a second soldier rode toward her. She jumped off her horse, ducked, and as the first soldier bent to swipe at her, she grabbed his arm and pulled him from his horse. Again, her sword found his heart.

She knew she wouldn't have time to withdraw her sword from the fallen soldier's chest before the other soldier was upon her. She took out her knife and stood her ground. Suddenly the soldier fell from his horse. Reva was looking at Nedir, who had appeared out of nowhere. A slingshot was in her hand. Reva knew Nedir was deadly with a slingshot. Then other Shamra appeared. Some had swords, others had knives, spears, or slingshots. Some attacked the Galvan guards with their bare hands.

Two of the Galvan escaped. The others lay dead.

Reva fell to her knees, too weary to stand. Nedir picked her up and carried her through another entrance.

"You're wounded, Nedir," Reva said, fatigue washing over her.

Nedir laughed. "You're one to talk."

"Dahlia finally gave in?" Reva asked.

Nedir stopped. "Dahlia's dead. I...I killed your sister. Later you can determine my punishment."

"What happened?" Reva asked.

Nedir told her of Dahlia's attack, the fight, and Dahlia's death.

"You protected yourself, Nedir. Dahlia betrayed us. And if our people had simply watched us die as Dahlia commanded, their morale would have been crushed. Kalin would have had his victory. He could have stormed Stone Mountain and met little resistance. So don't speak to me of punishment, Nedir." She smiled weakly at Nedir. "You're my hero."

◆◆◆◆◆◆◆◆◆◆

All the Shamra were gathered in the one cavern that could hold them all. All eyes were on Reva, who sat with one arm in a sling and numerous bandages covering her other injuries.

SHAMRA DIVIDED

Nedir sat on her left and Allegra, Janis, and Darcy on her right. Only Dyann was missing. Her wounds had been grievous, yet she stubbornly clung to life. Reva knew why. It was the reason she had assembled her people today.

She had never wanted to lead her clan. Yet, like her grandmother, Drea, events had conspired to force her hand. For the first time, she felt she understood Dahlia's frustrations. As her sister had experienced before her, a good portion of Reva's life was now plotted for her. There were no longer options that she had had several days earlier. She would have to find a mate and bear children. She was determined that her family's leadership of their clan wouldn't end with her. One day, when a child she bore could assume leadership, she would be able to travel like her mother. Her thoughts turned to the present.

"I have a story to tell. Many stories, actually," Reva told all who had gathered. "They are part of our history and will be passed down from generation to generation. I begin today, but the telling will take weeks, even months." She held her journal in her hand but didn't open it. She would *tell* her story, not read to her people. "Let me tell you about Chaos…" she began.

CHAPTER 17

~ *The Present* ~

"How could Dahlia turn on her own sister?" Dara asked when Briana had finished. She didn't expect an answer. She didn't need an answer. Heber, after all, her most trusted ally, had turned on her for the same reason.

"Jealousy, plain and simple," Briana said, as if unaware Dara wasn't expecting a reply. "Reva had spent years on a remarkable odyssey meeting all sorts of creatures and civilizations. Reva may not have spoken about her adventures, but there is no doubt that her time away from Stone Mountain had been wondrous. Meanwhile, Dahlia remained on Stone Mountain. She ruled, but she was a prisoner of sorts."

"Still," Dara said, "to betray her sister and help plan her death."

"Not all Shamra are noble. You told me about traitors in your midst when your homeland was invaded. We have a different culture than your Shamra, but we are far from perfect.

We can be as petty and trifling as any. We can turn on one another. It hasn't happened often. Dahlia's treachery is the most shocking example. It's a story, though, that must be told so you don't put our clan on any pedestal. You take the bad with the good. Bravery and deceit. It's *all* part of our history."

"You must tell me more when we escape," Dara said. "I hunger to hear everything."

"There's precious little else to tell," Briana said. "Our ancestors have lived on Stone Mountain and occasionally engaged in battle with the Galvan. Some of our leaders have left to explore like Anis did. None returned. Nothing truly remarkable has occurred until now. Chaos returning, and your appearance."

"My visit is hardly remarkable," Dara said.

"Time will tell," Briana said. "Now it's time to go to the horses," she said and rose.

Dara grabbed Briana's arm. "You haven't told me about you."

"What's to tell?" Briana asked. "The youngest child in a family Chaos is out to destroy."

"There's more to you than meets the eye," Dara said. "It's as if you have a death wish...or feel invulnerable. You're the last of your mother's children. I've already told you I won't rule the clan. Won't stay more than another week or so. Yet you seem to embrace death. You couldn't know for certain your whistle would succeed against the Fangala. You had no idea how I'd respond when they attacked. There's a dark side to you, Briana. It's almost like you carry a burden. You want to confide in me, but you refuse. Tell me I'm wrong."

"You've a vivid imagination, Dara," Briana said. "I'm what I am. No more. No less." She rose. "We have a long trip. We must be out of the forest before dawn."

They walked in the darkness, wrapped in their own thoughts. A quarter of a mile from where they left the horses, the horseless Galvan who had escaped from the mud river jumped from a tree, knocking Briana down. Briana rolled away from the Galvan, but needn't have bothered. His eyes were on Dara.

"Whether you rule the clan or not, you are our future," Briana called out. "Run, he's after you, not me."

Dara ran. As Briana predicted, Chaos followed Dara as if Briana didn't exist. It made no sense to Dara. If Dara escaped and returned to Stone Mountain, she would leave almost immediately. She and the clan she had just found had no future together. Yet, given a choice, her pursuer desired Dara's capture…Dara's death.

Dara stumbled over a fallen tree and hit her head on a rock. She opened her eyes expecting to see…

♦♦♦♦♦♦♦♦♦♦

Rain pummeled her. Thunder reverberated through the trees. Lightning lit the sky. Dara remembered what had happened. The creatures from the mud had been intent on her joining them. Pilla and another had fought them off. Then lightning had struck her. Other than a bump on the head and a headache, she was uninjured.

As suddenly as the storm had erupted, it abated. The downpour became a drizzle, then ceased. The clouds seemed brushed aside by an unrelenting sun. There was no longer any thunder. No lightning.

Dim remnants of a dream remained. Hairy creatures with razor-sharp fangs. Expressionless figures with black eyes. The presence of another, whom Dara couldn't recall at all. Then these memories, too, were washed away as Dara realized she was a Shamra warrior from a clan left behind when the rest of the Shamra had fled their old homeland. She remembered Drea, Anis, Reva, Dahlia, Mya and, most of all, Atyra.

She recalled Drea had prophesied Dara leading the resistance to an invasion two hundred years before it occurred. She somehow knew the prophets didn't exist. Drea and other Shamra didn't die but left one existence for another. She realized Drea, considered the greatest of all Shamra leaders, had been summoned in times of peril. Dara despaired that Atyra, who had been equally heroic, had never achieved the stature of Drea in their new homeland. Atyra had to keep a low profile, and the clerics were intent on dismissing a female as their savior. Which meant that even the new holy book Dara's soldiers had found hidden in the temple was a sham. The holy books made no mention of a banished clan led by females. And there were no passages of Atyra's exile or of her paving the way for the rest of the Shamra to safely get to their new homeland. There *was* one version of the original holy book hidden with Atyra's sword in a cave in the swamps. But the swamps, to even someone as familiar with them as Dara was, were still a maze. There might be a hundred caves, possibly more. The book was lost. And, even if found, its discovery would lead to further...further chaos, Dara knew. Her people's belief system once again ripped apart would not go unchallenged by the clerics and their supporters. Maybe it was for the best that it remained unattainable.

Finally, Dara vividly recollected her ancestors had lived in a lush valley surrounded by forests teeming with life. Then, later, her ancestors had been driven to a mountain of stone. Stone Mountain.

Dara finally understood why she was different from other Shamra. Pride flowed within. Her people...her clan, had been warriors and hunters. And Dara was descended from a group of Shamra who would rather face banishment than give up their culture and beliefs.

Dara was now more intent than ever to continue her journey to find her former homeland. Her clan had probably succumbed to the Galvan, who far outnumbered them. Or maybe they had fled, more intent on life than defending Stone Mountain. Regardless, Dara's pilgrimage wouldn't be complete until she set foot on her ancestral homeland.

Dara would always be indebted to this forest of lost memories, as she called it, as for the first time, she felt truly whole. An offering was required. Dara dug a hole and buried her most prized possession, the necklace that bore the red wood her mother had given her. She now that knew Atyra had fashioned it for Mya after her first kill. It had been passed down for two hundred years.

The forest, in return, offered delectable fruits Dara instinctively knew would not harm her. She fed her Bauble, Tyler. As she walked through the forest, she told Tyler all she had learned. For once, Tyler listened in silence.

When Dara exited the forest, she felt a profound sadness. She instinctively touched her neck to feel her necklace, which she had buried. She was surprised to find the necklace back on her neck. A smile lit her face. The forest hadn't rejected her offering, she somehow knew. No token of appreciation had been required. The forest gave selflessly. Dara had now learned one more lesson. Not everything demanded a price for what it offered. This forest had given her her heart's desire and relished in Dara's newfound sense of self. It wanted nothing in exchange. Dara's happiness was its own reward.

EPILOGUE

Briana spent the entire night agonizing over Dara. When the Galvan had pursued Dara, Briana had escaped. She hid within shouting distance of the horses. Every fifteen minutes, she'd second-guess herself. She should have followed the minion of Chaos to be by Dara's side if Dara were captured. They should have forgotten about the horses and fled the forest on foot under cover of the night. She should have told Dara to fight Chaos rather than run. Briana only had had the wind knocked out of her. She could have helped defeat the enemy. Should have done this. Should have done that. But it didn't matter what she *should* have done. She had told Dara to flee, and Dara hadn't returned. Briana feared the worst.

As the night tucked itself away, Briana saw four Galvan on horseback in the distance. The one who had lost his horse and pursued Dara must have been given the horse of the Galvan she and Dara had killed. Within twenty minutes, they'd be upon her. Reluctantly, Briana fled. It would do no good if they were both captured. Briana refused to consider the possibility Dara was dead. Maybe she had escaped in the darkness. Dara had told Briana of her many adventures. If she had eluded her enemy, she could well have made her way out of the forest.

When Briana entered Stone Mountain, Dara came running out to greet her. "What happened to you?" Dara asked. "You promised to take me hunting yesterday. I searched high and low—"

"What are you talking about?" Briana asked. "We *did* go hunting."

"Maybe in your dreams," Dara said. "You may have gone hunting, but I sat around all day waiting for you."

Briana looked at Dara carefully. The day before, she hadn't been seriously injured, but she'd had numerous cuts and abrasions. Now she appeared unscathed. "How many days have you been here?" Briana asked.

Dara looked at Briana oddly and shrugged. "Today is my sixth. Did something happen to you? You look a sight."

Briana suddenly knew this wasn't the Dara who had accompanied her to the forest the previous day. That other Dara had sworn she hadn't been at Stone Mountain for five days. It was a puzzle, made more complex by what Dara said next.

"You'll never guess, Briana," Dara said. "I woke up this morning, and my head was filled with stories about my...*our* heritage. It was like I suddenly remembered all my mother had told me...and far more. Anis, Reva, the final battle with Chaos, and Atyra's death. My mother knew none of this. So much of our history is so tragic. But even at the worst of times, our clan prevailed and made the best of a bad situation. I've finally found what I've been after." Dara paused. "Listen to me ramble on. What happened to *you*? You look like you took on the entire Galvan army yourself."

"I...I couldn't find you," Briana said, stunned by Dara'a revelation. "I went hunting on my own. Impulsive and foolish. I'm sorry. I should have waited for you. I'm going to wash up. We'll go hunting tomorrow. Promise."

Dara shrugged and ran to a wall where she could see the entire valley. Briana noticed a bounce in Dara's step. She wouldn't stay, Briana knew. Stone Mountain was too confining for the likes of Dara. But with Dara's memories of her heritage, she was no longer a freak or an outcast. The Shamra of Stone Mountain were her people. And whether she wanted to or not, Dara would one day lead them. For a fleeting moment, Briana wondered what had happened to the other Dara. Then she shook her head. It was one too many Daras for Briana to dwell upon. *This* Dara was safe, and that was all that mattered.

Briana walked up to Dara and put an arm around her shoulder. "You are truly one of us," Briana said as they both gazed at the land that had once belonged to the Shamra. "You are no longer a minority of one. You'll always be welcome here. And great things are in store for you."

"A prophesy?" Dara asked, teasing Briana.

"Call it what you want," Briana said. "Dismiss it if you wish. But like you, I have the Gift of Sight. Your journey has only begun."

THE SHAMRA CHRONICLES

by Barry Hoffman

Discover Where It Started...
Curse of the Shamra

Discover What's Next...
Shamra Divided (2010)

Chaos Unleashed (2011)

Curse of the Shamra:
CRYSTAL CAVE STORIES
A short story collection (2009)

Curse of the Shamra:
LIFE LESSONS STORIES
A short story collection (2010)

EXPLORE THE WORLD OF THE SHAMRA AT

www.ShamraChronicles.com

~ Sign up for Our Newsletter ~
Includes contests with unique prizes like Shamra t-shirts, bookmarks, bandanas & more!

~ Educators ~
Check out the website for free classroom sets of *Curse of the Shamra* in the 10,000 Copy Giveaway!